AND THEN
I Heard
THE Quiet

A NOVEL BY

ALYSSA HALL

FriesenPress

One Printers Way
Altona, MB R0G 0B0
Canada

www.friesenpress.com

ISBN
978-1-03-830344-8 (Hardcover)
978-1-03-830343-1 (Paperback)
978-1-03-830345-5 (eBook)

Fiction, Mystery & Detective

Distributed to the trade by The Ingram Book Company

"There is something awful about
the terror trapped behind silence.
About the latent emotion that can't be acted out."

Maggie Stiefvater

The Quiet

She knocked softly. Putting her ear to the door, she held her breath and hesitated. Nothing. With a sigh of frustration, she knocked again, this time louder. The sound echoed down the deserted corridor. Again she paused.

"I know you are in there." Her voice was just above a whisper. But the waiting created impatience. "Just open the door, dammit!" Her tone grew sharper, angrier than intended. She sucked in her breath at the hollow sound of her voice against the walls.

She exhaled, her forehead pressed into the grainy wooden door, hands resting on her head, fingers clasped. She was gasping for air. Did this building have no ventilation? Then she heard a sound, confirming his presence. She barely heard it, but it sounded like "Go away." Then she heard another sound. This one was muffled like a sneeze, or maybe a groan. Was he crying? This was too much, she decided, and she turned to leave.

As she turned away, she heard a bang, like something being dropped, or thrown. He was in there, but likely angry and was not going to talk to her, that much was clear. Her resentment was increasing as well, thinking about the time and effort she had put into being here.

"Okay, suit yourself. I'm leaving now. So don't ever bother to call me again. This has gotten beyond ridiculous. I never wanted to come here in the first place, but I always get sucked in, don't I." She tried not to shout, for fear of drawing attention from other apartments.

With that, she stamped her feet and headed towards the exit door, feeling inadequate. She had come unprepared for any of this. As the fire door slammed behind her, she blinked away the darkness in front of her. The unfamiliar stairway was poorly lit and she stumbled quickly down the steps and into the light, anxious to escape the stench of the building. She threw open the door and, emerging into the street, took a deep breath.

But as she walked down the alley towards the main road, something else was bothering her. Why wouldn't he speak to her? She shook it off, and kept walking. All the way to her car she fumed, angry enough to kick at the next thing that came near her. She opened the door and seated herself behind the wheel, but rather than start the engine, she just sat there.

She had no idea what she was waiting for. Perhaps she thought he would come outside. The time ticked on, until, much to her dismay, she realized she had to go back. It was that searing pain again, in her gut, and suddenly she knew. Maybe she had known all along, and that was why she fled the building. Her mouth was dry, and she tried to remember when she last had something to drink.

Exiting the car, she ran back. The fire door was locked, so she made her way around to the front door, throwing it open so hard it hit the wall, and she worried the glass might shatter. She climbed the stairs two at a time, and ran down the corridor. Reaching the door, she pounded, calling his name. Then she heard it-the silence. The feeling was profound, and it overcame her like a sickness.

Hearing a creaking sound behind her, she slowly turned around. A woman across the hall had opened her door, just enough to reveal her gnarled, down-beaten face. The smell of urine escaped the apartment and wafted into the corridor. A man's face appeared above hers. They were both frowning.

She stepped away from his door. "Please," she whispered. She took a few more steps sideways until her hand felt the wall, then she hurried past the two, head down, and left without another word. For the second time, the heavy exit door slammed shut behind her, the sound adding a touch of finality as she ran, two steps at a time, down, then out into the alley.

She ran all the way back to her car, the sick feeling returning. She was shaking by the time she climbed behind the wheel. Starting the engine and shifting the vehicle into gear, she heard the sound of her tires squealing as she pulled away from the curb. Yes, the feeling was there, and it frightened her. She had no intention of stopping until she reached home.

One Year Later

1

As Valerie opened the front door, a slight breeze wafted through the entrance. She held the door open with her knee as she wrestled the last box outside and down the front steps to her car. She packed it away, closed her eyes and inhaled deeply before shutting the trunk. The breeze picked up, cooling the heat from the morning sun. Climbing the stairs one last time, she paused at the top step and gazed to the sky, then smiled. She was beyond glad to be finally moving out of this cramped apartment and couldn't wait to see the back of Burnaby. The place had never been ideal, but at the time she had been desperate to find somewhere to live. Now ten months had passed since her hasty arrival from Calgary, and she had never learned to like it. Not even a little bit.

She walked into the kitchen, where she had left the open trash bag. Valerie had one last chore–cleaning out the fridge and cupboards. With unexplained haste, she mercilessly tossed everything into the trash bag. Out with the old. Make a fresh start. She certainly didn't want to show up at her new job carrying a bag of half-eaten food. When nothing remained in sight, she closed the bag. She then paused. Stomping her foot and rolling her eyes, she opened the bag again. Digging around, she retrieved half a jar of peanut butter, a box of granola, her almonds, a jar of olives, and a few crackers that she had placed into a zip baggie. Digging deeper, she found what she was looking for-a small block of cheese. Surely it would be okay if she brought these things along, discreetly stored away in a box. She could keep them in her room until she had the place to herself. Satisfied, she tied the trash bag firmly and carried it to the back porch for the morning collection. She then locked the back door and carried her edibles to her car.

Valerie had moved too many times in the past three years, and was hopeful that this move to Fort Langley would be a place where she could at last settle down. Surely British Columbia would be the ideal place to make her home. After all, this was supposed to be the best place on earth, according to the slogan on the licence plates. That was not the reason she came here, but hopefully it would be the reason she would stay.

As Valerie stashed her goods behind the driver's seat, she heard a door slam. She looked up. The man living across the street, who for the entire time of her being there had acted like she was invisible, had suddenly looked at her and lifted his hand in a wave. There must be some sort of comfort in this type of acknowledgement– the safety in knowing you will never have to engage in an actual conversation now that the person was leaving. Valerie waved back unenthusiastically before redirecting her gaze back to the small house.

Without looking around, she bounded up the steps, ascending two with each stride. She wondered what went through the man's mind each time he looked at her. She certainly appeared aloof, unapproachable. She lived alone in this ugly clapboard rental duplex, with its peeling paint and missing shutter. There were weeds in the yard and she had never made any attempt at making the place look more presentable. Perhaps if she was in a less traumatized state she might have tried. She locked the front door, pushed the keys through the mail slot, and ran down the stairs for the last time.

The steering wheel was hot to her touch, as the sun had been beating through the windshield all morning. Starting the car and putting it into gear, she held the wheel with her fingers until it cooled enough to hold on to. Driving towards the freeway, Valerie began to feel excitement about the new position that was waiting on the other side of the river. She had learned of it quite by accident while working for Anna at the agency. When Valerie had moved to her crummy little duplex and had gone to look for a job, it was down the road to Anna's agency that she had first gone. Based on Valerie's resume, Anna had hired her on the spot to work in her office. It was only a temporary position, but it lasted all this time and had been a good experience. The real bonus was that it proved invaluable to now have Anna as a connection.

Anna previously worked for the government, a position that she had held for over twenty years. She had considered her career in public records and freedom of information an interesting and informative one. She was able to retire at the age of fifty after banking every spare cent. Her goal had been to open her own employment agency and it was thus far doing very well. She had seen something in Valerie and had hired her without hesitation. While Valerie was grateful, she frequently expressed to Anna her desire to move on and find a better job. And then this opportunity came along.

It was nearly a month ago, on a Sunday, and Valerie had been dog walking at the time. This was her other occupation which she had also discovered quite by accident. Walking other people's dogs, she found, was a very good way to earn extra money to support herself—a far cry from her previous career, but this was out of necessity until she could get herself back on her feet. She needed to keep a low profile so that she wouldn't be found, as she was sure someone would still be looking for her. A high-profile job might have attracted more attention, and she needed to wait a bit longer, to make sure no one actually *was* looking for her. Meeting Anna on the street that day had altered the course of her life.

"I hadn't realized that you looked after animals," sang Anna, in the lyrical way she had of speaking.

"I also do gardening for my landlord, if that excites you as well," had been Valerie's response. "I'm just asking you to please understand, Anna, I do love working for you, but we both know it's temporary and I need to get myself settled."

Anna had smiled and said, "Give me a few hours. I think I have the perfect solution for you. I had a very interesting conversation with a client just this morning.

Let me call you this evening, and I'll explain." Valerie had walked away, her curiosity piqued.

That evening Anna had called, her voice elevated as she delivered the news. "Okay, I might just have the perfect thing for you. I have a good friend, Denise, who lives in Fort Langley. She and her husband need a house-sitter, dog-sitter, and gardener to move in for five months. I've been wracking my brain trying to come up with someone."

"You are making this up," Valerie snorted. Valerie would have taken anything if it meant getting away from this apartment and this side of town, but this actually sounded really good. Only this time it sounded like she might actually need to tackle the gardening.

"I'm not making it up, I swear. Well, actually, the request was for a house-sitter, but you have now ticked all their boxes. Obviously I wanted to check with Denise before I said anything to you. She and her husband are going on a sailing adventure. Crazy girl, but they are taking their forty-foot sailboat to Hawai'i. I know it's still a temporary job, but this will be good for you, Val. They are taking five full months. And Val–they will love you. I told them so."

Valerie had been surprised at how little effort was required by Anna to convince her. All she needed to do was insist this would be the perfect job. Anna said that she had given a strong recommendation, for which Valerie felt grateful and relieved. Anna herself sounded excited. "Denise is feeling fortunate to have found one person to fill all three positions. You really are the ideal candidate."

Valerie looked up from the road as she realized she was crossing the Port Mann Bridge. She slowed down to better catch a glimpse of the water and, to her left, the mountains in the distance. This place was beautiful. But it was beautiful in a different way than Calgary, and definitely very different from Montreal, where she grew up. As she reached the other side of the water and saw the sign that said Surrey, she felt her entire body begin to relax. She had no idea what lay ahead and was trying really hard to move on in this new direction. But what had happened was absolutely her own fault and she had no one to blame but herself.

As she made her way east, she couldn't help but notice the mountains in the rear-view mirror. It seemed the further away she got, the larger the mountains appeared. She chuckled at the illusion. Noting the instructions on the sheet of paper lying on the passenger seat, Valerie took the exit at 200 Street and headed north, towards the river, and then turned east to make her way into the village community of Fort Langley. How she had waited for this day!

Entering the village she was instantly taken by its quaintness. It was as if she had been transported back in time. This place reminded her of some of the small villages in Quebec that she had visited as a student and again as a young adult. The historical buildings with their colourful facades and picturesque storefronts sat along the main street, which was lined with stately trees. People were walking along the sidewalks, chatting and shopping–a sight she had not seen for a long time. She was more accustomed to deserted streets, with cars everywhere but no people. Usually a garage door would open, a car would pull out and drive away, and the door would close. That was the extent of neighbourly contact. But not here-this place felt like an actual community, complete with engaging pedestrians.

At the end of the road, she noticed a row of vehicles queuing off to the right. A sign over the road pointed to the bridge ahead, which indicated a ferry terminal on the other side of the river. Aside from the random shoppers she witnessed only some light traffic. She slowed the car and rolled her window down. From somewhere she heard music and wished she could dance. So far this felt good.

Over the past few weeks, Valerie had spoken many times with the Carters regarding this position. They had asked her many questions and in the end, based on Anna's reference, had announced their satisfaction with the arrangement. While this was not the life Valerie had envisioned, she was happy for the opportunity to earn money and have a place to live at the same time. And it might have to stay this way for some time, until she got her dream job and could afford a place of her own. She had given up a lot to get here.

What she was hoping for was a job working for the 2010 Winter Olympics, which were coming up in the next year and a half. Applications were being accepted now. She would waste no time in applying, as she was unsure how long the process would take. She was more than qualified, and surely by then no one would be looking for her-not here in B.C.

Glancing once more at the paper lying on the front seat, she turned the corner and spotted her destination. Surprisingly, Valerie was not the least bit nervous or apprehensive as she pulled into the driveway. She quickly shut the engine off, exited the car and walked briskly towards the front porch, pressing out the creases in her shirt. As she climbed the few steps to knock on the door, her eyes combed the stately character house. There was an immediate sound of barking followed by the squeaky turning of the knob. A smiling middle-aged couple greeted her, introducing themselves as Bill and Denise Carter. They introduced their dog, Hank, as he stood quietly wagging his tail.

"Please come in, Valerie. Come and meet our family," stated Bill, stepping back and extending his arm in a welcoming gesture.

As Valerie walked into the spacious entranceway, another couple approached them. Denise spoke. "This is my daughter, Karen, and her husband, Hamid. They live in Abbotsford with their two kids, Danesh and Anadia, who unfortunately couldn't be here today to say hello." As Denise was speaking, Hamid smiled warmly and stepped up to shake Valerie's hand, his eyes shining like onyx. Karen stood behind her husband and smiled, making good eye contact with Valerie. She too leaned forward to shake Valerie's hand. She was taken aback at the way they had gathered to greet her, like long-lost friends.

Bill Carter motioned for the group to follow, inviting Valerie to walk ahead of him to the rear of the house. He pointed the way, and they soon entered a spacious, upscale kitchen. Bill walked around to the far side of the granite island.

"Coffee?" he asked. Valerie nodded while Karen motioned for her to sit. Karen sat beside her and began talking nervously.

"I would have stayed here while my parents are gone, but I am very busy, you know, with both kids in hockey. And Hamid owns a busy bistro, which you can imagine takes up a lot of his time. You will have to come and try it. Do you like tagine? It's a spicy North African stew. It's his specialty."

The four seemed relaxed and casual, moving about the room in an easy-going way, which made Valerie feel comfortable. But as Karen spoke, Valerie sensed that she might be feeling guilty about not looking after her parents home while they were away. Her mom looked at her kindly and shook her head. "Karen, stop. Your father and I realize you already have a lot on your plate. You promised you wouldn't do this."

Karen appeared to be only a few years older than Valerie, and she found herself somehow envying this woman. Her life seemed quite nicely settled. Here she was, with a nice family, a handsome husband, and already two children. It drove home the awkwardness of her own situation–housesitting and walking a dog for a living, at her age, when she could have been settled by now.

Bill looked at Valerie with concern and said, "You doing okay? So are you thinking this will work?"

Valerie sputtered, "Oh my God, yes!" She couldn't get over how young and fit they both looked. It was hard to believe these two weren't around the same age as her. They could easily have passed for older siblings.

"Okay then, how about we get your things moved in and we show you around? We thought it best to spend these three days with you, to get you up to speed on everything before we leave. I'm sure that will be enough time." Turning to Hamid, he cheerfully called, "Let's get this lady moved in then, shall we?"

Together the three moved the contents of the car into what would be Valerie's new quarters. She felt a twinge of embarrassment at her few possessions, and she discreetly grabbed the bag of food from behind the front seat and carried it in under her arm. She really should have left it in the trash bag. What was she thinking? Valerie said very little as they moved her paltry few boxes into the house. She certainly had little to show for a life and was grateful nobody mentioned it. But that was also another story.

She followed Hamid up the stairs and through the doorway at the end of the hall. She gasped. Her new private space was wonderful. She stood in an oversized room with a large alcove in front of a bay window. The window overlooked the yard next door but was partially obscured by a large leafy tree. To one side was an adjoining private bathroom, which was larger than Valerie's kitchen in her previous apartment.

The men placed Valerie's belongings in the corner beside the bed. "We'll just leave you for a bit. You get yourself sorted, showered, or whatever you want to do, and we'll see you a bit later. No rush, take your time." Bill nodded, and with a smile, the men were gone, closing the door behind them.

Valerie put her palms together and touched them to her chin. She wanted to cry with joy. She stood in one spot, taking it all in. Things were starting out just fine. She hoped they would stay that way.

2

Valerie spent the next three days getting to know Bill and Denise, and them her. And while they were considerate in allowing her time alone to get her bearings, many of their hours were spent going over the running of the house. The dog followed them everywhere, which made Valerie a bit nervous. She really knew very little about dogs and this one already seemed to be judging her. She didn't like the way he looked at her, as if he was smarter than her and could see through her. She was very careful to avoid eye contact.

She thankfully spent a part of each day alone, familiarizing herself with both the house and garden. The house, while not big, was very grand. It stood tall on the slightly hilled lot, a deep shade of green framed by pale green trim. Although the neighbourhood was very well treed, casting the house in a shadowy chillness, the inside exhibited light and cheeriness, in part due to big south-facing windows. Adding to the ambience were the pale-coloured walls and neutral earth tones of the furnishings. Here and there she saw bold splashes of blue and gold in large paintings and big patterned area rugs.

The gardens began at the street, winding upwards on either side of the wide driveway, past a large storage shed and opened into an ample green space displaying a good variety of shrubs and blooming flowers. It would take Valerie some time, she guessed, to become accustomed to all of the plants, many of which were unrecognizable to her.

The days seemed to fly by, each bringing a new level of comfort. Their evenings were spent on the front porch, a glass of wine in hand. It was a civilized way to end their busy days, was Bill's way of putting it. While the music played, usually Fleetwood Mac or something classical, Bill and Denise would sit talking to Valerie about their plan. The goal, once they reached the Hawai'ian Islands, was to spend some time on the island of Oahu. Their destination was the Makani Kai marina, which Bill showed Valerie on a map. Bill periodically pushed his eyeglasses up, as they seemed to constantly slip down. The setting sun cast a bronze glow on his curly blond hair. Denise, also fair, wore her hair in a high ponytail. How old were they? Valerie guessed maybe fifty.

Denise sipped her wine. "We have rented a condo there and are understandably a bit nervous, having never seen the place." Bill smiled at his wife. Their faces glowed as they spoke of the journey ahead. Valerie couldn't help but wonder if they would survive the ocean and if she would ever see them again. But her prophetic ability was not telling her anything about that, so perhaps they would be safe.

"If all goes as planned, we will fly home about half a year from now, once we have hired someone to sail our boat back to British Columbia. Of course, it would need to be next season. And we won't stay longer than agreed." Denise looked at Bill and they both nodded in unison, to themselves and then in the direction of Valerie. "We realize you have your own life beyond your commitment to us. And we will be in touch regularly once we arrive there, so we can gauge how things are going for you."

Valerie shuddered at that comment, because she really had no idea what lay beyond this position, although she would never admit such a thing out loud. She was snapped out of her reverie by Denise's next question.

"We have said far too much about ourselves these past days. We'd love to hear a bit about you, Valerie. Where had you been before you arrived here? And what brought you to BC in the first place?"

Valerie attempted to provide a very brief and vague description of the preceding few years. She tried hard not to stammer as she fumbled through the untruths and omissions. She had never considered herself a liar, but by withholding so much, she felt like one today.

"So you see, I had been living in Calgary, working for the Stampede. As I mentioned, I'm an international events coordinator. A facilitator. It's been a wonderful gig, but my dream job has been to come here and work for the 2010 Winter Olympics. My superiors understood that I was ready for a change. I realize it's still a year and a half away, but I knew it would be good to get myself settled, as the jobs will be starting soon. So it felt like the best time was now."

The dog, Hank, who had suddenly barked and sprinted from the porch, interrupted Valerie. Bill turned his head sharply and Denise stood up.

"Squirrel," Bill announced.

"Not again," Denise uttered, a soft moan in her voice.

Valerie let out a huge sigh of relief. Now, if she could just avert questions for one more day, then these two would be on their way. And she just might make it, as Karen and Hamid were returning in the morning, which would provide another distraction. While Hank proceeded to tree a squirrel, with Bill and Denise in hot pursuit, Valerie excused herself without the necessity of faking a yawn.

She crawled into bed, exhausted. She lay listening to the sounds of the Carters scolding their dog as if he were human and could understand what they were actually saying. In Valerie's mind, *"Bad Dog!"* should have sufficed. Valerie had hardly slept those first three nights. One would think this was a normal reaction to being in a strange home, with unfamiliar creaks and sounds in the night, and with strange people in the next room. But for her, it was other things that kept her awake. Other sounds. Or more precisely, it was the absence of sounds. It was that disturbing noiselessness from what seemed a lifetime ago that continued to haunt her. From somewhere a train whistle blew, and she was soon asleep.

Early the next morning, the sound of a car in the driveway indicated that Karen and Hamid had returned.

Valerie was still in her room when she heard their voices outside. She remembered Karen had mentioned bringing the children, Danesh and Anadia, to spend the day and see their grandparents off on their journey. She quickly dressed and headed down the stairs, eager to meet the kids. Seeing her, Karen walked towards the staircase smiling, her children in tow.

"Good morning. We are just taking Hank outside. Why don't you grab a coffee and meet us out on the porch?" she said, pointing towards the door.

Still sleepy, Valerie obliged and was soon outside seated in the Adirondack chair next to Karen. There was no sign of the Carters or Hamid. She was barely seated when two small children bombarded her. The first to greet her was Danesh, an energetic boy of about seven. He was full of sparkle and wouldn't stop talking, as if he'd known her for his entire life. Not to be ignored, Anadia walked up beside her brother. She was quieter, but seemed somehow tougher. Valerie imagined she was a bit of a tomboy who loved her brother but wanted to be able to keep up with him, no matter what he did. Valerie remembered Karen saying she was five. Or was it six. Nonetheless, the children stayed only a few minutes before running off to find Hank, who had wandered off towards the shed.

The day was a flurry of activity. Valerie had offered help but it became clear that the family was on a mission, helping the Carter's pack their things, and Hamid was being given last-minute instructions for various technical issues to watch out for. She found the best thing she could do was take Hank for a long walk to keep him out of everyone's way. When she returned a short while later, nothing had changed, so her next move was to take the children for a walk, for the same reason.

That evening after dinner, while sitting outside watching the kids play with Hank, Hamid leaned over to Valerie and asked, "I can't help but notice your accent. May I ask from where it comes?"

"I guess it's a mixture of Italian and French. I'm Sicilian but I grew up in Quebec."

"Small world, I did as well. I was born very near to Quebec City. Ah, wonderful, we have something in common. But you said Sicilian. Is that not in Italy and are you not just Italian?"

"Oh no, Sicily is quite different than Italy. There's a whole different dialect and culture thing going on. It's a long story."

So Valerie and Hamid spent a bit of time discussing their roots. Hamid told Valerie his descendants hailed from North Africa, although he had never been there himself. His parents, along with his grandparents and children, had moved to British Columbia from Quebec. Just then Karen came out to join them. She touched Valerie's shoulder softly and smiled at her as she took a seat next to Hamid.

Valerie asked, "What kind of dog is Hank?"

Karen smiled. "Isn't he beautiful? He's a mix of cocker spaniel and golden retriever. A cogol, I've heard them called before. He's great with kids and with adults as well. He's easy to train, he's quiet, and he doesn't mind the heat. Mom lucked out when she found him. Although I should warn you, he can be a handful."

Valerie was enjoying the way the dog was teasing the two kids. Hank actually seemed the smarter of the three, although she dared not say so.

"We are so glad you are here, aren't we, Hamid? My parents seem so relaxed and less afraid of leaving for the journey that's ahead of them."

Valerie's heart warmed to this gentle and friendly family. They sat in silence and watched as Hank chased Danesh around a bush. A Frank Sinatra song played softly from somewhere inside the house.

The next morning, Denise and Bill said goodbye. The two were in jocular chaos as they scurried about making sure they had everything. The dog, Hank, was whining quietly, aware that something big was happening. Anadia and her brother followed their grandmother around the house, offering moral support. Bill was once again going over last-minute details with Valerie.

"I'm very grateful to you, Valerie. It's surprising how comfortable we feel leaving you. Anna was right when she said you were the one for the job. She has much faith in you, as do we." Denise's eyes sparkled in the wetness of her tears as she hugged her grandchildren. And then they were gone. It seemed to happen so fast.

Later that morning, Karen and Hamid and their children left as well. Karen hugged Valerie warmly, which took her by surprise. She had not known such sentiment so quickly.

"Promise you will call if you need anything at all," she said kindly. With rolled-down windows, they waved as the car drove away. Valerie waved until they were out of sight.

Finding herself alone at last, she walked around the house, as if for the first time. She realized she might well love this job, and the house-although she was not yet too crazy about the dog. He grunted all the time, even more so now as he followed her from room to room. She hadn't noticed the grunting before. Perhaps she could hear him more clearly with the house so quiet. She wondered if it was his need of a proper diet, which she vowed to look into. But first, she planned on getting settled into her new temporary life.

That night, Valerie had another nightmare. They were always of Julian. She had been searching the streets for him when, suddenly, she spotted him ahead, walking around a corner. She started to run towards him. When she reached the corner, he was nowhere in sight. But then she saw him again, just ahead of her. He appeared to be walking really slowly, his head hung down. She ran as fast as she could, yet somehow she couldn't seem to get any closer to him. The pavement was uneven and she was terrified of tripping. When she looked up again, Julian was gone. Running to the next corner, she saw him just as he disappeared again, far ahead around the next corner. Again, she ran, calling his name. She started to cry, and as she did, she stumbled and began to fall, but she wasn't falling onto the sidewalk. There was now a huge hole in front of her and she was plummeting into the blackness. She tried reaching her arms out to catch herself and at that moment, she woke up.

3

The first week consisted of finding where things were kept. Valerie had been shown, but it would have been impossible to remember everything. The rooms were big, cupboards were plentiful, and every time she found a new room, she found more cupboards.

The house itself was a thing of beauty. She walked outside to view it again, now that she was alone. The driveway was large, easily accommodating four vehicles. The detached garage on the left held everything but vehicles. Bill and Hamid had spent a lot of time in there the previous day, and now she understood why. It was the one place Bill had not taken her. She walked to it and slowly opened the creaky door. This was the heart of everything boating. On the hooks hung ropes, rubber fenders, fishing lines, an anchor, dock lines, lanterns and a host of other accessories. There was a small boat and more boating gear, plus two kayaks suspended from the beams, a shelf full of oil and lubricant cans, and a few bicycles.

Coming back outside, her eyes wandered to the right, to the house itself. The green-grey two-story building was accented with many light green framed windows.

No other trim, leaving a clean look. Three steps led up to a covered front porch where sat two grey Adirondack chairs. Massive double front doors opened up to a spacious foyer, which was filled with natural light from the many windows. Valerie loved the simple yet tasteful décor. The kitchen beyond was as well equipped as any she had ever seen.

She eventually made her way to the yard shed that she had been shown, but she wanted to see it again now that she was alone. The shed was also filled with shelves and drawers, containing everything from tools and gardening equipment to more cycling gear and most everything in between. A huge wooden cabinet revealed oversized light bulbs, batteries, bits of rope and chain, old, rusted hinges, and an assortment of shower heads. How the hell could people accumulate so much stuff! She laughed when she came across a box that contained a deflated blow-up doll and a plastic skeleton. That was enough snooping for her!

Many nights, she lay awake, unable to forget the events that had brought her here to BC. They would play over and over again in her mind, but she was slowly learning how to let go of them. She couldn't forget, but hopefully she could see the past becoming less and less important to her–something to be left in the past. She felt grateful that these thoughts didn't plague her during the day as well.

Valerie was born Katerina Valeria Russo in Nicosia, Sicily. Her only memories of that period in her life were of her grandmother's house and of the big, angry mountain. It was because of that mountain that her papa moved the family to Canada. Mount Etna had a significant eruption in 1983 that lasted for months and was eventually blasted with dynamite in an attempt to divert the lava flow. Her papa, having grown up there, always hated that mountain and grew tired of the eruptions. Most Sicilians seemed to embrace it, but not him.

That year, her papa had had enough and packed the family up. She was six years old when he relocated her family to Montreal. He had told her she had some sort of prophetic ability-an uncanny way of knowing when the eruption was going to happen-and that he actually believed it was something inside Etna–the magnetic pull-that had made her this way. That was the one and only thing they were taking with them, he had said. At the time she was too young to understand what he was talking about.

But as she grew older, he would occasionally refer to her *curse*. He called it her "Etna." Now understanding what he meant, she dismissed this notion, telling her father all she had was a keen case of intuition-instinct, perceptiveness, ESP or whatever-but certainly not any magnetic pull from Etna. Her father never did agree.

She remembered the day they left. It was deeply ingrained in her memory. As they stood at the train station, her papa held her in his big arms. Her arms were wrapped around his neck and she remembered crying. She held on tightly, peering over his shoulder at her grandmother, who was weeping into her apron. It was the last time Valerie had seen her grandparents.

Etna did erupt again, and not just once. The most recent was around the same time Anna had offered her this job. The summit crater had exploded, leaving in its wake a very altered landscape. The eruption was followed by at least a hundred earthquakes. Did she sense the eruption? Did she feel something here in BC? If what her father had thought of her powers was true, was this somehow a sign? She wondered what he had thought of it and how grateful he would be to have left.

Growing up, her name had been Katherine. She had always quite liked her name, having thought there was nothing wrong with it. But even before she graduated, she had become Valerie. It was the name given to her by her best friend Alice. All of their friends had seemed to accept it and so it had stuck. Alice seemed most pleased with the change. Although it was never quite clear to her why it happened, she was now Valerie and would remain such, although her parents and brother still called her Katherine.

She tried not to think of Alice and her family-tried to not wonder how they were managing in their flawed, sick dysfunction. Her life would have probably turned out better if she had never met the woman. This was just one of the things she was learning to let go of. She had to live with the consequences of having been involved with them in the first place. But right now, Valerie found herself thinking of her own family in the Montreal community of Brossard. She hadn't spoken to any of them since leaving Calgary. She would need to call them soon, but which one to call was the big question. Perhaps her brother would be the best bet. He would be the least likely to patronize her and the most likely to spread the message to everyone else. She was undecided whether or not to disclose her current situation, and he would respect that.

Most of the time, Valerie was happy and had a clear mind. Before long, she had created a nice routine for herself. Actually, it was more Hank's routine than hers. There were the early morning grunts at the door, letting her know he wanted to go outside. Then it was feeding time, followed by a walk. Then he pretty much slept and lazed around for the rest of the day, but by three he was ready for something a bit more ambitious. Hank, being a cogol, needed lots of activity, so walks were frequent and brisk.

She had never lived with a dog before and was finding it more enjoyable than she imagined it would be. Maybe because Hank knew what he was doing, his routine already established. Now he was merely training her to go along with his plan. At this juncture, she really needed someone to guide her, so she followed the dog's moves. It made things easy. And the fitness was definitely not hurting her. She had been inactive for quite some time, and it felt good to be moving again.

So on most days, Valerie would take Hank to the river's edge around three. They would cross the tracks to the pier where the long rowing boats were kept. From there, they would walk along the river on the Derby Reach trail. Often the longboats would go by. Hank would stop and wag his tail, and thankfully for Valerie, he wouldn't bark.

Valerie so enjoyed exploring this delightful little village called Fort Langley. The main street was lined with large old trees, having grown a wide enough canopy to create a tunnel effect down the street. In the opposite direction, towards the river, lay the train tracks. If in town and if she was near enough, she found it exhilarating to hurry to the tracks whenever she heard the signals at the train crossing. She would arrive as the arms went down over the road and would stand as close as she could to feel the ground shake. She would squeeze her eyes shut and turn her face towards the oncoming train to feel the "swoosh" of wind.

Valerie was also surprised to discover there really was a fort! The Fort Langley National Historical Site was a former fur trading post and had been built by the Hudson's Bay Company in the early eighteen hundreds. This was, she had read, the second location of the original fort, which had been built further up the river in Derby in 1827. This fort was completed in 1839. A section of the palisades still remained along the front of the grounds, and inside were small buildings that had served as stores, barracks, as well as blacksmithing and barrel-making quarters. And while most of the buildings had undergone reconstruction, there remained a few original structures. The fort now served as a tourist destination, and Valerie made a promise to herself to go and see it one day soon. Periodically the fort held events where they converted everything back to a working fort, with residents in full period costumes, replicating the time. Perhaps she would wait for that occasion to visit.

Part of her days consisted of household chores, usually mornings, as the rest of the day she preferred to be in the garden. There was always something to do. She laughed to herself. What would her friends think to see her so domesticated? The days were warm, and she found herself constantly watering, which in turn brought weeds. Something else new that Valerie discovered was that she actually enjoyed pulling weeds. Inspired by the well-tended gardens in town, she found the entire gardening experience to be very therapeutic, and yes, that included weeding. It gave her a sense of satisfaction to stand back and see the result afterwards. This was something she had control over.

She found solace in the yard, except for one thing. Occasionally she noticed a man at the house behind her property. The first time she noticed him, he seemed to be merely walking around his yard. But after a few weeks, little by little he seemed more interested in Valerie than in his yard. It seemed odd, and she tried hard to ignore it. She needed to stop imagining anyone was looking for her. Perhaps he was a friend of the Carters and was wondering who she was. If that was the case, why not just come to the fence and say hello?

The past few times she spotted him there, it actually sent chilling warning signals throughout her body. He was there now. She picked up her bucket with trembling hands and slowly went into the shed. A few minutes passed before she took a breath, left the shed and walked briskly to the house, not looking back.

Later that afternoon, as Hank was indoors sleeping, Valerie decided this was a good time to walk into the village to pick up a few things at the grocer's. The air had cooled slightly, and she was in the mood for a stroll. Walking out onto the street, she noticed a woman at the house next door. Up until now, there had been no sign of life at the property. Valerie had assumed the people next door were either away or very private. In truth, she had not bothered to pay attention, as she rarely saw any of the neighbours, now that she thought about it. In this case, there was a fence between the properties and a few shrubs shielding the view to the front door. So it was easy to go about her day and not see any activity. But today she noticed.

The woman was about her age, possibly a bit younger, and she was sitting on the top step, quite vocally moaning in pain. Valerie timidly called out to the woman as she walked by.

"Are you okay?" she asked.

The woman winced and seemed genuinely injured. "I tripped and sprained my ankle, stupid me. I had hurt it before, but I thought it was getting better. As soon as I came outside, I almost fell off the step."

"Can I do anything to help you?"

"No, I'm fine, but thank you." She then seemed to change her mind. "Well, actually . . . I do need to get this package to town, and I'm already late. I don't know what to do. My dad is waiting for it."

"Can I please help you?" Valerie asked again. "Can you stand?"

"I just need a moment to catch my breath. Say–do you suppose you could take it for me? You look like you are on your way out."

Valerie hesitated for a moment. "I still don't know the area very well."

"It's the antique store, you see it as soon as you get down the hill." The young woman lit up at the prospect of having her parcel delivered. "It's the big one, with all the stuff out on the sidewalk. I'm sure you've seen it. I'll give you forty dollars if you take it now. Like I said, I'm so late, and my dad will be furious."

Valerie laughed and she said, "Don't be silly, I don't want any money. I'm going anyway so I'll take it now. I'm having a good time getting to know my way around here, so will enjoy finding the store."

She leaned forward and placed the parcel into Valerie's outstretched hand. "You can't miss it. And thanks again."

Valerie waved as she continued down the street. Normally she would have lingered, taking in everything new, but today she felt a sense of urgency, as the young woman had seemed upset and anxious to get this package to her father. She quickly made her way to the antique store, where she spotted a man standing outside looking her way. As she approached, he eyed the package and reached out his hand. Valerie smiled at him.

"I think this is for me, isn't it?" he said as he took the package. Without another word, he got into a car that was parked directly behind where he stood. The car was running and he put it into gear and quickly pulled away from the curb.

"Oh, fine. You're welcome and have a nice day," Valerie muttered under her breath. The man drove away without looking. Not giving the matter another thought, she went about her day. She continued exploring the surrounding area before picking up her groceries at the only market in town. One day she would need to venture further out to find more shops, but for now, this was fine.

Another hour had gone by before she walked back up the hill towards her home. As she passed the neighbour's house, the young woman was no longer sitting on the step. Valerie climbed the stairs to the front door and rang the bell. No answer. Assuming the woman had perhaps gone to have her foot examined, Valerie went home. As she put the key in the door, she heard Hank's grunt turn into a bark. Maybe she should have taken the dog with her, but she had really enjoyed the time alone to linger. She paused at the door, reaching into her bag to find the new bone she had purchased, knowing this would soothe the beast. She turned the key and went inside.

4

That night it rained. Perhaps rain was too gentle a word. It was more of a torrential downpour complete with thunder and lightning. Hank seemed mildly agitated, but only during flashes of lightning. Valerie felt like the house would get washed away in the deluge. The windows shook with each thunderclap. Turning the lights out, she cupped her hands around her eyes and pressed her face to the glass. She could see the water rushing down the street, bubbling over the curbs. Then came the pelting hail. This was becoming ridiculous. Feeling tired and slightly unsettled she went upstairs to brush her teeth and wash her face. She was too tired for much more than that.

Sleep didn't come easy. Valerie tossed and turned, but eventually fell into a fitful slumber. She dreamed she was standing on a beach. Rescue workers were standing in the shallow part near some rocks, and had just hauled three bodies out of the ocean. She walked over to have a closer look. The bodies were those of Bill and Denise Carter, bits of seaweed in their hair and in their mouths. She stood staring, afraid to move. As the workers turned over the third bloated body, she screamed in horror, but no sound came out of her mouth. It was Julian. His eyes were fixed on her. She sat upright, her heart pounding. Still only half awake, she pulled the covers over her head but lifted them off again as she heard the rain had abated. Within seconds she was fast asleep.

Valerie woke up with only a vague recollection of the details. She remembered fragments of people on a beach by the ocean. Something told her it wasn't a good dream, as her covers were strewn across the bed. She had no desire to dwell on it, as often in the past, she did remember the dreams, and they were usually unpleasant. The sunlight was streaming into the window, hitting the wall at the far side of her room. She could still hear moisture dripping from the eves onto the roof, and the sound of car tires as they swished on the wet asphalt. She heard the distinct cawing of crows in the distance.

She heard Hank moving around downstairs. His dog tags were clinking as he scratched his ears. She smiled, feeling very much like she had landed somewhere safe. This was good. Technically, this shouldn't even qualify as a job. This was merely living a life and was a walk in the park compared to her usual demands.

Valerie learned quickly that a happy dog was key to a good day, and this one had started out well. After a simple breakfast, she gathered a few things in preparation of taking Hank outside for his walk. Most important was the plastic bag of dog treats that went into her pocket when Hank wasn't looking. She turned towards the front room at the sound of a car pulling up in the laneway. Making her way to the front window to peek outside, she gasped when she saw a police officer walking towards the door. Why was he here? Did they somehow find her? She moved quickly to the door and opened it before he had a chance to knock.

"Good morning," she said to the man, unsmiling, her eyes glued to his. She started to shake. What the hell did he want?

"Good morning, miss. My name is Officer Clarke. Do you live here?"

"Well, yes, temporarily I am living here," she attested, not breaking eye contact.

"Are you the owner of the house?"

"Well, no, I'm not. The owners are away. I'm the house sitter. How can I help you?" The officer was of medium height and slightly pudgy, and he didn't appear at all confrontational.

"I'm looking for a bit of information. Did you by chance carry a package and deliver it to a man outside the antique store yesterday?"

His voice was calm and friendly, and Valerie sighed with relief. The package. He was here about the package. She smiled.

"Yup, that was me. I delivered it for my neighbour. Would you care to step inside?" She spoke enthusiastically and maybe a bit too cheerfully.

The officer stepped into the foyer but made no attempt to venture further into the house. He stood rooted, his eyes fixed on the notepad in his hand, his pen poised. Hank stood at a distance, watching him but making no attempt to come closer.

"Would you like to sit down?" she offered, and behind her Hank promptly sat down.

"I'm fine here, ma'am. So what is your name, please?"

"Oh–of course. My name is Valerie Russo."

"Thank you, Miss Russo. And are you living here alone?"

"Like I said, I'm the house sitter and yes, it's just me living here. Is there a problem, officer?"

"The package that you delivered to the man at the antique store. Can you please tell me about this man and how you two are connected."

"I don't know that man. I took the package for my neighbour, a young woman, who was hurt and was late to deliver it. I was going out anyway, so I offered to take it."

"So tell me about this woman. Is she a friend of yours?"

"I don't know her either," she answered awkwardly.

The officer was suddenly frowning. Valerie's eyes brushed his face then she looked away, towards Hank. "She lives next door. Like I said, I was just on my way out and stopped to help her. She'd sprained her foot or something, and was upset, so she asked if I could please take the package for her."

"And what did this woman look like?"

"Gee, I don't know. She looked younger than me. I would guess maybe about twenty-five. Brown hair, thin face, she had on a big sweater and black leggings."

"Okay, I'll check it out next door, but please don't go anywhere, I will likely have more questions for you." He nodded and turned to leave, then turned again to face her. "Is there anything else you'd like to tell me before I leave?"

"No, not really," she answered, a faint tremble in her voice.

He left, and Valerie watched him out the window as he walked back to his vehicle. She noticed a second officer seated inside the car. Officer Clarke got back into the drivers seat. Hank nuzzled Valerie's leg as she watched the second officer get out of the car and walk to the neighbour's front door. After a few minutes, Valerie saw him disappear into the house. She remained glued to the window, although she wasn't quite sure why she was so interested. Hank was beginning to whine, and she looked at him apologetically.

"I know, buddy, you want to go out. Hang on, just a minute more." She bent over and scratched behind his ears.

After a few minutes the officer emerged from the house next door and returned to the patrol car. Valerie couldn't wait any longer. She snapped Hank's leash onto his collar, put on her shoes and walked out the front door. Officer Clarke, seeing her come outside, quickly got out of the cruiser and walked towards her.

"I'm so sorry," she stammered. "It's Hank. He has to pee, and, you know."

"My partner has just been next door, ma'am. The elderly gentleman who answered the door says he knows nothing of a lady of your description. He said he and his wife live alone and that they had been away for a few days. Actually, ma'am, he said he doesn't even know who you are."

Valerie stood silent, not sure what to say. So the mystery woman doesn't live there. What the heck?

"So let's start over. Can you tell me about the man at the antique store and the package you gave him?"

"So is this about the woman or about the man? Or is it about the package? I'm confused." Valerie could feel her cheeks colour.

"You told me about the woman. I was actually asking you about the man, and the package." The officer studied her face. "Are you sure you are telling us everything?"

Valerie gasped at this. "And why wouldn't I tell you everything? What's this even got to do with me? Okay, aside from the fact that I helped someone out."

Officer Clarke simply said, "Well, to re-cap, you carried a package of you don't know what, for a girl you've never seen before and gave it to a man who was waiting for you, yet you don't know him either. Or so you say. Who does that?"

Valerie said nothing. The officer then said, "Can I please see some ID?"

Valerie was shaking as she walked back to the house to retrieve her driver's licence. The police officer followed her as far as the door. She handed him Hank's lead and shrugged her shoulders as she disappeared into the house. Coming outside, she took the lead back from the officer and handed him her licence.

"Just have a seat for a moment while I check this out," he replied. He had changed his stance, his soft voice sounding empathetic and non judgmental.

Valerie moved to the porch and seated herself in one of the chairs. Hank once again began to whine and she stared at him helplessly. She spoke through her teeth. "Gimme just a tiny break, will you?"

Within a few minutes, the officer returned with her document. "This is an Alberta licence. Didn't you say you lived here?"

"I've just moved here, and was planning on changing it this month," Valerie lied. In truth, she had completely forgotten about changing her licence over. "I'm sorry," she added with a generous smile, in hopes of smoothing things over.

"You only have ninety days to switch, so please be sure you do it right away," he instructed. "Also, know that we will need to speak with you again. Please make sure you will be available. Are you planning any trips?"

"No. Like I said, I am house-sitting. The owners are on a trip."

"Okay, so we will check this out a bit further. Just make sure you don't go anywhere. No sudden urges to leave, okay? One of our detectives will be in touch very shortly." He eyed her up and down suspiciously before turning to walk back to the patrol car.

"A detective?" she called after him, her voice anemic. "Why a detective?" Was he ignoring her or didn't he hear? He shut the car door and the two drove away.

Valerie stood rooted, feeling profoundly humiliated. As it was, the culmination of past events had left her feeling perpetually rattled. She had really wanted this move to be untroubled and conflict free. She wanted to live in peaceful anonymity, not be thrust into the center of more chaos. The officer saw nothing more than a house-sitter-and a lying one at that. Turning in the other direction, she let Hank pull her down the lane towards the river.

Watching the dog on the end of her lead, she began to understand why people had pets. The diversion was almost immediate, with Hank snorting and sniffing, and occasionally looking up at her with what seemed like a smile. Before long she was smiling and speaking to the dog as if he could understand her. It was more than an hour before they found themselves back at the house, and only then did she start thinking of the visit from the police. She walked into the living room and turned on the stereo, loud.

It was becoming harder and harder for Valerie to live with total quiet. She found she needed constant sounds around her. Even the hum of the refrigerator and the ceiling fan were welcoming. During the day the radio was always on. She slept with her window open, to hear the wind rustling the leaves, the sound of a passing car, a plane flying overhead and occasionally, coyotes in the distance.

Valerie hoped before long she would hear from the Olympic Committee. It was time to get on with that, and she was feeling impatient. That and her licence; tomorrow she would see to her drivers licence.

5

Valerie was up early, and by seven she was sitting near the big window in an easy chair. She sat drenched in sunshine as she glanced through a large, hard-covered pictorial journal of Fort Langley. This impressive little town of a mere 2400 people was situated on the southern shore of the Fraser River. The town was oozing with history, and she was eager to explore areas around the fort and the railroad museum. Her mind, for once, was surprisingly clear. No demons plagued her today. She stopped reading and put her head back to stretch when Hank, who had been lazing luxuriously on the carpet nearby, looked up at her imploringly.

"Okay, okay, I'm moving," she said as she stood lazily.

By mid-morning, Valerie was walking down the hill that led into town, Hank happily walking in front. He was nonchalantly sniffing his way along the grass, stopping once in a while to bury his nose into the base of one of the gnarled old horse chestnut trees. A few crows had gathered in the tree above and were cawing at Hank. She had never known crows to be as big or as loud as these. Valerie walked around the corner towards the shops. Suddenly, Hank looked up at the sound of voices coming from the coffee shop ahead, and began to pull frantically at his lead. He let out a bark, and a man standing outside the coffee shop looked over.

"Hank, you old dog. Where the hell have you been?" The man stooped as Hank dragged Valerie towards him. He gave Hank a pat, his eyes gazing up at Valerie. His face broke into a smile as he stood up. He wasn't tall, but he exuded confidence. His smile was big, his chestnut hair windswept. A rumpled T-shirt thinly veiled his muscular frame.

"I saw you the other day, in front of the antique store, with that man. I didn't realize you were the sitter, because you weren't with his highness here. Hi, I'm Garret." His crooked smile revealed a wee gap between his front teeth. "It's nice to meet you."

Valerie seemed confused. "So you know who I am?"

"Well, I do now. I had heard from the Carter's that the new house-sitter was coming to town." He turned his head and nodded down the street to the left. "I run the bike shop down there, and I look after Bill and Denise's bikes for them. I see them a lot and got to know Hank pretty well too." He bent and patted the dog on the head again as Hank bounced around and wagged his tail. "I think he likes you. He's being very good. Either that or you've drugged him." Garret smiled widely as he scratched his head and brushed some hair from his eyes.

Valerie felt herself relax as she smiled back. "Nice to meet you, Garret."

"Hey, pardon my manners. Would you like a coffee? I just grabbed this and was about to sit down. Here–you sit and let me go grab you one. Is a latte okay?"

Valerie's resistance fell on deaf ears and so she sat in the chair that Garret had pulled out for her. He placed his coffee cup opposite her and disappeared into the bistro. She sat nervously, not really wanting to be there. A group of cyclists had arrived and were busy parking their bicycles behind her. Before long, Garret reappeared with a second cup of coffee. He moved the chair slightly and sat down opposite Valerie.

"Cheers," he said as he lifted his cup to his lips.

Valerie smiled but said nothing as she took a sip of her drink. It was her first latte in some time and it tasted wonderful. She greedily took a bigger gulp.

"I'm sorry, I didn't get your name. I don't think Bill mentioned it."

"Valerie," she said awkwardly. She loosened the clip in her hair and tossed it back before re-clipping it in place. It was a warm day. She looked around. Why had she never noticed this place before? It seemed really popular and frequented by people her age.

"You don't say much, do you?" Garret looked like he was the type to talk enough for the two of them. "I saw you at the antique store the other day. What was that all about?"

Valerie sighed. "You've already asked me once. Why is everyone making such a big deal about that? And why are you asking me again, as if that's the most important thing about me? I was just bringing a package to town for my neighbour."

"A package! How interesting. So who's this everyone you are talking about?"

Valerie said nothing. She was still trying to figure out if this was some kind of sick joke. Who was that girl who had sat on the porch step, and where was she now? She still couldn't figure out if this was about the girl, the man or the package.

"It's nothing," she casually replied.

Garret continued. "The police have been watching that shop for some time now, didn't you know?"

"I'm new in town, I'm dog sitting. How am I supposed to know what's going on? I haven't been here for more than a few weeks. I couldn't care less what the police are or aren't watching. I'm more upset at being accused of lying, and I have no way to prove I wasn't."

"Whoa, who's doing that?"

"Just this police officer that came to the door the other day. He asked what was in the package and I said I didn't know. He acted like he didn't believe me. Besides, I don't really want to talk about it," she said, as she bent to pet Hank, who was lying beside her chair, licking the concrete.

Now it was Garret's turn to say nothing. Sensing her discomfort, he tried changing the conversation. "You have a bit of an accent. What is it?"

"I call it 'Frenglian'. A wee bit of French mixed with English and Sicilian." She emitted a small chuckle at her made-up word.

"Frenglian, eh? That's interesting. I like it. So where are you from?"

"I come from a lot of places, so it really depends on when. I don't really want to talk about that, either. I'm sorry, but I do have to get going," she said, standing slowly. "But thank you for the coffee."

"But you just got here."

"And now I'm just leaving. Listen, Garret is it? I appreciate the coffee, really. Thank you for such a nice welcome, but I do need to go."

"Let me walk with you part way." He stood and was instantly at her side.

Reluctantly, Valerie began slowly walking, unclear in which direction to go. Garret insisted on walking alongside her, but to his credit, he left a good distance between them. Hank was pulling on the lead in order to get closer to the man.

After a moment of silence, Garret turned to her. "Can I do anything to cheer you up?"

"Who says I need cheering up? she replied, maybe too quickly, trying hard to relax and not sound too fierce.

"Come and see my bikes. It's just there, up ahead."

"Maybe another time, really," she politely declined.

"No, too late, we are going there now. Come on, Hank." He turned left and Hank followed, wagging his tail and dragging Valerie along.

Within seconds they arrived at the front door of the small, historic-looking building. The shop was small, but upon entering, she saw it was well equipped. The racks were crammed with bicycles of all types. She saw road bikes as well as mountain bikes, trail bikes, tricycles, and tandems. A few customers were milling around, and the cashier was busy with a few more. Off to the side, Valerie spotted another room where a man was heavily involved in repairing a bicycle. A woman with a thick auburn braid that ran halfway down her back sat on a stool watching him carefully.

"I don't really know much about bikes, so I don't know if I should be impressed or not. But there certainly are a lot of them," she said.

"Oh, you can be impressed. These are damn good bikes, and my guys are good at their job. These bikes over here are a very popular brand," he boasted, pointing to a rack at the front of the shop. "My customers come from all over the region. We not only sell bikes, we also do fittings, take exchanges, and there's always a shitload of repairs. We also sponsor races and different cycling events in the summer."

Valerie really had no interest in any of this. After a hasty look around, she had seen enough. As she excused herself, she tried hard to avoid any eye contact. Hank seemed restless, giving her another reason to leave. "I'm sorry, but we have to go now. Hank needs his walk and some privacy to do his thing." She felt stupid using this excuse. Since when does any dog require privacy? They seemed to squat wherever they pleased.

Garret held the door for her and made a sweeping gesture for her to exit. He winked at her as she passed him. She looked away. The doorway was narrow, and she was trying hard to avoid any physical contact. Although she didn't look at his face, she could almost feel him smiling, which annoyed her. Valerie felt she couldn't get away from him fast enough, yet she could not deny a small attraction to the man.

"I'll see you around, Valerie," he called after her. She waved her hand but didn't turn around. Hank had already headed for the nearest tree.

6

The sun had just disappeared over the rooftops and the house was slowly losing light. Valerie walked into the pantry and flipped on the light switch as she looked around for a snack. Finding nothing that appealed to her, she went to the refrigerator and cut off a few slices of cheese. She then grabbed her paper bag from the counter and headed to the sofa. She sat down in front of the TV, landing hard, and began cracking pistachios that she had bought earlier at the farmers market.

She placed the plate of cheese in front of her. She could almost live on cheese, if she let herself. Her dad had always said it was the Sicilian in her. As she chewed, she realized she was completely uninterested in the program, but Hank seemed glued to the screen. His head was darting from side to side, watching the action. She laughed to herself as she popped a handful of nuts into her mouth. At the sound of the telephone ringing, Valerie stood and licked the salt from her fingers before she picked up the handset.

"Hi Valerie, it's me. Karen. I can't believe it's been over three weeks already. We were wondering how you were settling in and thought now was a good time to invite you for dinner to our home in Abbotsford. I know it's short notice, but could you come tomorrow, say, around five?"

Valerie switched on the light. "Tomorrow? What about Hank?" The call had caught her off guard.

"Please bring him! The kids love him, and they will keep him occupied. You could probably use a break from that dog. So will you come? Grab a pen, and I'll give you directions. There's a nice back road route so you can avoid the freeway. It can get stupid busy, and it might take you forever if there's been an accident."

Valerie decidedly welcomed the distraction, agreeing right away. She wrote down the directions, thanking Karen for the invitation. After hanging up, she found herself feeling restless. She walked out to the porch and called Hank, who looked up but seemed unwilling to venture outdoors.

"Party pooper," she called to him. She gazed at the empty chairs on the porch and they suddenly looked uninviting. It would be nice if Hank had come out with her. So she decided to call it a night, and she locked up the house and went upstairs. She was hoping she would not dream. Not tonight.

Valerie woke early and began the day with a bowl of Cheerios and almond milk. By mid-morning, she started her yard work but found she couldn't concentrate. After a few chores, she spent a bit of time in the shed exploring the contents, inventing ways to pass the hours. Eventually she retreated indoors to check the clock. The time was dragging, so she decided to slowly get ready for her trip to Abbotsford. After taking Hank for his midday walk, she came home and had a long, luxurious shower. She had plaited her hair back into a braid and was now rifling through her clothes looking for something to wear.

With Hank settled into the back seat, Valerie grabbed a fresh bottle of water, locked the front door, and got into her car. She realized that since her arrival, this was her first time driving anywhere outside of this little town, and it felt good to be on the road. She rolled the window down and let in the fresh air. She smiled as she felt the breeze swirl around, bringing unusual scents with it. She felt free. She leaned back and turned up the radio to hear Bobby Bazini singing "I Wonder." She sang along loudly. Hank rested his chin on the console and wagged his tail.

Karen's directions were very good. Valerie found herself driving along a pleasant winding country road. The drive took her past a game farm, with llamas and goats visible in the pens. Next came a berry farm displaying big signs beckoning people to come and pick their own blueberries. Although she didn't have time to pick, she did stop. At the open stalls, she found baskets not only of fresh blueberries and raspberries but also an abundance of fresh cakes, pies and jams. She purchased some fresh berries and a small berry cake before continuing on her way.

While driving, she couldn't believe the extent of the fields. Along both sides of the road sat acre upon acre of berry shrubs; she guessed raspberries and blueberries. Most fields were full of eager pickers, many with children running up and down the rows, carrying small plastic buckets. In the distance she could see a red tractor and turban-clad men hard at work in the fields, picking berries.

Next she passed an outdoor equestrian arena. The lot attached to the show park was a bustle of activity with cars parking their trailers. She caught glimpses of trainers walking their horses around, likely preparing for a competition. The sight of this activity gave her a heightened sense of excitement. She loved horses, and perhaps she could some day attend one of these events.

As she crested the hill, she gasped in astonishment. There in the distance was a massive mountain peak, covered with snow, even though it was summer. The bottom wasn't visible, giving it the look of a ghostly apparition hovering above the earth. Mount Baker. She had been told about it, but one needed to see it in person to appreciate it, and she was humbled by its magnificence. How odd that since running from a volcano as a child, she once again lived near another–albeit one that hadn't erupted in about 6,700 years. It would be just her luck if it erupted now that she was here.

During the remainder of the drive, she hardly saw another car. The country roads wound around and up and down, past expansive estate homes and well-kept farms and took her over small arched bridges. It was a wonderful route, and Valerie was appreciative of Karen steering her away from the freeway.

When she arrived, Karen was sitting on the front porch waiting to welcome her. Valerie shut the engine off as Karen walked towards the car. "You're right on time," she said with a smile. At the sound of her voice Hank sat up and barked, which summoned the children from the house. Karen opened the back door and Hank sprung out of the car towards the children. Valerie had not seen him move this fast in a long time.

It felt so good to be greeted with such kindness. Karen seemed genuinely warm, and hopefully she had invited her with no agenda. Valerie hated herself for feeling any kind of suspicion, but still, she preferred discretion and low visibility at this point. She vowed not to say anything about the package and the police. They entered the house, and instantly her senses came alive from the aromas of spices coming from the kitchen. Anadia surprised Valerie by taking her hand and guiding her in to the sitting room.

The home inside was impressive, with vaulted ceilings in the living room, exposed beams, and floor-to-ceiling peaked windows. The sofas and chairs were all pale blue leather and were accented with a cream-toned carpet and dark wood tables. The very modern interior was decorated in the complete opposite of Karen's parents, which was more country rustic and cozy. Here was the feel of elegance. How did Karen manage to maintain such luxurious surroundings with two young and very boisterous children?

Hamid emerged from the kitchen wearing an apron and a big grin. As he walked towards the sofa he held up a bottle of wine and three glasses.

"Welcome to our home, Valerie. Let's have a glass while my meal rests, shall we?" he announced. He sat the bottle and glasses down on a side table before retrieving a bottle opener out of the pocket of his apron. Hanging the apron on the back of his chair, he deftly opened the wine with his long slender fingers and poured three glasses before sitting down. His motions were quick and precise, like a conjurer displaying the most impressive sleight of hand. She likened him to the Canadian master, Dai Vernon, whom her father had often spoken of. She remembered seeing him on the television when she was very young. Hamid seldom looked up and appeared consumed by the task at hand. But he smiled warmly as he handed the glass to Valerie. Karen had disappeared to the kitchen and had returned with a small plate of cheese and crackers as Hamid motioned for Valerie to sit down. By now, Anadia had disappeared with Hank.

The conversation was light. Mostly there were questions about how Valerie was settling into small town life. And of course, asking how things were at the house. Valerie would have preferred to be the one asking questions about their lives-maybe to know something about Hamid's roots. She would have loved to know about his restaurant. Or perhaps she would ask Karen whether or not she worked outside of the home. But it was not to be, as Karen seemed to be directing the conversation.

When her husband stood and announced it was time to eat, Karen called the children in, and the conversation was moved to the dinner table. Hamid brought three casserole dishes from the kitchen and placed them in the centre of the table. Valerie watched him, his fingers deftly manipulating the utensils. Intense serious eyes contradicted his smiling mouth. He handed the first plate to her.

"I know we should have asked, but I hope you are okay with spicy food. I did scale it back considerably, so hopefully it will agree with you," he said, as if expecting a thank you for doing so.

Valerie stared at the food, disappointed that she wasn't given the opportunity to plate it herself. She would have avoided that one brown-looking thing. But she responded with an air of optimism. "Well, my grandfather was from Calabria, so I do recall a few meals being a bit spicy. But I moved away when I was very young, so I can't really remember how well I liked it. I was raised on a blend of French and Sicilian, so more simple flavours. So let's give it a try and see how it goes."

Now Valerie had never considered herself a fussy eater, but she did disguise her dislike for the taste. The piquancy was intense, the seasonings were undistinguishable and this had caught her completely off guard. And while not unappetizing, it was indeed too spicy for her. Not to mention there seemed to be things on her plate that she didn't recognize but was not prepared to ask what they were. She managed to mask the flavours with big pieces of flatbread, which was very good. She smiled a great deal and drank more wine, which seemed to solve the problem.

After dinner, Hamid took the kids and Hank for a long walk. He invited Valerie to join them, but she chose to stay and help Karen clean up. Once the house was empty and they were on their own, they fell easily into conversation, this time about the progress of her parents at sea. Karen seemed a different person when her husband wasn't in the room. She seemed relaxed and cheerful as she quickly rinsed the dishes while Valerie cleared the rest of the things from the table. Dishes rinsed, she shut the water off and wiped her hands on a towel.

"Anna had spoken so highly of you, it's easy to see why my parents jumped at the opportunity to hire you. And she seemed to find you from out of the blue. Had you lived in Burnaby long?"

"Nearly a year. I started working for Anna almost right away," Valerie answered between large gulps of water. The meal had left her incredibly thirsty.

"How did you meet Anna?" asked Karen.

"That's how I met her. I went into her office looking for a job and she hired me right away." She really was tired of questions.

"Well, lucky for Mom and Dad. It makes me feel less guilty."

"I think your parents knew you had enough on your plate and couldn't possibly be in two places at one time," she said reassuringly.

Karen turned to the dishwasher where she began loading the dishes that Valerie was passing to her. "You are actually very beautiful, if I'm not embarrassing you. Where are you from?"

"I was born in Sicily." Valerie was feeling more comfortable opening up, as Karen clearly had no real interest and was just making conversation. She gave Karen a brief history of her family's move from Italy and her upbringing in Quebec. Beyond that, she kept it vague.

"I moved to BC from Alberta. I had been working there for a few years."

"I've never lived anywhere but here. I met Hamish in high school, and that was it for me. You are lucky to have been so many places."

"Well, there's good and bad in that. There's a feeling of discontent at having never settled. And I'm not good at making new friends. But I hope I can settle here."

"What will you do when my parents get back?"

"Well, I have applied to work at the 2010 Winter Olympics. I worked as an events planner for most of my adult life. Fortunately, I had always landed good jobs. I've organized some pretty big, important gigs. Many were political and others were extravagant galas like winery promotional events. I'm super anal about organization but not always good at delegating. So while trying not to micro-manage, I often end up doing too much myself. And there were also some bizarre gigs. I went to scout a location for a corporation that wanted to have a Blue Tattoo party, and I had a staff shortage so I went out alone. I got beat up-assaulted by a couple of street people who tried to rob me. Took me a while to recover. It was a very tough year financially."

"Is that why you came here? But it sounds like you gave up such a good job."

"Well, I actually have time to decide whether I want to go back. But I'm not sure Calgary is the place for me."

Valerie felt like a liar. The truth was, if she did decide to go back, she would have to crawl on her knees and beg for the job back. And she worried about having to face the music about that other thing that had happened. She was also thinking of her belongings, still in storage. She had less than a year left on the lease and would have to make a decision soon or lose her possessions.

"I am really just here to work for the Olympics. In the meantime, I will just focus on finding a home and a job. I will speak to Anna soon, even though I still have a few months to be at your parents' home. But I know the time will go quickly. Maybe she'll have another temporary job for me, once I decide where I want to live."

She left out the part about a plan B. What if she wasn't hired for the Olympics? Valerie knew that no matter what happened, she would not go back to Calgary. She needed to think seriously of a backup plan.

Just then, Hamid came back into the room. Valerie took this opportunity to change the subject. "I met a guy in town named Garret, do you know him?"

Karen rolled her eyes. "Not well, but Dad always talks about him. He's their bicycle guy and they love him. I think he sells them too much crap that they don't need, but they seem happy with him. Plus he is definitely motivating them to ride, which keeps them busy."

Hamid cut in. "I don't like him, and I don't trust him. He's too cheerful. Too cocky, if you ask me. I think he pretends to like Karen's folks just so he can keep their wallets open."

"Stop it, Hamid." She turned to Valerie. "I think Hamid is jealous of him," she said, as she poked her husband in the ribs.

Valerie was tired. She'd had a good time but was not one to linger when the evening was clearly over. She surprised herself by thinking about Hank and feeling the need to get him home. And it felt good thinking of the Carter place as "home."

"I better get going. It's been wonderful, really. I can't thank you enough." She called Hank and made her way to the door. She couldn't explain her sudden discomfort. The family followed after, to see her off.

"It's been nice getting to know you. Please don't be a stranger," Karen called after her. Valerie backed the car out of the driveway and waved goodbye. Hank was already curled up on the seat. Valerie wished she could curl up as well. The drive seemed long and she'd had wine. Her mind started to wander, going over the events of the past few hours. Just then, she remembered about the berries and the small cake in the trunk. She had completely forgotten to give them to Karen.

Once back home, Hank walked into the house and collapsed in a heap. Valerie knew he was tired and would not be very ambitious for the remainder of the evening. She went out to the porch and sat down, setting a bowl of berries and her water on the side table. She was still thirsty after that meal, whatever it was. As she reflected on the evening and the conversations, she began mindlessly picking yard dirt from under her nails. Yuck. Why hadn't she noticed it before? How embarrassing that she went for dinner with visible dirt. She was realizing it really was impossible to get it all out, as Denise had tried to warn her. Tomorrow she would start wearing the gardening gloves that the couple had left for her.

7

It had been raining all morning, and Valerie had debated staying indoors. She had eaten half the berry cake for breakfast and was now eyeing the second half. Hank was sitting by the door, his restlessness increasing. Valerie had hoped the weather would improve, but she quickly learned that dogs don't necessarily care about the rain. While reluctant when she opened the front door, Hank soon began wagging his tail. He climbed down the porch steps and began sniffing around. She shrugged her shoulders and grabbed one of Denise's rain jackets from the back room. The cake would need to wait.

She was surprised at how little the rain affected people's everyday lives. Someone had told her that if people here let the rain stop them from doing things, they'd never do anything, as the rain was frequent and unpredictable. The streets of the town as well as the trails were full of people, many hurrying somewhere, others lingering along the river walk-laughing, talking, some holding hands and kissing. It made the rain enjoyable in a way, and it made her feel alive and a part of something. She found herself smiling.

But after being out for this length of time, she was surprised at how cold she had become. She pulled the hood up over her head and stuffed her hands in her pockets, quickening her pace. Hank, too, looked like he had enough and was happy to move faster. Valerie was impressed at the distance they had covered, but it had been a long and muddy hike. Her shoes were quite wet, despite her best efforts to avoid the puddles.

Approaching home, she immediately spotted a car parked in front of the house. Nearing, it looked to her like it might be an unmarked police car. They did send someone after all. She walked past the car and headed straight for the house. She felt her heart pounding in her throat as she walked up the drive and towards the front porch. She really needed to stop being so paranoid.

She was cold and needed to dry off. The car door opened, and a tall man emerged. He gave a slight smile as he walked up to her and nodded in greeting. He checked his notes.

"Good morning. Are you Valerie Russo?"

She nodded as she pulled the hood from her head and wiped the rain from her nose. "Are you the one they said would be coming?"

"I'm Detective Tobin from the RCMP, with the Special Enforcement Unit. Can we talk inside?" He looked vaguely familiar, and for a moment, Valerie almost thought she knew him, but she knew that was impossible. Still, something about him seemed so familiar that she almost asked him if they had met before. But his businesslike demeanor prevented her from doing so.

Something about his face and the area around his mouth, was teasing her memory. He was smartly dressed and had a full head of light brown hair, worn short and slicked back. His eyes stared at her with intensity, and his voice sounded grave. A hint of stubble covered his squared jawline. Too much in a hurry to shave, Valerie guessed. His bronzed, healthy looking complexion suggested he spent a lot of time outdoors.

Valerie's voice was hushed in response to his aloofness. "Yes, please come in." She walked to the front door while he followed a few steps behind.

"It's a good thing you are here. I was trying to reach you yesterday. I thought maybe you'd decided to take a holiday," he said as Valerie invited him into the hallway.

"I was in Abbotsford. Is that against the law? I told the officer I wasn't going anywhere." His attitude annoyed her. She dried Hank's feet, and he trotted off happily. "I need to change quickly, if you don't mind."

He didn't reply, but merely stood looking at her, compelling her to move quickly. She bounded up the stairs and was back within a few minutes, nearly tripping on her way back down the staircase. The detective hadn't moved from where he stood.

She cleared her throat. "So how can I help you?"

"Can you tell me again about the package? We have cameras on that building and have been watching it for some time now. We were able to watch the handover to your associate. You weren't very careful." He remained in the hallway with no attempt to move further into the house.

Valerie noted his hardnosed composure; his feet spread and planted firmly on the ground. "I didn't know I needed to be careful. And stop calling him my associate. I have never seen the man before. Plus you don't need cameras or witnesses. I'm telling you I was there, and I was the one who handed the package to the man. I was helping out my neighbour."

"Yes, you said that," he commented as he again checked his notes. "The neighbour that you didn't know. 'A favour for a stranger' is, I think, how you put it." He was quiet for a few minutes, reading over the pages of his pad.

"Don't make assumptions, Detective. Don't they teach you that in detective school?" Valerie began shifting from foot to foot. She crossed her arms defensively across her chest. She wished she could sit down. She inhaled shakily. "I just don't get it. None of this makes any sense."

He acted as if he wasn't listening to her. Finally, he spoke. "Okay, so let's start here. I need you to come to the station to look at mug shots. Oh-and we may have more questions. Is it convenient for you to come? Just see if you can recognize either of these people from the photos."

She instantly relaxed. Was he really going to believe her? "I could come, yes."

"Good. If it's convenient, I would like you to come today. They've transferred the mug shot files to us at the Langley RCMP station, and it would be better to do it right away, in the hopes these people are still in the area." Then he added, "And before you need to be in Abbotsford or anywhere else in the next little while."

Valerie was frustrated. "I'll come if you stop looking at me that way, as if I did something wrong." Her blood was beginning to boil.

Detective Tobin continued without reaction. "According to neighbours, the owners of the house next door were away, which confirms their statements. And no one else saw this so-called girl you mentioned."

"Why is it my fault that these owners weren't home? And stop saying so-called girl. There was a girl sitting on their step, whether or not anyone else saw her. And why is it my fault that there is some weirdo watching me from the backyard behind my house? Is he not real either? Let me guess—he's not real, and the owners are away too. Is everybody from here always away?" she lamented.

Unfazed, the detective answered, "Can I drive you?" He placed his hand on the doorknob and began to turn it.

"No thank you. I will take my own car," she shot back.

Wanting to get this over with as soon as she could, Valerie grabbed her car keys and ignoring Hank's whines, she followed the detective out the door, slamming it behind her. Brushing past him, she climbed into her car and started the engine.

Valerie composed herself as she followed the detective's car to Langley, to the RCMP station detachment. Watching him pull into a parking lot adjacent to the building, she opted to park across the street. She parked in front of a small house situated on a treed lot with open fields on all sides. She had no idea such beautiful country existed such a short distance away. She exited her vehicle and saw the detective waiting for her at the entrance. Locking her car, she ran across the road. There was no traffic to speak of in this quaint, out-of-the-way part of town.

Valerie followed the detective into the building. The quiet reception area was spacious, well lit and minimalistic. They walked down a corridor, past rooms filled with state of the art equipment; employees were quiet. Heads down, fingers busily clicking away on keypads. Valerie's legs were shaking. Here in a police station was the last place she wanted to be. A year ago, she worried she would be arrested and dragged into a station because of what she had done, but somehow she had avoided detection from the Alberta authorities. What the hell was she doing here now?

At the next corridor, they turned and entered a small conference room. At the far end of the table sat a woman with an open computer on the table. She looked at Valerie and, with a nod towards the chair, directed her to sit down. Valerie obediently sat down and began nervously chewing her nail. She looked down at it and saw more dirt. *Damn*, she thought to herself. The detective took the seat beside her, moving his chair slightly back and behind, so that he could look over her shoulder.

After some brief instructions, the woman took out a stack of photos and placed them in front of Valerie along with a pen. "Look at each one closely. If you do recognize anyone, please mark your name and signature on the back of the photo. Take your time," she said.

The detective added, "We will be recording you, if that's okay."

Valerie mumbled an okay and moved her chair forward. She kept her head down and slightly away from the camera. At each photograph, Valerie shook her head. It seemed to take hours. She paused at last, at an image of a woman.

"You know, this could be her, but I really can't say for sure. It happened so fast and I was more worried about her ankle. Plus in this photo her hair is pulled back and the woman I saw had her hair loose."

"But it could be her," the woman stated, not in the form of a question.

"Yes, I think it could possibly be her, but I won't say with certainty."

"Can you sign the back, please," instructed Detective Tobin. He then rolled his chair back around the table.

The woman made a few notes, shut the laptop, and with a nod to the detective, left the room without a word. Valerie watched her leave. Betty Boring. She was again alone with the detective, and he was again writing notes, but not from his pad. These were larger pages, out of a file. He then gathered the photos from the table and put them back into a file box.

"What's your story, anyway? Where are you from, and how did you end up here?"

"Do I have to? This isn't about me, it's about these people." Valerie was resisting, and the detective noticed.

"Do you have anything to hide? Perhaps I should talk to the Carters about you. For example, how did they hire you? Why you? Where did you say you were from?" he asked.

She sighed and decided she'd better play nice. "I'm just frustrated, that's all. This whole thing is unreal. Anyway, I'm from Montreal. That's where I started my career as an events planner." She mentioned this because, for some reason, she wanted to impress him. After all, he just saw her as a dog-sitter. "But I'd been living in Alberta for the past few years. I had a fabulous job working for the Calgary Stampede. But I felt I needed to get out of there, have a change. I loved my job, but I had been injured and wanted a break. I only moved here recently, first to Burnaby and now here."

"So you had a–let's see, how did you put it–a 'fabulous' job as an events planner and yet you decided to move here. I see. To be a house-sitter."

"It's more than that. Anyway, it's personal and I don't feel like discussing it with you. And if I'm not under arrest, I'm sure I don't have to tell you." Her tone was abrupt, her face twisted into a scowl. She didn't really care how she came across, as the man annoyed her.

The detective reached into the drawer and handed a pen to Valerie. Unfazed, he asked again, "You decide to come to Fort Langley and house-sit for strangers?"

"Why are you so interested? This has nothing to do with why we are here."

Detective Tobin looked at her squarely. "Now that's an interesting thing to say. How do I know it has nothing to do with it? Can you please write down your last place of employment and a reference?"

"Because I'm telling you it doesn't. I have things I don't need to discuss with you. My personal life is just that.

It's personal, and it's not like we don't all have demons. What are yours?" Valerie bristled. She was angry now. She took the pen and wrote down Anna's information. That's all the man was getting. She left the paper and pen on the table.

The detective remained unruffled. He looked at his notepad, and without looking up, he asked her, "Do you have a record? I really don't understand your anger and your unwillingness to cooperate, Miss Russo. This is why I am likely to suspect something. You seem very nervous right now. That's not on me, you giving me cause to wonder. And your reluctance to talk about this package also makes me wonder."

Valerie thought it would be best if she calmed down and answered his questions. "No, I do not have a criminal record. Yes, I left a good job to come here. This is transitional, and I need a break from the stress. My job as an events planner was a very good job, but intense. I was covering everything from weddings to political rallies and such. My last project in Montreal, before I moved to Calgary, was for the 2005 Montreal World Aquatics Championships–the XI FINA. I worked closely with the Marketing Department, and as part of the Organizing Committee, I was chosen to oversee the planning and coordinating of the opening ceremonies. We almost got Cirque de Soleil."

Valerie now seemed to be talking more to herself than to the detective. "And we did, but not until after the championships were over." She sat up straighter. "But I had a personal issue with a boyfriend and I wanted a change. So I moved to Calgary. It really is very personal, and painful, so you can check me out, and then leave me alone. Can I please go now?"

"You are free to leave, but like I said, don't take any vacations."

He remained seated and watched as Valerie left the room. Heading towards the exit, she saw the same woman, Betty Boring, seated at a desk just down the hall. Walking up to her, Valerie spoke loudly. "Is he always like that?" She was almost snarling.

"Like what?" the woman asked."

"Never mind," Valerie mumbled, and she stormed away. She needed cake and she needed it now.

8

Valerie had reasoned with herself while lying in bed last night. It was obvious the police were not looking for her, so perhaps she was safe after all. This new life seemed light years away from her life in Calgary, and she had fallen asleep with a new sense of positivity. She woke up feeling refreshed and clearheaded. This new day brought with it a sense of calmness. The air was still and the birds were singing. Luckily today there were no crows. She had decided she didn't much like the crows and their disturbing caws, which at times seemed endless. She had come downstairs to a happy dog, which warmed her heart.

Having spent the past two hours deadheading the rhododendrons, she was nearing the end of the gardening project. She had no idea if deadheading was a necessary task, but the plants looked so much better after the spent flowers were removed. She found that she would do anything to keep her mind off the events of the past few days. Humming a tune, she dragged the last bag of bark mulch out of the shed.

Having raked up all of the yard debris and filled the paper waste bags, the last step was to spread fresh mulch in all the garden beds. She spread a few handfuls and then stood up to stretch her back. She took a few steps back to see the effect of the mulch. The redness added a wonderful contrast to the greenery. It was important for her to keep busy, as she felt otherwise she would go mad from boredom.

Valerie proudly felt she had blossomed into a gardener, and while she did enjoy keeping plants alive, she knew she could never see this as an occupation. But it was definitely enjoyable. Thanks to Denise, she had started wearing the gloves and her nails were no longer black.

She moved to the front yard to retrieve her trowel. As she knelt to pick it up, she noticed an elderly gentleman approaching her. Valerie recognized him, as she had seen him in town on a few occasions. And gentleman was definitely the right word, as he looked very dapper in his light brown dockers, tweed jacket and flat cap. He walked towards her with intention, a smile on his face. She stood to greet him as Hank walked around the corner wagging his tail.

"I was hoping to catch you," the man said, his eyeglasses steaming up with the warmth of the day. Valerie was certain he was overdressed. "You are doing a lovely job with the garden. Since my Carolina died, I have had a hard time with mine. My body isn't as adaptable as it once was, with all the bending and lifting. I thought I would stay here in my home forever but I realize it's too much for me." He gave a soft chuckle.

Valerie smiled at him. She thought he seemed a lovely old man, but found it odd that here she was, dressed for July in shorts and a T-shirt, yet he seemed dressed for February.

"Mostly the gardens, of course." He continued, "I do manage with my cooking and cleaning. I'm just not as flexible anymore, and I don't have the strength to do any digging. I do have a lady who comes once in a while to clean inside, but she doesn't do the yard. I just need to get it into shape for a sale. I must sell it, you see." He had a way of finishing each sentence with that same little chuckle. He was still smiling as he held out is hand. "How do you do? My name is Gordon." Valerie detected a slight British accent.

They talked a bit about the house, her temporary job here, and Hank the dog, who had grown bored and retreated back to the porch. Their conversation was unhurried. Here she was, dirty up to her elbows with bark mulch, but she found the man quite enchanting.

"I can tell you everything you need to know about these plants. I know about them but I just can't care for them any longer."

Valerie smiled. "Well, I would like to know what this curious little tree here is." She pointed to a small white-leafed sweeping tree at the side of the house.

"Easy. That's a Nishiki willow. And that is Canterbury Bell," he said, pointing to a very tall, elegantly pointed plant covered in blue bell-shaped blossoms. "And that over there is a hosta." He let out another little chuckle. "But you probably know that. Maybe you are just humouring an old man."

"No, I actually did want to know the name of the tree." Valerie was enjoying their conversation when she realized she was actually quite lonely and needed to talk as much as the man did. "Hey, if you like, I could help you with your garden."

"I couldn't ask you to do that, and I apologize if I sounded like I was hinting."

Valerie smiled. "I don't mind popping over one day to have a look." She had another reason for wanting to befriend him. Maybe he would know of someone who could use her services when this job ended. Then she had a thought. "Do you happen to know the people who live there next door to this house?"

"Well, yes, I do know who they are."

"Do you know if they have a friend or maybe a relative about my age? A woman?"

"I don't think they do. To tell you the truth, since your coming here, I think it's been quite some time since we've had anyone around your age living in this neighbourhood."

"Thank you, it's not important. I was just curious." Valerie was determined to prove she was not lying. She would need to try something different, but she didn't know what. Saying goodbye, the man went on his way. After watching him disappear down the street, Valerie returned to her work.

Meeting the elderly man somehow made her feel more at ease. At the same time, it increased her curiosity about the man who had been watching her from the back of the property. She wished she had asked Gordon about that place as well. She decided to take Hank for a walk past that house, just to see what it looked like from that side. She put her tools away and walked into the house. She could finish the mulch later. Washing her hands, she grabbed the leash and called Hank. She knew he would never say no to a walk.

Making her way around the block, she discovered that the street was in fact a cul-de-sac, and there was only one way out. She found she had to enter from the other direction to gain access to the street. Hank was happily sniffing his way along, oblivious to her mission. Exiting the area, she made her way around the block.

Arriving at last on the right street, Valerie walked slowly, peering into people's yards trying to look as though she wasn't. Soon she could make out the backyard of the Carter house. As soon as she recognized the cedar fence at the back, she knew she had found the right place. The house sat in darkness. Leaves and debris covered the lawn and the driveway, indicating nobody was home. On the front lawn, she noticed a for sale sign. She took note of which way a car would need to travel in order to get here, as many of these small streets ended in a cul-de-sac. It always surprised her how quiet the streets were on this side of town, compared to the hustle of Glover Avenue.

She carried on to the end of the cul-de-sac, unhurried. If anyone were to see her, it would appear as though she was walking the dog and nothing more. However, it wouldn't have been suspicious to walk to the empty house, stare into the yard, then turn around and leave, thanks to the sale sign. She continued at a slow pace, peering into each yard with a casual indifference.

Walking back towards home, she discovered an access path halfway down the street. She took it, curious to know where it led, and found it came out at the end of her street. This was good, as it meant if necessary, she could get back here in a hurry. Or get there in a hurry. Although she had discovered nothing, it somehow made her feel more in charge of the situation. She at least knew where the house was and how to get there if she needed to. Maybe next time she would get up the nerve to knock on a neighbour's door or to run over if she saw the man there again. Whether or not she would confront him was a different story.

Hank was enjoying this walk, so Valerie decided to walk past Gordon's house, if she could recognize it from his description. She found it right away and did see his gardens sorely needed attention. Poor guy. She walked quickly, hoping he wouldn't see her. That stupid girl was on her mind again. Who was she, and why had she chosen Valerie? Also, what was so important about that package? No one ever did tell her what was in it. She still had no idea if the issue lay with the girl, the man or the actual package. She would eventually find out, as she had little doubt that detective would be back.

On the way home, she stopped at the community mailbox. Much to her excitement she found a letter from the Olympic Committee. Pleased at how quickly they had responded, she tore the letter open, not waiting until she was inside the house. It was the typical blanket correspondence sent to all applicants. Thank you for your interest, and so forth. To her delight, she had been shortlisted. Although she had only applied for one of the positions as events coordinator, the letter was asking if she would be willing to take another position, such as office manager or even working in the information booth. Enclosed, she found a supplementary form to fill out. She let herself into the house and decided to fill out the form right away. Hank must have wandered off to sleep in another room, as he hadn't come into the kitchen with her.

By the time Valerie had finished filling out the form, Hank had emerged from somewhere and lay by her feet. He flopped heavily to the floor and as he did so, Valerie noticed little mounds of dog hair wafting across the floor. Looking at the clock, she thought she'd better feed him before it was time for his last walk of the day. But first she needed to brush him, as it was still days away from his visit to the groomers. She had come to the conclusion that this job was more about the dog than the house. She felt she had been duped and not for the first time in her life. Conned by the Carters.

This particular breed of dog required endless brushing, as the coat was long and could mat. It really did create a mess inside, and it was the one thing she disliked about Hank. The Carters clearly didn't mind, but as this was their dog and not hers, she found it unpleasant being covered in hair all the time. And his grooming was an arduous chore as well. So the brushing was something she did out on the porch and was grateful at least that Hank enjoyed it and would sit still throughout the process. He looked sideways at her and she couldn't help but smile. He had a big white patch on his nose and throat, and his big cow eyes shone like granite. She kissed him on his forehead.

Valerie sat back and admired her handiwork. Hank stood up and had a good shake. By the time she had grabbed his leash from the hook, it had begun to rain. She groaned loudly. Not only had she left the mulch out, but Hank's coat would also get wet. She didn't care so much about the mulch. Spreading it wet might not be a bad idea, as it would be less dusty.

Hank sat still, his eyes glued to Valerie. No way he was going out in the rain. Not now. "Hmmm," she mused aloud. "Are you reading my mind, Hank?" She retreated into the house to put on some music, grateful for the delay. She could wait, as she had all the time in the world and knew they would have to go out eventually. She would let his bladder dictate the situation.

9

Despite her mild case of nervous delusion as to whether or not she was being watched, Valerie was beginning to enjoy the home and the yard. She also quite enjoyed the short walks into town. As it only took her a few minutes to get there, she found herself going every few days to pick up fresh meat and produce, or often just to browse. On her outings it was easy to forget about her past and focus on what was happening now. Not that what was happening now was really much better, but she was trying to deal with that.

Occasionally she would stop at her new favourite place for lunch, which happened to be a small Japanese restaurant that served amazing sushi. The restaurant was off the beaten path at the end of a small alley that intersected at Mary Avenue. Two brick walls lined the historically delightful alley. Three large colourful wooden doorways of small businesses were situated along a brightly painted red brick wall. The opposite wall was skillfully painted with large murals. One would never have suspected this restaurant would be tucked inside one of these doors.

Valerie had come upon it quite by accident, having been following a woman that way. She was convinced this was the person from the front porch, so she had turned around to go after her. She had followed her right into the restaurant before realizing this was not the girl she was looking for. Finding herself inside the restaurant staring at a stranger, she didn't miss a beat. She had walked around the girl, eyes down, and stood in line to wait for a table. Once seated, she had awkwardly ordered the first thing she saw on the menu. Her lunch consisted of a dynamite roll, gomae and a Japanese beer. Even though she wasn't hungry, it actually tasted pretty good, and after trying it a few more times it had become her go-to place for a midday meal.

Valerie was annoyed with this obsession in wanting to know the identity of the woman. She found herself looking at everyone who even remotely fit the girl's description, looking for the tiniest hint of recognition. And she was trying for astuteness in the hopes she wouldn't need to be discovering any new restaurants in the foreseeable future. Another thought persisted-the girl could well have left the area. But somehow, she couldn't stop looking.

She also had profound moments where she thought she was being watched. Not necessarily followed, but just watched, as she went about doing things. Whether she was selecting produce or buying a newspaper, or just throwing a stick for Hank, there were moments when she felt eyes on her. She wasn't comfortable with this added layer to her already ridiculous and likely unwarranted paranoia.

On the upside, Valerie had recently invested in a decent pair of hiking shoes. This was a luxury she could ill afford but deemed necessary given the increase in her walking. This was of course brought on by Hank's incessant need to keep moving. Yes, it was new to her, but the newness was a catalyst for this fitness kick. She became as enthusiastic as the dog and often found herself on the fort-to-fort trail, following it all the way to Derby Reach Park. This walking route followed the banks of the Fraser River and connected the Fort Langley Historical Site with the site of the original fort in Derby Reach Park. It then continued past the Huston Trail, through open fields and on to the park and campsite at Edgewater Bar. The winding trail, a combination of forested stretches of gravel trails, boggy terrain along the river's edge, and rural green fields, was never empty. This was nature at its finest, and the area attracted dog walkers, runners, cyclists, and young families alike. Omnipresent were the birds, ranging from herons to flycatchers.

She was grateful to have landed in a town so rich with nature and a sense of community, but it also increased her awareness of how alone she was. She missed the company of co-workers and friends. Because of what had happened, she was terrified to contact anyone from Edmonton, or even from Montreal, in case word got back to Alice. If word of her location got out, she didn't think she was ready to handle what might happen, or who might find out. She still wasn't sure if people were looking for her.

Having a lack of human companionship, Valerie had slowly begun to develop a real relationship with Hank, feeling an increased understanding and knowledge of the dog. Not just as a pet, but as a dog. And she had decided that dogs were pretty cool. If she was honest with herself, the idea of another similar gig didn't sound so bad. She was realizing that caring for someone, whether person or pet, was actually fundamental to her well-being. As long as she had a good schedule with Hank, could do whatever she pleased, and set her own agenda, she felt happy and fulfilled. Perhaps this might be a good time to begin putting out the word of her availability for other such positions. Perhaps she could begin by speaking to people she had been meeting, like Gordon and even other dog owners on the trail. They may know of someone looking for a house-sitter. There certainly seemed to be enough vacant places around.

On her way home from the morning's shopping excursion, Valerie decided to stop in at Garret's bike shop. She arrived in no time at all and found the shop to be very quiet. Not like the bustle of her first visit. Oddly enough, the technician was working in the back, and the same lady with the long red braid was in the room with him. She either had a very shitty bike or she was a friend of his. Again, they seemed focused on each other. Garret was not there, but she did ask the technician if they might put a notice on the bulletin board, asking anyone for leads on house-sitting jobs. He promised to mention it to Garret next time he came in. Nodding to both of them, she left the shop. On her way home, she checked the mailbox and there it was. Valerie had received the official letter. She tore open the envelope, and it was the news she had hoped for. She was in! She climbed the stairs to the front door, a spring in her step.

By late afternoon, the weather had turned significantly warmer and Valerie needed to finish her outdoor job. The mulch that had been left in the rain was again dry but unfortunately the grass beneath the bags had yellowed. Once she had completed spreading the last bag, she realized how stiff and thirsty she was. Standing up, she brushed the hair from her face with the back of her hand and examined the garden. She had to admit, it looked good. The hard work had paid off. She walked gingerly into the house to get a drink of water. Her leg had fallen asleep from kneeling and she was limping like an old lady. Hank lifted his head as she walked through to the kitchen. After a cursory glance, he dropped his chin back to the floor, uninterested.

As she was running the cold water tap, Valerie happened to glance out of the kitchen window, and she saw him. The man was in the yard again, looking in and no longer pretending not to look. She shut the water off and ran to the back door, grabbing one of Brian's hats off the hook before rushing outside. She could hear Hank's nails on the wooden floors as he ran to the door behind her, but she had shut it quickly before he reached it. He began barking, wondering where she had gone without him. "No time for that now," she muttered to herself.

Putting on the hat and her sunglasses, she quickly made her way into the alley. She felt this was an advantage knowing it was the only exit from that street. She slowed once she reached the corner and began dawdling along the road, hugging the edge of the adjoining properties, trying to look like she knew what she was doing.

Up ahead, Valerie watched as the man emerged from the yard. He lowered his hat and began walking towards her. She darted behind a tree, feeling foolish and praying nobody was looking. As the man neared, she could hear him breathing heavily. Once he had passed, she waited until he was a good distance ahead of her before following. He made his way along the streets, down Queen and across Francis, finally emerging onto Glover Road. She had no problem keeping up while staying a good distance behind. He was nearing the cemetery. He crossed the road and walked up the narrow street, coming to a stop in front of a small white car. He got in and sat for a few minutes before starting the engine. She crossed the street and again tucked herself beside a tree (she was grateful for all of these lovely big chestnut trees). She positioned her phone so that she might get a good picture of the car and the licence plate as it passed. She was fairly certain he had not seen her.

While waiting, she turned and faced the cemetery. This was the closest she had come to this city of the dead. Gravestones intermingled with neatly trimmed shrubs and surrounded by black iron fencing. As her eyes scanned the rows of headstones, a chill went up her spine. Once again her thoughts took her back to that day. Had anyone seen what she had done? She wondered what had happened afterwards, but quickly shook the feeling off. She had to think about here and now.

The car had started to move. It slowly travelled to the end of the street, and, after a poorly executed U-turn, headed back in her direction. She shielded her body from the driver. As the car turned the corner, she leaned out to take a few pictures. She wasn't sure if she was able to properly capture an image, as she was afraid of being seen.

When the car was completely out of sight she turned and ran all the way back to the house, stopping only when she reached the alley. But as she was waiting to cross, the car passed her again, very slowly. She turned away, afraid to look, although she knew he had seen her. Once the car had driven by, the man intentionally applied the brakes, making sure she knew that he knew.

At this precise second Valerie no longer felt safe, and she cursed the situation. But this would not rattle her. She would not allow it to. Although this was different than the other, it was nothing she couldn't handle. She stood rooted to the spot and defiantly stared back, head high, until the car drove on.

"Screw you," she said aloud, but not too loud.

She arrived to a very happy dog that nearly fell sideways wagging his tail. He had not left the door since she bolted out.

"Sorry about that, boy." She went to the cupboard to fetch Hank a doggy snack.

Sitting down, Valerie took her phone out of her pocket and looked at the photo. The image was good enough. It was blurry and most of the car was outside of the frame, but the licence plate number was legible. Without delay she found the detective's card, picked up the phone, and called the number. After pushing what seemed like a thousand buttons, she reached his voicemail. At the prompt, she left a message.

She kept busy, wondering if the detective would return her call. As it grew dark, she gave up hope of hearing from him today. She locked the doors and turned out the lights. Before retiring upstairs, she turned the music on low. Again, she planned to leave it on for the night. As she walked past the front door, she caught a glimpse of someone moving. She jumped and then calmed as she realized it was her own reflection. Berating herself for being so skittish, she retreated up the stairs with Hank on her heels. It had been a challenging day.

10

Valerie would be fooling herself if she pretended yesterday hadn't worried her. How on earth had she managed to get caught up in this? It made her wonder about the Carters. Were they perhaps involved in something that she inadvertently got swept up in? Did Denise Carter carry packages? Did she know the man in the yard behind the house? Did she forget to tell people she would be away, or was that intentional? Questions came flooding to her and if she let them get to her they would surely drive her crazy.

But perhaps the Carters were not involved, and Valerie was just profoundly unlucky. So she was steadfast in her resolution to deal with it. Just like she was trying to overcome that other thing. Her current situation here at the house was proving to be quite glorious and she wasn't about to give in to negativity.

The morning was an unusually lazy one. Valerie sat perusing her employment package for the Olympics when she was distracted by the sound of the morning paper being thrown onto the front porch. She had come to recognize the thud of the paper against the door. She jumped up to retrieve the paper, welcoming the distraction. Switching chairs, she moved in front of the TV. Flipping casually through the paper, Valerie's eye was drawn to the section entitled Upcoming Events. One event in particular had caught her eye. A cranberry festival would be held right here in Fort Langley, apparently an annual event. Not much information was given, but she would be sure to ask about it. Perhaps she would ask Doug at the grocery store. He seemed to know everything about the community, having lived here most of his life.

It was late in the afternoon when the Detective Tobin finally showed up again. Valerie was actually happy to see him, assuming he had received her message and could maybe do something. Again, as in the previous occasions, when she invited him in, he chose to stand inside the foyer. His dreary disposition almost made her sorry she had been happy to see him.

"I thought I'd pop over rather than call, as I was in the area this morning. Thanks for leaving the message. My team has been looking into it. Then on my way here, I received word the car is licenced to someone out in Richmond, but we think the car may have been stolen, and these are dummy plates. What I mean is, the plates don't match the car. They will get back to me with a confirmation once they check further. But I have a few more questions. Is there anything more you can tell me about the package, and have you seen the woman since?"

Valerie shook her head. "It was just a box wrapped in brown paper. It didn't weigh a lot. And no sign of the girl, I'm sorry to say. I've been embarrassing myself looking for her. People here think I'm nuts, the way I stare them in the face."

"What about the man from the antique store? Could the man in the yard have been the same man that you handed the package to?"

Valerie thought about it before answering. "Yes, someone had asked me that before. And I'm sorry, but I really can't say. It happened so fast, that day at the antique store. I barely had a chance to look at him." She finished with, "Should I be afraid? What was in the package?" Then added, "I'm now assuming this is about the package. I think since I was the one who carried it, I should know what was in it."

The detective let out a sigh and leaned against the doorframe. He pinched his nose at the corner of his eyes, indicating frustration or maybe a headache. He straightened his posture, his height once again glaringly evident. "If I tell you, I'd have to ask you to please keep it to yourself. Can you do that for me, Miss Russo?"

Valerie didn't smile, despite the fact this probably meant she was no longer a suspect and she really, really wanted to smile. With checked demeanour, she responded.

"Of course I can do that. Like I said, I'm new here. I don't know anyone, so I don't really have anyone to tell. Um–not that I would, of course, even if I did know anyone." She kept her tone serious.

It was the first time she had seen him smile, although she wasn't exactly sure if it wasn't more a grimace than a smile. Maybe he did have a headache. He was opening up to her. Did this mean they were now on the same side?

"We believe the packages are full of drugs. Local busts have been revealing MDMA. Ecstasy. This has become all too typical. Smuggled drugs can now show up anywhere. People order product, and these are drop-off points. Despite our best efforts, we have developed a serious drug problem in the Township area, and it's not just here. Our guys just found over 100,000 pills in Princeton this month. Frankly, we are surprised it got here this quickly. These guys keep looking for more out-of-the-way locations. It's a good way for them to avoid detection." He had resumed his stoic stance.

The distress showed on Valerie's face. "So you thought I was a pusher. It makes sense now, the questions. I don't like drugs, they make me nervous." She rubbed her clammy palms up and down her thighs.

"The good thing is that they haven't avoided our detection. We know they are here and we've had cameras set up for some time now. If this guy is who we think he is, we know him and it's only a matter of time before we find him. There's a serious problem with cocaine coming in and ecstasy going out. Hopefully we can shut them down before this thing gets out of hand." He turned and put his hand on the doorknob, turned towards her again and cleared his throat. "Don't go too far. We will be in touch when we need to talk to you again. And thanks for the call." His tone was astringent, his eyes steely.

As he was reaching his car, Valerie hollered after him, "Let me guess. You are just showing me your humorous side, right?" He didn't respond. Perhaps he hadn't heard her. This guy was rigid beyond belief.

Valerie stepped out to the front walk and watched as he drove away. Although it was a balmy afternoon, she crossed her arms across her body and shivered. She was concerned at the news that she had handled a package full of drugs. She really didn't like drugs as they had destroyed people she loved, and could very likely have destroyed her as well. Throughout the evening she felt no less troubled. She retired early and took her book to bed with her. Before climbing the stairs, she turned the radio on softly, again planning to leave it playing all night, making downstairs feel more alive. She also found comfort in knowing Hank would bark if anyone came near the house.

She slept in fits and starts. Again, dreams plagued her. Alice and her mother stood over her. Was she lying on the ground? It was raining. Suddenly Alice was screaming. There was something behind her. She rolled over to look, and it was Etna, erupting. A huge lava flow was headed towards them. She woke up and was not able to fall back asleep. Fortunately it was already five in the morning.

After lying for a spell and listening to the sounds out her window, Valerie pulled herself out of bed feeling very tired. Her energy slowly returned with her morning coffee and a smiling Hank, awaiting his routine. It seemed funny how the same routine of feeding Hank, then walking, was almost soothing. She and Hank moved rhythmically through their motions as though they'd done it forever. She only wished the dreams would stop. Why these constant images of Alice and Julian?

She ran upstairs to dress, welcoming this morning's walk. The sun was shining and the only sound was that of the birds. Snapping the lead on to Hank, Valerie heard footsteps on the porch followed by a knock at the door. "Now what," she lamented.

When Valerie answered, she was surprised to see Garret standing there, a small speckled dog sitting at his feet, wagging its tail.

Garret was grinning from ear to ear. "I haven't seen you in a while. I wanted to make sure you were okay. Hey, would you and Hank like to come for a walk with me and Sadie?"

Valerie smiled. "Is this your dog?"

"Yes and no. She's actually our shop dog. We take turns looking after her. It might sound like chaos, but she actually loves her three homes."

She bent down to pat the little dog. Hank was rubbing his nose against Garret's leg; a very friendly Garret, she was quick to note. This was a welcome contrast from the stuck-up detective that she had met yesterday.

"I got your message about the notice. It's a great idea. If you can write something out for me I'd be happy to post it."

"I'd appreciate it. You do seem to have a lot of people coming and going. I thought I'd ask at the coffee shop as well."

"Sounds like a good plan. Maybe we'll get to keep you here a bit longer after all."

Valerie blushed. "I'd love to walk with you. We were heading out anyway." Slipping on her runners, she closed the door behind her.

As they walked towards the river, Garret immediately fell into casual conversation about his bike shop and the latest news from the folks at the coffee shop. It didn't take more than a few minutes before Valerie realized she was quite attracted to him, although she still wasn't sure this was a good thing. She had long ago learned not to trust, not to like too quickly and not to let her guard down.

A man across the street hollered a greeting, and Garret suddenly handed Sadie's lead to Valerie. "I'm sorry, I'll be right back."

Valerie took a few steps forward as she watched the two men interact with one another. Garret wasn't a big man, and the other loomed above him. Yet Garret was the one who stood out. He was animated, laughing and gesturing, the other smiling and nodding in response. He occasionally swept his hand across his eyes, brushing the hair from his face, as it was breezy. She remembered what Hamid had said about him. He did seem a bit cocky, but she wasn't sure this was a bad thing. The men ended their brief discussion with a handshake and Garret returned to where Valerie stood. As they walked on, she at last mentioned the previous day's visit from the detective.

"That man came again." She then remembered her promise to the detective that she wouldn't talk about the package to anyone, so she changed the direction of her comment. "And he's not a very friendly one at that. He seems to not like me, or not trust me, or something. I'm not sure what his problem is, but something about him just rubs me the wrong way."

Garret looked at her, winked, then tapped the side of his nose. "Let me guess. His name was Detective Tobin."

She looked up at him, her mouth breaking into a smile. "How did you know that?"

But even as she was asking, Valerie suddenly realized why she thought she had known the detective the first day he showed up. He looked very much like Garret.

"I thought he looked familiar." She ventured a guess. "Are you two related?"

Garret laughed. "He's my brother. We don't see a lot of each other. Haven't had more than the occasional conversation for many years." He cleared his throat. "Now it's my turn to say that it's a long story. But he *is* my brother."

"I'm stupefied, Garret! Okay, well, he may be your brother but he's not like you at all. He's rude and abrupt and he never smiles." She paused as Hank slowed, having taken a particular interest in a dandelion. He was gently prodding it with his paw. She added cautiously, her eyes still on the dog, "Sorry to say that about your brother. Did you know he thinks there might be a drug problem here in Fort Langley?"

"He's exaggerating. It's his job to make sure there's a problem, otherwise he'd be out of work."

"Do you think there's a problem here?"

"If there was, I'd know about it. I think I'm pretty central to what goes on. I've told him before that everything here is fine. He just doesn't want to hear it."

Garret took his phone from his pocket and looked at it. Smiling at Valerie, he said, "Hey, I'm sorry, I need to shorten this walk. Duty calls. Come on, I'll walk you back."

They took a different route along a small side street, where Garret pointed to a clearing with a gravel drive leading to a large lot.

"Look at that. They took down some of our redwoods, which is a damn shame. Those trees are historic, man. Just to build two big houses in there. I think we will see a lot more of that in the coming years."

Once back at the Carter house, Valerie thanked him for the walk. She bent down to pat Sadie. It was abundantly clear the conversation about his brother was over.

"Would you like to ride with me some day?" Garret looked serious.

Valerie laughed and shook her head in refusal. "You mean ride, as on a bike? I'm really not a rider, Garret. I haven't ridden since I was a kid. I'd probably kill myself."

"Come on chicken shit, we'll take it slow. There are a lot of flat stretches of road around here. There's a ride just down along River Road to a place called Glen Valley. It's a nice ride, beautiful farmland. We just need to get you on a bike and see what happens. Think about it and I'll be in touch. See you." He gave her a two-fingered salute and walked away, calling out to Sadie. "Come on, girl. Chop-chop!"

Finding herself back at the house so early, Valerie wasn't ready to go inside. She opened the door for Hank and locked it again. He started barking as she walked away, smiling at his neediness. She spent the next two hours exploring, clearing her head. She felt better although she still couldn't shake the feeling of being watched. And although she tried hard not to, she still found herself searching every young female face in hopes of recognizing the girl from the porch. Occasionally she looked away in embarrassment as some of the females caught her looking at them for a bit too long.

11

Valerie had left the house early with Hank in tow, but once he had finished his morning business, she had taken him home. He had been in a mood and was moving too slowly for her. She knew he loved the route along the main street past the grand yellow community hall, but today she would enjoy walking it without the repeated pee stops. She listened to the sounds around her and observed the interactions of the people on the street. Summer was passing too quickly, and she could already see the change in the length of the shadows.

Glover Road was lined with stately old horse chestnut trees, which was a sheer delight for dogs. These magnificent trees dated back to 1921 and had been planted, oddly, by the village's first physician. They were now tremendous in size, and Valerie lingered to have a better look. The trunks were gnarled and twisted strangely out of shape with age, giving them a fairy tale appearance. The shade that the canopies offered was very welcoming on sunny days, although it was still early and the sun had just appeared from behind a light cloud covering the morning sky.

She heard him before she saw him. There was an old man with a guitar on the street corner. Standing with a small amp beside him, he was playing "While My Guitar Gently Weeps." Valerie found herself thinking of her family. The music faded into the distance as she reached the 1920s railroad museum. She carried on walking along the path to the railway platform, where she stopped to admire the peonies in the heritage garden. She had read that these bushes were descendants of those originally planted by the wife of the first stationmaster. Her father had loved peonies and would have really enjoyed seeing these. She had no explanation as to why she had not reached out to her family. She didn't know what to tell them, she supposed. She'd better get that straightened out in her head before they sent out a search party.

The smell of fresh bread wafted in her direction, tantalizing her taste buds. Tempted, she headed in that direction. She knew exactly where it was coming from, and today she wanted pastry.

Carrying her goods, she purposely took her time walking back to the house. The paper bag rustled in rhythm with each step. Again, the quiet of the morning was interrupted, this time by loud voices behind her. Then the whoosh as two cyclists came by her, fast. One shouted, "On your left," but it was almost moot, as they had already brushed past her. Valerie slowed down even more.

The bicycles were a reminder of why she was not in a hurry to get back home. Undeterred by Valerie's objection to riding, Garret had appeared at her door last week, insisting she ride with him. This was the day, and noon was the time.

"We'll drive to Murrayville. It's not far from here. We'll park in a small shopping centre and cycle from there. The ride is along one straight country road. It will be easy, Valerie. Just some gentle rises in the road, no real hills and very little traffic. The road will take us to Zero Avenue. There's a fabulous winery there and I thought we could grab a bit of lunch at the outdoor eating area there."

Although still reluctant to get on a bike, she didn't mind the idea of spending some time with Garret, so she had unenthusiastically said yes. Yet she did, in fact, say yes. Her curiosity regarding Garret was, as it turned out, greater than her misgivings about riding. And the idea of lunch at a winery sounded most appealing. Now walking up the driveway, she saw that Garret had already arrived and was waiting for her.

She smiled, her anxiety replaced with a sense of calm upon seeing him standing there grinning his grin. "You wasted no time in getting here. Do you live far away?"

"Just a short distance from here, in a small community called Walnut Grove. It's literally just up the road. You had me worried. I knocked, but just heard the dog."

"You are a bit early. I just have to take him out for another pee," she called over her shoulder. At the sound of her voice, Hank began barking. "I'm coming, master," she wisecracked.

Before long, Hank was settled, and they were on the road. Valerie loved this stretch of Glover Road and on towards the small airport. True to his word, it was only a short drive to Murrayville, where they were to start the ride. It seemed that Garret had thought it out wisely, knowing she wouldn't be able to cycle a great distance. After an awkward reintroduction to mounting a bicycle, they were on their way. The country road was splendid, and Valerie was pleased with how she managed to stay upright and steer in a relatively straight line. Following Garret, they encountered only a few slow-moving cars; otherwise, the ride was peaceful. The sights, smells and sounds reminded her of childhood–freshly cut grass, cow manure, meadows in bloom, farm vehicles tending to crops–it was all so beautiful. She felt like she was in a different country.

She was snapped from her reverie when Garret stopped his bike and announced they had reached their destination. He pointed further down the road.

"Zero Avenue is at the end of this road," he explained. "It's the first street on the Canadian side of the US border and runs parallel to the actual border, although you can't see anything through the bushes. It sits on the forty-ninth parallel, I believe. We are now in an area close to Campbell Valley. This is a good place to start, as this winery is new to the area."

"I can't believe how quickly we got here. You were right, it was a good ride," she chuckled proudly as Garret pointed left and headed towards the entrance.

Only a small sign was visible from the road, but as they approached she could see the building and the modest grounds. Beyond the building, she could see the vineyards. Garret directed her to the side of the parking lot, where he dismounted. Valerie was only too glad to be getting off the bike. She hadn't noticed that her bum was sore and her legs wobbly. She hoped the ride home wouldn't be too difficult. Garret locked the bikes to an old wooden fence at the end of the lot as Valerie removed her helmet. They left their gear on the bikes and walked over to the counter to order lunch. While they stood waiting for their order, Garret shifted his weight onto the left leg and then shifted to the right in a footloose manner. Valerie had noticed that Brian had stood with both legs firmly planted, his body balanced to the center. No shifting involved. Garret seemed unpredictable; his brother tense and restrained.

Taking their food, they moved to one of the picnic tables near the vineyard. There were only a few patrons lunching aside from themselves. The setting was beautiful, and Valerie was glad she had come. She appreciated the shade offered by the generous umbrella.

"The owners just recently opened this place, and it's now the third in the area." The conversation was light, and she was grateful that Garret didn't pry and ask too many personal questions. He chatted a bit about the Carters and their sailing expedition. Valerie didn't have much to add. Then unexpectedly, Garret asked Valerie, "Has there been any development in the mystery of the girl with the package or the man in front of the antique store?"

Unprepared for this question, Valerie replied, "Uh, no. I haven't heard from the detective since. I mean, your brother." She still felt she should keep her word and not disclose anything. She had promised, and that meant something to her. Brother or no brother, if Detective Tobin had wanted Garret to know, she figured he would have told him.

Valerie looked up and observed two young men standing next to their bikes. "Is that guy doing something with your bike? Look, Garret."

Garret stood up, shading his eyes with his hand. He started walking towards the bikes, saying, "What the" Then he stopped and said, "No, look. He's gone. Looks like he just dropped something. It's okay, Valerie. The bikes are locked, and I was sure to put them within eyesight. Besides, I didn't bring my good bike." He winked at her.

As they turned back to their lunch, Valerie couldn't help delving further into his brother. "Speaking of the detective–your brother-what is it with you two? You never talk about him. Are you not close? Is there a big difference in age?

"Well what do *you* think the difference is? Brian's a hotshot detective and I fix bikes. Anyway, it's too long a story to go into right now. We grew apart years ago. Different interests, you know? Plus there's a big age gap. I guess he was more driven than I was. Being older, he was pushed. I was younger and was spoiled to some degree."

"So what is his story?" I can't help it, I'm curious. You two are so different."

"He's in a better place now than he was before. I think he's trying to get his life back together. His wife left him because he got messed up. Something like PTSD."

"What happened to screw him up so badly?" she asked.

"Well, okay. I'll tell you. Have you heard of the pig farm murders?"

Valerie shook her head, a curious expression on her face. "I'm not sure but it kind of sounds familiar. I haven't lived here long."

"You would have heard of it. It started back around 1997 and they just sentenced the guy last year. This pig farmer guy was driving to Vancouver to pick up women. Many were drug addicted sex trade workers, but never mind that. He was picking them up and bringing them back to his farm in Port Coquitlam, just across the river from where you live. He used to have some type of charity parties there until he was shut down. But that was likely just an excuse to bring them out there. He was having fun with the girls, but he was also slaughtering them, Val. He might have killed fifty of them, they estimated. But he didn't get caught for something like five years. By the time they got him, there were body parts buried all over the place."

Valerie suddenly wasn't very hungry. "Those poor women! Why?"

"I guess he thought he was doing the world a favour, I don't know. There had been reports of these women running and screaming, trying to get away, but the cops had no proof. Nor did they have any real evidence to nail the guy. They finally got him, but then the cleanup and court case also took years. Brian had worked with the Special Investigations Unit, along with the forensics team, so he was up close and personal. His unit had worked on scene at the farm for months on end, and it was really hard on him. The poor bastard didn't expect to be one of the guys doing the digging. They were uncovering things that nobody should have been subjected to. They were finding bits of faces, and ears and things. I think the time working on the pig farm really messed with Brian's head. This asshole was a serial killer, and he was getting away with it."

Valerie pushed her plate away. "Nobody deserves that," she cried.

Garret shrugged. "When it was all over, Brian needed to get away and do something else. It changed him, as well as other cops who were working there. Personally, I think he snapped. The papers didn't let go of the story for a long time. They said the whole thing was sloppy. Heads rolled, police were scrutinized for conducting such a shoddy investigation. The guys involved took a lot of shit. Some of the crime scene cops who worked there committed suicide, I heard."

"But surely someone cared more about the girls than to waste time chastising the people involved with trying to solve the case." Valerie was mortified. She thought of a young woman from her past.

Garret looked at the sun. "Yeah, well that was then. No point in looking back on it. The damage has been done." He checked his watch. "We'd better move, girl. It's getting late."

The ride back was quiet but tough. She had enjoyed the ride here, but it felt longer going back, and her legs were burning. By the time they had returned to the car, she groaned in relief.

"I could cry I'm so sore." She fell stiffly into the passenger seat, relieved to be off her feet. She closed her eyes while Garret loaded up the bicycles. She doubted she could ever come to love this activity. She preferred both feet on the ground, thank you very much. Driving back to Fort Langley, her head was swirling with the pig farm story she had just heard.

12

It took Valerie only a few days to get over the stiffness from the bike ride. All that was left was the pleasant memory of cycling along the country road. The days were passing by, and Valerie realized that things were going well. She wasn't certain at exactly what point in time everything had changed, but it just seemed to happen. One day she woke up, and life was good. All misgivings lay behind her. Demons safely tucked away. Thoughts of Julian no longer sent her into panic. Most on her mind these days was her furry companion, who now lay sleeping on the carpet, his hind leg kicking as he snored. Valerie had accepted the fact that her roommate was a boy named Hank, and what amazed her more was the number of conversations they had. Although to be fair, they were pathetically one-sided, except for the occasional bark or grunt. The irony was that when she had arrived, she thought the Carters were idiots for talking to Hank as if he were human. She was now the proverbial pot who had called the kettle black.

Valerie had been worried there wouldn't be enough for her to do, given what she was accustomed to, but to her credit, she worked hard here, cleaning, sorting, gardening and, of course, looking after Hank. Most recently she had been spending time digging through a box of recipes she had found in the pantry and often kept herself busy trying new recipes, having never been much of a cook. But this! What a treasure trove. For example, salmon! Who would have thought there were so many things to do with a piece of fish? Today she was trying lemon garlic salmon with potatoes, olive oil and fresh herbs, all roasted together on a cookie sheet.

The next few days would be busy as she watched the town ready itself for the festival, and the day was rapidly approaching. She had already decided she would go into town alone and leave Hank behind. She wanted the luxury of browsing and perusing all the artisan's wares, and she wanted to dig into the food without having a drooling dog staring at her. Her first stop would be to sample some local cheeses she had been hearing about.

She awoke before dawn and was having coffee by the time it was light. Although it was early, she could already hear the sounds coming from town. She pinned up her hair and quickly added some blush. Grabbing her blue sweater and her sunglasses, she cheerfully left the house. Valerie walked down the hill, excited about the chance to explore the long-awaited festival. She could hear music coming from below, from one of the many buskers who were expected at various locations throughout the festival. She was so excited she found herself running.

By the time she arrived, the festival was in full swing. This was the third year that the festival had been held, the purpose being to celebrate local cranberry farming.

The paper said that after Fort Langley had been established by the Hudson Bay Company, here on the banks of the Fraser River, it had become an important trading post. Since the 1850s, cranberries were traded with the natives and packed into barrels and then shipped to San Francisco for sale. Cranberries grown in the Fraser Valley and Vancouver Island made up a good portion of the North American crop.

Valerie smiled more than she had smiled in a long time. This little town had come alive with food vendors, live music, and crowds of people walking past the tables and tents that had been set up by artisans, and they were selling everything imaginable. Fort Langley being a small village meant that every street was jam-packed with musicians, food carts, and crowds of shoppers. She marvelled at people's creativity as she checked out some tiny birds carved out of wood, and some very unique pottery. She grinned appreciatively at the canned goods, the soaps, scarves and funky retro clothing. She hadn't even found the cranberries yet! But even in her excitement she kept a wary eye out for the girl and for the man from the yard. Although unlikely, they could be lurking around here somewhere, avoiding detection while making contacts.

Up ahead she spotted the British man Gordon, and tried to make her way to where he stood. Just then, she heard someone call her name and turning, she spotted a smiling Karen walking towards her. Valerie hadn't seen her since having dinner at their home. Feeling embarrassed for letting so much time go by without contact, she was relieved when Karen began chatting, no hint of having felt ignored.

"I was hoping I'd run into you here." Karen smiled. "I tried calling but no answer. I'm sorry I haven't called in such a long time. Busy, you know?" She hugged Valerie. "I've been to Langley on errands and had almost forgotten about today's festival. I wanted to see you, but would have come anyway, as I had a few hours to myself this morning."

They walked along for a short time, Valerie stopped occasionally to purchase some pickled beans, a hair tie and some homemade soap. Karen, who seemed on edge, was saying very little. Valerie had suddenly lost her momentum, feeling tension from Karen. She anxiously kept her eye out for Gordon, as she had now lost sight of him. He was another person she had been neglecting and she badly hoped she could find him. Karen eventually lost interest in the booths and suggested lunch at the pub by the river. Valerie agreed, so they turned and walked back towards the water.

The pub was located inside a very rustic, old building, set away from the town. Valerie had seen it many times but had never been inside. She went past it regularly on her walks to the river with Hank, and although it was very close to the shore, Valerie found it strange that the patio was on the front and didn't overlook the water. The lineup was short, much to their surprise, and they stood in relative silence waiting for their table. Again, Valerie turned around and scoped the area for a glimpse of Gordon.

Upon entering the building, the first thing she noticed was the darkness of the interior. While the pub was very old, she had expected the inside to be–how to say it–refreshed. The antiquated wooden floors looked drab and worn, as did the big wooden beams overhead. The same went for the tables, seemingly made of the same worn wood, amalgamating everything into one big piece of wood. The music as well seemed dark – and loud. It reminded her of an old cowboy saloon. This was obviously the look they were going for, as it was representative of the time period in history.

Valerie ordered soup and a white wine, while Karen opted for a sandwich and a beer. After a few sips of alcohol, Valerie had begun to relax, and it seemed as though Karen had as well. They were soon settled into a somewhat awkward conversation, as the music was loud and comprehension difficult. When their meal was finished, they ordered a second drink. Valerie heard John Mayer in the background singing "Waiting for the World to Change", and started to tap her foot, glad to hear the music somewhat toned down. With the quieter music, Karen also seemed more relaxed.

"Mom and Dad called again. They are in Hawai'i and are doing well. They asked about you. They didn't want to call you and make it sound like they were checking up on you. I told them we had been together and that I'd see you again today. I assured them that all was good."

"Great, thanks for that," answered Valerie, trying to sound enthusiastic. But something seemed off, and their conversation seemed strained compared to the last time they were together. Valerie was almost regretting running into her, as she feared she had now missed Gordon. She would go to his house later this week. She looked over at Karen and smiled, not wanting to appear distracted. Fortunately, the waiter came with the bill. Valerie watched as Karen stood from her chair and reached into her purse.

"Let me get this. I insist. You go outside and wait for me, it's too loud in here," she said. Valerie thanked her and gratefully walked out into the bright outdoors. Karen came out a minute later, just a few steps behind her. She walked out the door smiling and lifted her hand to retrieve her sunglasses from the top of her head. Valerie noticed for the first time how tired Karen looked. Although young, she seemed more like a middle-aged woman. Tiny creases were beginning to form on her forehead, and she seemed unconcerned with her appearance or her hair. Even since Valerie had first met her, she seemed to have put on some extra weight around her hips.

"I went by the house first. Have you been working too hard? The yard looks better now than it ever did. Take a break, Valerie." The women began slowly walking back towards the crowd. Karen suddenly touched her hand. "I mean it. Take a break. Come with me to the island. I'm taking Danesh to Nanaimo, on Vancouver Island for a summer hockey camp. They have an event the day we arrive, so I am only dropping him off. After the picnic, he will stay with friends for the week. It's the second year that he's attending this camp, and he's very excited. You can come with me so I won't have to come back alone, and Hamid will go pick him up next week."

Valerie looked at her in surprise. "I have never been to the Island."

"Seriously? Then you *have* to come. I have already asked Hamid if he could pop by the house later in the day to walk Hank, if that's okay with you. He has a few things to do in the shed that he had promised Dad he would do before they got back." Karen's spark seemed to be coming back. "I could use some girl time, Valerie."

Valerie thought it might be a good opportunity to do some digging into Karen's mom and dad. Did they know anything about carrying packages or about the man in the backyard? She now wondered what exactly Hamid would be doing in the garage, but then she stopped herself. She was letting her imagination run wild, and that wasn't good.

"Okay, I'll go with you. Just tell me what day."

13

Karen drove to the ferry terminal, the three of them laughing and talking and listening to the radio all the way. They arrived in good time, bought their tickets, and queued near the front of the line. Valerie watched as the massive ferry approached the terminal, glad that she had agreed to come. It had been a while since she had seen such activity; loudspeaker announcements, vehicles offloading, and people rushing back to their cars in preparation to board. Once the ferry was empty, they were waved on, and Karen followed the cars as they slowly made their way up the ramp. After they parked and walked up the stairs to the passenger decks, Danesh grabbed Valerie's hand.

"Come on, let's go outside. There's a whole deck up top." Together they ran up the stairs. Once on the top deck, they moved to the back of the ferry and watched the rest of the cars file on. She couldn't believe how many vehicles kept loading on to the ferry. The line seemed endless. Valerie watched as everything from huge transport trucks to pickups hauling boats boarded the lower deck. A multitude of passenger vehicles began boarding the upper deck. She even noticed cyclists walking their bicycles aboard.

Finally the last vehicle was loaded, and the ramp slowly moved away. Hamish ushered her inside before the ship's whistle sounded, which would indicate departure.

"It's a good idea to go inside now. The whistle is very loud, Valerie. Dad says it's best to cover your ears," he said, as he put his hands up to his. Valerie smiled and did the same. Once the vessel had pulled away from the terminal, Danesh escorted her back down to the passenger deck and together they found Karen, who was holding seats for them near the front.

"We are headed to Duke Point, which is very close to Nanaimo," Karen announced. She proceeded to give Valerie a brief history of the ferries. "This one is quite new. You'll find this interesting, Valerie, because it was actually built for the 2010 Winter Olympics. There are three main terminals. Two do the routes to Nanaimo and one goes to Victoria. We had a fiasco some years back, with the so-called fast ferries. They ended up costing about five hundred million dollars, which was way above budget, and were three years late being delivered. And then it turned out they used far too much fuel and had repeated breakdowns, meaning ongoing cancellations. There were other problems as well. Not enough outdoor space, the wake was too big when they were coming into port... but never mind. This new ferry works well for us."

Karen seemed more like her old self, so Valerie wasn't sure what was going on that day at the festival. Karen insisted that Valerie take the seat by the window, saying she had seen it all before. Danesh took out his Game Boy and busied himself right away. He, too, seemed to have seen it all before. Sitting quietly by the window watching the water, Valerie started to get a funny feeling. As she was occasionally affected by premonitions–sixth sense or whatever-she tended not to ignore them. This feeling was often a sickening silence in the pit of her stomach, but this one was just a nagging feeling that someone was behind her. Stretching her arm across the back of Danesh's seat, she turned her body around slightly to have a look. There, a few rows behind her, sat the young woman who had asked her to carry the package. She was alone and seemed preoccupied with something in her lap.

Valerie's heart started to pound. What were the odds of this happening? She excused herself as she brushed over Danesh and out into the aisle. She then, surreptitiously, approached the girl. Her covertness was a waste of time, as sensing someone nearby, the girl looked up and stared right at her. Recognizing Valerie, she seemed to become panic-stricken. She stood from her seat and tried to move quickly away. Valerie grabbed her by the wrist and forcibly steered her down the aisle, grateful that the couple seated behind were engrossed in their books and didn't notice. Spotting a rest room sign, Valerie directed the girl through the doors.

Staring directly into her face, Valerie saw that the girl was much younger than she first thought. She stood and stared back insolently, her lips taking on a sneer. She was taller, which Valerie found a bit intimidating. Nonetheless, she held her grip and spoke quickly.

"Who are you? Why did you do that to me?" She didn't try to hide her anger. She straightened her shoulders and spoke again. "Say something, dammit. Do you realize the shit you got me into? I'm going to report you right now, to whoever is running this boat."

The girl suddenly softened her stance. "Please, I beg you, don't do that. They will hurt me. The reason I gave you the package is that I was afraid they would catch me there. I got sloppy last time and was seen, and I'm trying not to piss these guys off. If they don't need me they will get rid of me and see that I don't talk."

Valerie looked into the woman's bloodshot eyes. "Are you stoned right now?"

"The man who picked up the package, he's dangerous and he's hurt people," the woman answered, ignoring the question. She looked like she could handle herself, yet sadly in need of some kindness.

"Are you doing this to support your habit? That much is clear, but do you need help with that? Is there another reason? Please, you need to come to the police with me. I want to help you."

"Deportation. He'll have me deported, or worse," the woman told her, wiping her eyes. "I don't know how to get away. I have no other place to go. I've already been caught once, in Vancouver. I need the stuff and I need them."

"There are people that can help you," Valerie cried. But the woman's demeanor changed again, and she pushed Valerie hard.

"You're just trying to trick me. Go away and mind her own business." She landed a swift kick to Valerie's shin, causing her to release her grip on the woman and double over in pain.

Caught off guard, Valerie called out. "Who is the man? What's his name?" Before she could stand up, the woman had disappeared through the door, bumping into a group of girls on their way into the washroom. Valerie didn't follow her, realizing she was in no position to make a scene on the ferry. She washed her face and hands before walking back to her seat, where Karen was reading a magazine. Danesh had fallen asleep.

Karen looked up at her and smiled. "Did you have a nice walk? It's great, isn't it?"

"Yeah, just lovely," Valerie replied, half sarcastically.

"Come on," Karen said as she led the way to the outside deck. Valerie was impressed. She loved the exhilarating feel of the gusty wind and found the surroundings intoxicating. The land was slowly coming into view. She was looking forward to disembarking, yet she had been hoping for another chance to get a glimpse of the girl. But she never saw her again. Ideally she would have liked to stand at the exit and watch each person disembark, but she knew that couldn't happen. She felt defeated as they left the terminal.

Danesh was more than happy to say goodbye to his mother. As soon as they had arrived at the picnic area, he waved to some friends and disappeared into a crowd of boys having a water fight. Karen had handed his luggage over to one of the parents, and after a brief conversation, she and Valerie had left. Karen seemed just as happy to say goodbye to her son.

It had been a long day, and the ride home was uneventful. Karen had chatted about her parents in Hawai'i and about Hamid's restaurant, and Valerie realized it would be impossible to ask any specific questions about parcels and drugs. Even at the mention of the man at the back fence, Karen simply shrugged. "I really don't know anything about their neighbours or neighbourhood. I'm not there long enough to notice, and my parents never talk about that sort of thing. It's pretty much just biking, boating, Hank and the garden."

Having lost interest in the entire affair, Valerie didn't push. She was sick of the whole thing and because she lost sight of the woman, she was also frustrated. She pushed her head into the back of the seat and dozed off a few times. Off and on she would wake up and sigh irritably as her eyes scanned the passengers looking for that face. She had handled everything so badly, particularly after it had taken her so long to find her. That alone was nothing short of a miracle, to think she had found the woman here, on a ferry, of all places.

Returning to the mainland, Valerie couldn't wait to get home, wanting to call Detective Tobin as soon as possible. She was still reluctant to share anything with Karen and hoped she was doing an okay job of hiding her agitation. She dismissed it as fatigue.

Karen dropped her off and quickly left, citing a hungry family waiting at home. She made her call quickly and then took Hank for what was certainly a much-needed walk. Valerie's lips were pursed, and her head was down. Tramping along with some sort of urgency, she intently took stock of the situation. Again, she knew she would need to wait patiently for the detective to get back to her.

As she neared the town shops, she saw a long lineup of cars waiting for the Albion ferry. She had noticed this a few times at this time of day. The rush hours could be terrible with a three to four sailing wait, on a good day, but this looked like another ferry had broken down. Most of the locals hated the ferries and couldn't wait to be done with them. A bridge was being built just up the river and would be completed within the year, but for now, the town would have to put up with it for a bit longer.

That night, she had another dream. She was sitting in a small room. Everything was dark. She tried to speak, but she was choking for air. Suddenly, she heard ghost-like sounds from the other side of the wall, almost like a wheezing sob. She heard a knock, but when she stood up, she was standing outside. It was raining, and she was running. It felt like she was running for her life but not moving. People were standing on the sidewalk, staring at her disapprovingly. She looked away, feeling ashamed. She woke up with a pounding heart.

She lay there blinking away the darkness. The breeze was rustling the leaves on the trees. She turned onto her side and closed her eyes again. Her thoughts returned to her family and her reluctance to call, mostly because she would be afraid they would let Alice know where she was. She had no doubt that Alice wanted to know where she was, and she couldn't let that happen.

14

"Can I please have another look at the mug shots? I might recognize the face after having seen her again." The phone call from Detective Tobin had woken Valerie from an overlong sleep. She tried not to sound groggy. "She looked different and much younger than I first thought. I tried to talk to her. I think she might be in trouble with these people."

"You might have been smarter not to approach her. Now she knows that someone's on to her. Besides, she could have hurt you if she felt cornered."

"But she said someone is already on to her. Her people are angry with her because of something sloppy she did. It's why she gave the package to me. Besides, she seemed more frightened than aggressive. I want to help her and I wanted to tell her that."

"Why do you want to help her? I would have thought differently, considering what she's putting you through."

"I do have my reasons. It's a kind of atonement."

"Atonement? For what?" Brian's tone wavered, from what Valerie could assume, somewhere between curiosity and annoyance.

"Let's talk about it when I see you," she quickly answered, avoiding the question.

"Okay then. Mug shots today. Everything is still here. I will set it up and someone will call you later this morning."

"Thank you, I will be here." Valerie hung up the phone.

At the assigned time, Valerie arrived at the RCMP station in Murrayville. She entered the building and was escorted to the same room, where Betty Boring sat with her computer. The woman was typing but was looking at Valerie strangely from the corner of her eye, perhaps remembering her erratic behavior last time they had seen each other. Valerie offered a nod as a greeting, sat down and remained still. Betty Boring made no attempt to smile or say hello. Valerie didn't have the energy to try to be nice.

Detective Tobin arrived a few minutes later. All around good afternoons and pleasantries were exchanged, then they got down to business. Like before, the photos were placed in front of Valerie and she slowly and carefully studied each image. This time she easily identified the young woman. As before, she turned the photo over and signed the back.

Pleased, Betty Boring and the detective exchanged smiles, then the woman gathered all the paperwork and placed everything back into the box. She closed her computer and left the room without a word to Valerie.

Detective Tobin crossed the room. "Can you stay and have a coffee, and talk?"

"Yes, I can stay, but no coffee thank you. Maybe some water?" She then added, "I know your brother," a big grin on her face.

The detective handed her a glass of water then sat opposite her. He said nothing, aside from letting out a short deep sound, something like a grunt. Valerie was certain he had heard her but decided he was deliberately not answering, so she changed the subject.

"I am worried about that woman. I have a feeling that something bad might happen to her."

"And why would you feel that?" He rearranged himself in his chair.

"I get, like, these weird feelings in the pit of my stomach. Maybe more like an electric current that goes through my body. Maybe not even that. I don't know-it's kind of hard to describe. Other times, it's kind of a nauseous feeling."

Standing, she slowly walked across the room, her arms crossed in front of her. She then returned and sat down again, her hand on her forehead.

"Let me try to describe it. Imagine its summer and you are sitting outside–maybe on a porch, or on the lawn. Or you could be lying in bed with the window open. It's dark, the stars are out, but it's not quiet. There's this overpowering, all encompassing sound of crickets. The rhythmic chirping that hypnotizes you and possibly even soothes you. The sound can be deafening. And then all of a sudden, all of the crickets go quiet, just like that. And you hear the quiet. It's their defense mechanism, so they only go quiet if they feel danger. Possibly something predatory–or threatening-is nearby. So you might get out of your chair and look around, or you might even go indoors. If you are in bed, you might get up and look out the window, to see if anything, or anyone is out there. Now imagine the same scenario, but not in the comfort of your home. You are all alone in a dark field somewhere, and the only thing that makes you feel safe is the sound of the crickets. But then they stop, and all you hear is the quiet. That's what I feel. And I get almost sick. It's the feeling that something bad is out there, and I have nowhere to go. That's when it gets in my stomach, and I know. When I hear the quiet, I know something is wrong."

Valerie sat back, unmoving, waiting for a response. The detective was looking at her but was making no attempt to speak. But then he said, "So you are telling me you have some kind of gift or something?"

"Oh, is that what you are calling it? A gift?" She went on to explain, "You see, I was born in Sicily. Technically it's Italy, but we are actually from Sicily. There was this volcanic mountain that erupted a lot and my dad hated it."

"Etna?" Brian commented, intrigued.

"Yeah, Etna. He feared another Pompeii would happen. It was why he moved us to Montreal. He said he'd put up with it for long enough and he couldn't get far enough away. Anyway, my dad says I was affected by Etna's eruptions. He thinks it had something to do with the effects of the magnetic field on my brain, or something stupid like that." She rolled her eyes. "To me, it's just a keen sense of intuition or telepathy. So maybe it's a curse, not a gift," she replied flatly. "I once told my mom something about a neighbour, and it freaked her out when it turned out to be true. Then my own mom wouldn't hug me for fear I would read something from her."

"Can you actually do that?" he asked her, a look of incredulity on his face.

"Of course not, that's my whole point. I don't know where the hell they got that idea. My mom isn't the brightest. She actually said I wasn't hers, and that I must have been switched at birth. So I'm not exactly rushing to call this a gift."

He leaned back in his chair, trying to absorb what she had just told him. After a pause, he said, "I hate crickets."

Valerie was only half listening. She sat at the table, leaning forward, her elbow on the table, her chin resting on her hand as she swirled the water in her glass and mumbled, "Yeah, crickets are like cilantro. You either love it or you hate it."

"Did you just say cilantro?" The look on Brian's face suggested that she had just lost her mind.

"Yeah, you know." She looked at him as if this was common knowledge. "When people talk about cilantro, they either totally love it or can't stand it. It's genetic and so not a choice. You never hear anyone say, 'Oh, I guess it's okay, I can take it or leave it.' I think it's the same with crickets."

Feeling the conversation was wandering off track, he said to her, "Okay, so why did you move to Calgary?

"Is this even relevant?" She started to object, then acquiesced. "I needed to get away from Montreal.

There were things going on in my life, but my instincts let me down that time. In truth, I had wanted to move to Calgary for some time. I had applied for a job at the Calgary Stampede as their Events Manager. And I was so surprised when I was accepted. So I found a place to live and moved there almost right away. I loved the job, I really did."

"So why aren't you still there?"

Valerie realized how ridiculous she must sound. "Well, just about a year ago, I asked for a time out. They wouldn't let me, so I left. It was unclear if I would have the job when I returned."

"So you walked away from a dream job?" The detective seemed to be judging her.

She shifted in her chair, feeling under scrutiny. "Please don't judge me."

"Hey, I haven't said a word." His words came out in a softer tone. "But it must have been something very compelling to make you leave." He pulled his chair closer and leaned forward, his elbows resting on his knees. His fingers were clasped. His eyes stared deeply into hers with a profound intensity. Valerie sensed a reprimand or something was coming, as he sat in an authoritative, almost scolding fashion.

He spoke slowly. "You know, you might think you are strong because you are holding on to all of this, but I think letting go of it might make you stronger."

"I'm not turning this into a therapy session." She took a big drink of water. Valerie was struggling to talk to this man, but she wouldn't be led into having this conversation. Again, she changed the subject.

"Okay, your turn. Why does Garret have such an unusual name?"

The detective sat back and shrugged, seemingly unprepared for this shift in the conversation. He unclasped his hands and placed them behind his head. A huge exhale escaped his lips.

Valerie let out a triumphant HAH. "So okay, you think it should be easy for me to talk about my shit, but you won't talk about your brother? What you are asking me isn't even relevant to this case."

Surrendering, he began speaking. "I wasn't really prepared to talk about him or my family. But if it will make you happy, our grandparents were both Irish. Garret was named after his dad, who was also called Garret, and my granddad was Brian. So both of our names are Irish."

"What do you mean by Garret's dad?"

"His name is Garret Murphy. We are half brothers. Did he fail to mention that? We have the same mother, but different fathers. I wasn't yet five when my mom left my dad in Ireland and came to Canada. She remarried and had Garret a few years later. So we aren't exactly close. My name means strength. I guess my mom somehow knew I'd need it, as my life started out one way and suddenly everything changed. Dad tried hard to keep me strong–I was confused and he didn't want it to affect me. So he said I had the name of some Irish warrior king who drove the Vikings out of Ireland."

Valerie laughed. "My name also means brave and strong. But look at us, both presumed strong yet struggling." She quickly added, in a softer voice, "What I mean is, I'm struggling." She realized she shouldn't reveal what Garret had told her about Brian's past trauma. It wasn't his story to tell.

"It's a nice name," he told her.

"It's actually my second name. Valeria."

The detective cleared his throat. "So now that our friendly bonding session is over, tell me about this atonement."

Valerie was playing with a strand of hair, sitting back casually in the chair, her legs stretched out front and crossed at the ankles. "I met a girl once who I might have had a chance to help. She was using and I did nothing. I have seen what drugs can do to someone, and I understand that often the person can't see their own erosion. Anyway, we all know that addiction is a disease. The girl I met was so young and perhaps not yet hooked. Maybe she didn't have anyone to help her, but I might have been someone who could have helped her."

"What happened to her?" Brian questioned.

"I haven't a clue. I brushed her off, and I don't want to think of what might have happened. I only know that I did nothing to at least try. Try to turn her around, convince her to get help. I think maybe it was new to her. She didn't really look like a user. I remember her looking back at me as she walked away. Stoned and confused. Anyway, I had told myself if I ever encountered that girl again, I would do something. Of course I never saw her again, and that was a long time ago," said Valerie, explaining her train of thought, "but for me, this woman I saw on the ferry could be her. And I don't know why, but I feel guilty."

The detective was looking at her and she felt his reluctance to say anything. She opened her mouth, then thought against it. She too felt reluctant to say any more.

15

Garret was walking slowly towards the Carter house, unsure how he would approach Valerie. She had so far been receptive to him, but he had to be careful and not crowd her, that much he could sense. He found her intriguing, her past shrouded in mystery, and he was eager to find out more about her. Hopefully she was harmless, as long as she was who she said she was. After all, the Carters would not have hired just anybody to stay in their home and care for Hank, never mind leave their daughter and her family exposed to a stranger. But then, who was he to talk about being who they said they were?

He reached the front porch, but before he could knock, he heard Hank bark, followed by laughter. The sound was coming from the side of the house. He walked around, just in time to see a squirrel climb a tree, Hank fast on his heels. He whistled, and the dog stopped in his tracks, turned, and ran towards Garret. Valerie, who had been on her knees pulling weeds, turned around, a look of surprise on her face. Then she stood up and smiled.

"What are you doing here?" she asked.

"I haven't seen you around for quite a few days, just thought I'd say hi, see if there's anything new. I was walking by the house anyway."

"I've been away with Karen." Then she added, "I was on the ferry." She laughed. "I loved the ride to the island. They even had bicycles and I thought of you."

"That's almost funny, because I was going to ask you if you wanted to take a ferry ride with me, only in the other direction. I want to take you to Swartz Bay, through the Gulf Islands, and we can cycle the Galloping Goose."

"The what?"

"It's an old rail line that was converted into a biking and walking trail. It's pretty cool. And the ferry ride through the Gulf Islands is much more interesting than the straight ride into Duke Point."

"Oh Garret, you know I'm not much into biking. Why do you keep insisting? Isn't there anything else we could do instead? Could we walk this Goose?"

"Well no, because you will love the ride. Some sections of the route are along the coast, and much of it weaves through farmland and a few residential communities near Sidney-by-the-Sea. We only need to go as far as Cordova Bay, to the market, but it's too far to walk. We don't have to go all the way into Victoria."

"I don't know. I don't like to leave Hank for that long."

"It's just a day. And Marie at the shop can come and let him out. She's done it before, when the Carter's have been away for a day. She can bring Sadie with her. Come on, Val, people come from all over the place to experience the trail. It's one of Victoria's biggest tourist attractions."

Against her better judgment, she agreed to go. "Just there and back, then. I can't be gone long. For Hank."

The ferry ride was all that Garret had said it would be. It was almost poetic the way the huge lumbering ferry wove its way through the narrow passes, swaying back and forth between the small islands. It was a glorious day, and they spent the entire trip on the outer deck. Garret named each island as they passed. That's Galiano, and that one there is Mayne. Okay, we are just heading into what is called Active Pass. It's very narrow, and there's always the problem of riptides through here. There have been many accidents with boats because of all the traffic coming though, combined with the tides. These big ferries have to pass each other really close, while also looking out for other boats, like freighters, fishing boats, and lots of yahoos whipping around in their power boats like idiots. Like that guy right there." He pointed to a small Zodiac carrying four people. They were moving fast and laughing loudly.

Garrett took her to the other side of the ferry to see the islands to the south. He stood behind her, his hand on one of her shoulders while he pointed over her other shoulder.

"There's another island over there. You can't quite see it, but it's Saturna. This little one is Prevost. That one there is Pender. Let's go back to the other side again, Val. The last one you will see just up there." He pointed ahead.

"It's the great big one. That's Salt Spring. And further up ahead–see it Val? That's the ferry terminal."

The journey took just over an hour and a half, but it seemed to go by quickly. She was pleased that Garret was able to tell her about the islands. He was right when he said this route was more exciting than the one to Duke Point. When the announcement came for motorists to return to their vehicles, Garret led her down to the lower deck where they unlocked their bicycles and prepared to disembark.

They started the ride directly from the ferry terminal, exiting the parking lot and cycling down a road that passed a small marina. Soon they were following the signs that read *Lochside Trail*. The first two hills caught Valerie off guard, and she silently cursed Garret for saying it was an easy ride. But the road eventually leveled out, and everything was peaceful. She loved the little community of Sydney-by-the-Sea with the sparkling sun-kissed water and the winding pathways, ambling past the waterside bistros. They stopped at the waters edge for a drink and a snack.

"Look at that big white mountain across the water. Tell me that's not the same one I could see when driving to Abbotsford. Mount Baker. It's the volcano, right?"

Garret laughed. "Yup. That's Mount Baker. I call it the ghost mountain because it seems to pop up everywhere." He stood and put his helmet on. "Come on, we better be going. You are on a time limit, remember?"

They carried on, but before long Valerie began to struggle with the ride, and again she tried to remind

Garret that she really was not an athletic person. She shouted ahead to him, but he appeared to not hear her. While still following the Lochside Trail, they were now cycling on a main road, and cars were passing by quickly and too close for Valerie's liking. Garret's speed increased and she had difficulty catching up to him. After what seemed forever, they approached an intersection. Garret stopped to wait for her. A large cement truck passed Valerie very fast and too close, and Valerie braked a little too hard.

Coming over a big curb, Valerie wobbled; her front wheel turned ninety degrees, and she and the bike came crashing down, sideways and onto the roadway. Garret put his bike down and slowly moved towards her to pick her bike up from the street, inspecting it for damage. Valerie stood up quickly, coloured with embarrassment. She tried to take a step but instantly realized she had sprained her ankle. Rather than be sympathetic, Garret seemed short-tempered with her. He held the bike as she brushed herself off and assessed the damage. Her ankle was scraped and her shin displayed a fairly serious contusion, but she was not bleeding. The entire leg was really sore.

"Can we please go back and try this another time? I think you may have overestimated my ability." She felt she shouldn't need to be asking this, that he should have figured it out by himself. He seemed disappointed that she didn't love it as much as he wanted her to. He stood looking at her blankly, as if expecting something.

Valerie was trying to recover mentally. "How about this. You go on, Garret. I'll go back to that little town of Sidney and wait for you." His lack of empathy dumbfounded her. He seemed like a different person.

He looked at her, frowning. "You'll probably get killed on the way there," he sighed. Are you sure you can't keep going? You look okay."

Valerie glared at him but before she could say anything, Garret held his hands up in surrender. "Okay you win. We will go back."

They turned around at the end of the trail, Garret not hiding his anger. Valerie rode behind him in silence, as he stayed just far enough ahead of her to make conversation impossible. Once they had returned to the terminal, they waited by the gate to catch the next ferry back to Tsawwassen. Three other cyclists were waiting there as well, and Garret quickly started up a conversation with one of them about his fancy bike and expensive accessories. Valerie stood there feeling inadequate and stupid.

The ferry ride back was disastrous in every way. Aside from this premature return, the winds had picked up and the ride was treacherous. The two sat in their seats without much conversation. Only once did Garret ask her how her ankle was. He seemed more upset that they didn't make it to the market at Cordova Bay. He kept looking at his phone, sending and receiving text messages. "Trouble at the shop," he explained.

"So maybe it's a good thing we are going back if they need you at the shop," she said, trying to better the situation.

"It would have been a nice place for lunch," is all he would say.

The drive back to Fort Langley was awkward and Valerie wished there had been a different way for her to get home-a bus or something. Garret made an attempt at an apology but it sounded hollow, as if he still believed it was her fault. He reached over to hold her hand but she pulled away. He stepped on the gas and the car roared forward. It wasn't until they reached Fort Langley and parked at the back of Garret's bike shop that Valerie relaxed.

As they were exiting the car, Garret again became agitated. "Do you always get your own way? Is that how it is with you?"

Valerie didn't answer him, feeling it was he who wanted his own way. As Garret was offloading the bikes from the back of the car, she carried the helmets into the shop, dropped them on the counter then turned to leave.

He had followed her into the building. "Hang on a minute, I can drive you. If you just help me with this."

"I'd rather walk, but thank you anyway." She did her best to smile and appear calm. Garret seemed almost antagonistic as he tried to block her when she walked towards the door. He stood really close, causing Valerie to take a step back. She had felt it. It was small, but it was there. A jolt.

"Why do you always want to do things your way? I can see why you are alone. Have you ever even had a boyfriend? Then again, maybe I have that all wrong." He seemed too intense for her, very unfriendly. It was no longer clear what was wrong, but it put her on her defense and she has no intention of continuing this conversation or answering any questions. She pushed her way past him, feeling confused.

"I get it that you were angry about ending our ride, I do. And I'm sorry I fell and hurt myself, it was clearly a great inconvenience to you. But I don't know what's going on here right now, and why you are acting so nasty."

"Maybe I am, but seriously, what is your problem, anyway?" he said to her. "You are always on edge, like a deer caught in the headlights. And you never talk about yourself. What did you do? Kill someone?"

Valerie froze. Why would he say that, of all things? "Goodbye, Garret. It's late and we are both tired." She quickly left the shop and began walking home. She heard him calling after her.

"Goddamit, Val. Get back here." His voice had escalated to a shout.

The sky was darkening rapidly. Valerie was fuming as she tried her best to walk quickly. She was limping and her head was down, bracing against the pain. It occurred to her that she almost deserved what had happened. She never should have gone with him. Something about him put her on edge. She knew damn well what it was. It was Julian all over again. She would have to think hard and seriously about that. The streets were quiet this time of night. The quaint chestnut trees under the streetlights now looked dingy and menacing. Once she got away from the main street, she sensed that someone was walking behind her. She slowed to let them pass, but as her steps slowed, so did the steps behind her. She quickened her pace in agony, as her ankle had swelled. She became alarmed as the steps behind her also quickened pace. She wondered if it was Garret, but doubted it, as he was still unloading the bikes. Valerie's heart began beating faster.

By now she was almost running, afraid to turn around. She considered knocking on anyone's door but couldn't see lights in the windows of any of the houses on her route. She decided her best bet was to just get home as quickly as she could.

As she neared the intersection where she would need to cross, she quickly peered over her shoulder. It was definitely not Garret behind her. The figure looked smaller and older under the streetlight. Without warning, Valerie started to run. She ran for her life as she heard the footsteps behind her break into a run as well. She was limping badly and her foot was throbbing. She could see the house ahead, but by now she was out of breath and hoped she could get there in time.

Valerie ran up the driveway with the last of her strength. She neared the front steps. They stood before her like a beacon offering refuge. All she wanted to do was climb them and reach the door when unexpectedly she felt someone grabbing at her ankle. She screamed as a hand brushed her foot. Inside, Hank started to bark. She began kicking at the man as he tried to grab hold. Valerie didn't notice the car coming up the driveway behind them, but she heard the blast of the car horn. She gave one hard kick and felt contact with something. The figure backed off, and she scrambled up the last few steps to the door. Only when the key was in the lock did she chance turning around to look.

There was Garret, running towards the house from his vehicle. Between Valerie and Garret stood the man. Was it the same man from the backyard? She wished she could be certain. He was turned facing Garret, looking like a deer caught in the headlights.

"Valerie, I've called the cops," Garret shouted at her. "Get in the house."

The man tried to run but Garret was younger and bigger. "Stay where you are asshole, or I swear, I'll drop you."

Ignoring the warning, the man tried to run around the car, the engine still running, the headlights pointed right into the man's face, and the car door still open. But Garret was faster, and he grabbed the man and twisted his arm behind his back. The man wriggled sideways and kicked Garret in the shin. The grip was loosened and the man broke free. He ran down the street, Garret hot in pursuit.

Once the men were out of sight, she went back out to the car, shut the engine off and closed the car door. She didn't know what to do, so she went back inside and waited. She sat in the big chair, her arms wrapped around her knees, pressing them into her chest. She was trying to figure out exactly what had just happened. Was this a random attack by some creep or pervert, or was she targeted? Her heart was pounding, and she had a headache. Gently rocking back and forth, Valerie closed her eyes and pressed her forehead into her knees. Hank stood beside her, whimpering softly.

Garret returned nearly half an hour later. She heard footsteps on the porch, then a knock on the door. Hank raised his head and cocked his ears. But she remained seated and didn't move until she heard his voice. She stood up from the chair and moved quickly to the door.

"He got away."

"Garret, I…"

"Forget it," he said. "I just wanted to make sure you got home okay. Oh –m by the way, I ran into the cops, and I've left it with them. See you later, Val." He avoided eye contact as he turned and walked back to his car. Without looking back, he started the engine and drove away.

That night, Valerie woke up covered in sweat. Was someone in her room? She'd heard him, loud and clear. "What did you do, kill someone?" If it weren't for Hank, she would have turned on the lights and searched. She was grateful that he was keeping watch, stretched out in the doorway to her room.

16

Valerie sat with her foot up. Today would be the last day of icing. The swelling was nearly gone, and she was anxious to get moving again. Hank had been miserable with the shorter, slower walks around the neighbourhood. Valerie, as well, was missing their treks along the river.

"Soon, buddy," she said to her friend. He wagged his tail and barked. He walked over to her and rested his chin on her lap, his big eyes gazing up at her. She smiled warmly.

The real comfort came from knowing she was leaving and would no longer need to worry about seeing Garret or the man in the back, who had been peering at her. Detective Tobin had been unsuccessful in finding the identity of this Peeping Tom guy. Added to her uneasiness, she didn't know what to make of the jolt she had felt when standing close to Garret, but she had no desire to find out.

The Carters had called, saying they would be home by the end of the month. During their entire absence Valerie had only heard from them three times. To her, three times was plenty, as she now knew they kept tabs on things through their daughter without the need to speak directly with her. She was happy to hear that their voyage was a success. The conversation wasn't a long one, as expected. Denise did remind Valerie that Karen and Hamid would be by occasionally to prepare for their return. Valerie was relieved she had given up the notion of them somehow being involved in these past events. She had really let her imagination run away with her.

The weeks passed slowly, and Valerie's packing was almost finished. She had kept clear of the town and had focused on walking Hank on the trails. It broke her heart, as she knew she would miss this little community and the people she had met. The leaves were slowly changing, the flowers in the garden were spent and days were getting shorter. Walking home, the wind gusts were swirling the leaves around her feet, covering the sidewalk behind her as if she had never been there. The symbolism wasn't lost on her.

She had been neglecting Gordon, the old man, and so decided to take a walk past his house to say goodbye. Nearing his home, she saw a woman on the front lawn hammering a For Sale sign into the front garden. Horrified, she hurried to the spot and asked, "Is the man moving?"

"Already moved. The house has been empty for a few weeks now." The reply was curt.

"Where did he go?" The disappointment shone through in her voice.

"Sorry, I'm just here to put up the sign. You will need to speak to the agent or the family."

Disgusted with herself for having put off this visit, Valerie walked away feeling impotent. Everything seemed to point appropriately to her leaving.

Valerie needed to make one last trip to the grocery store to replace some things she had used up. Despite her better judgment, she felt it would only be right to stop in at the bike shop, one last time, to say goodbye. She has been thinking of Garret, feeling maybe she had been too hard on him. He could have been nervous? Or stressed? Or was she again making excuses for a bad fit?

But to her dismay, as she approached, she heard him before she saw him. Garret was having what she could only describe as a temper tantrum while speaking with someone just outside the bike shop. As Valerie looked closer, she gasped for air. Horror-struck, she looked closer as Garret continued his intense conversation with the man. It was the same man from the backyard, and the man who had chased her home. The same man, she was sure of it and now here, in a very heated and very personal conversation. Valerie quickly left the scene, her head spinning.

Valerie struggled with this revelation. That shit Garret had obviously known more than he let on. He was in on it the whole time! Should she tell Brian? She felt she had to call him. All this time they had been trying to identify this mystery man, and his own brother had been in on it. She took out her phone as she walked around the corner. She headed towards the grocery store and dialled the number while moving. The man who answered her call identified himself as Desk Sergeant Lee.

"Please, I need to speak with Detective Tobin."

"I'm not sure he's available. Who is this calling?"

"My name is Valerie Russo. He knows me, and it's important that I speak with him."

Sergeant Lee answered her calmly, "I'll see if I can get him for you." The line clicked as she was placed on hold. It seemed like she had been on hold forever, and she began to pace back and forth, not wanting to go into the store until she had finished with her call. Then another voice was on the line. "Whom are you holding for?"

"Detective Tobin," she said, her voice somewhat elevated.

"I'm sorry, he's not here. Who is calling please?"

"Valerie Russo. Can I leave him a message please?" She sighed with relief as she was patched over to his personal voicemail.

Valerie was in a trance as she did her shopping, only too anxious to get home. She walked the long way around town so as to avoid the area of the bike shop. Once home, she locked the doors, as if being pursued by something she couldn't see. She felt something churning in her stomach. She had no idea how long she would need to wait before Detective Tobin called her but she hoped it wouldn't be long.

During that final week, as she cleaned her way through the rooms in the house, her mind often wandered to Garret. Different things that had happened slowly began to make sense. Why had he been so upset when she couldn't finish the ride to the market at Cordova Bay? What had been so important about going there? And why had he appeared out of nowhere that night when she was followed home? Did he know the man would be following her? He said he had called 911, but why had she never heard from anyone? Surely they would have wanted to speak to her, to get her version of events. Maybe he didn't call them at all.

Suddenly other things came to mind. She thought back to the first time she met Garret. The very first thing he had mentioned was having seen her at the antique store, handing over the package. Why would that be the first important thing? Before even acknowledging it, he knew she was the new house-sitter for the Carter's. She had thought nothing of it at the time, but it now seemed odd. Was he involved, and had they picked her specifically to carry the package? And when they had cycled to the winery, she was certain she had seen someone tamper with Garret's bike pack. The person had either put something into it or taken something out. But Garret had waved it off, perhaps not expecting Valerie to notice what was going on. She also recalled the day she arrived home from a walk and Garret was at the house, having arrived early. Was he deliberately early? What did he do while there?

That led her to Detective Tobin. He had not been returning her calls, and that also made her curious. He was usually pretty good at getting back to her. Why the sudden change in habit? She found his silence disturbing.

Her desire to leave was now overwhelming. Although she would miss Hank, she no longer felt safe here. Anna had come through and was sending her to another house-sitting job, and she was looking forward to the change of scenery. She had taken this new position out of necessity, vowing it would be her last temporary job. Valerie well realized the need to get a real job and a home of her own, and soon.

Valerie spent the morning doing nothing, but now that her ankle was back to normal, she needed a long walk. Hank was almost crying with joy as she fastened his leash. After days of isolation it felt good to be out in the open. The air was crisp but the sun was warm. She had called and left another message for the detective, but still had not heard back. Again, it seemed very odd. It made her wonder if he already knew, and had always known.

They quickly made their way down to the water's edge. Valerie stumbled as she felt Hank tugging at the lead. He had suddenly become interested in a lady who sat on a bench overlooking the water. The lady looked up and smiled, and she extended her open palm towards the dog. Valerie smiled and approached the bench.

"Wow, Hank seems to like you."

"It's only because he smells the pastrami in my bag. I have a half-eaten sandwich." She put her head back and let out a warm chuckle. "What's his name?"

"Hank. He's not my dog, I'm just watching him."

"But look how much he loves you." She slid over a bit. "Would you like to sit down for a minute?"

"He loves me? Do you think so?" Valerie sat at the far end of the bench, turning to face the woman. Hank immediately lay down and rested his head on Valerie's foot, his eyes never leaving the beautiful stranger. Her mannerisms were elegant, her voice soft and velvety. She wore sunglasses and a big hat over her long blond hair. It was hard to tell her age, but she was clearly older than Valerie. She had a strong jaw line and smooth skin.

"Dogs are honest. They love with no agendas. If they don't love you, they won't pretend."

"But he likes you!"

She laughed again, her smile showing off her white teeth. "Yes, but only because I have pastrami. He's clear about that. There are no illusions."

She looked around and sighed. "It's beautiful here, isn't it? Look all around and you'll see we live a charmed life." Leaning over, she rubbed Hank's ear. "Don't we, Hank?" Her entire being radiated calm.

Valerie sighed. "If it were only true. It doesn't always feel charmed."

"Your accent–where does it come from?"

"It's French Italian, I suppose. I call it Frenglian. Born in Sicily, raised in Quebec, now speaking English." Valerie was losing enthusiasm for telling this story, which no longer seemed charming to her. Nothing charmed her right now.

"That's a cute description." She leaned back and rested her arm across the back of the bench. In the warmth of the afternoon, she looked cool in her pale green linen outfit. "I love Sicily, and I love their food."

Valerie agreed. "I love all good food. I've really been expanding my tastes, being here. But come to think of it, I can't remember the last time I've had some good Sicilian food."

"I don't come over here often, but when I do, I have a favourite place to eat. Do you ever go to White Rock? If you do, there's a little Sicilian restaurant, right at the end, on the hill on the waterfront. Go in and order the Parmigiana di Melanzane."

"Okay, thanks for the tip. I will go."

After a minute, the lady spoke again. "So this isn't your dog?" She casually bounced the foot of her crossed leg.

"I'm actually in between lives right now. In this one, I am house-sitting. I've been here for nearly six months, and Hank here is part of the package. I didn't think I'd still be re-inventing myself at this age."

"Listen, we can re-invent ourselves many times in our lives. It's not always bad. But what was wrong with the old you?"

"I don't even remember what she was like. I got talked out of being her a long time ago."

"Well, maybe you should find her again and just be who you are. Or who you were. Either way, you seem like someone who will bounce back and find your way. Something must have led you here."

"I moved here in the hopes of working for the 2010 Winter Olympics. I finally got my letter, so it looks like I'm in."

Hank looked at Valerie, surprising her with a loud bark.

"Oh, I'm sorry. I guess I'm interrupting his walk. But you see how he's lost interest in me? No pastrami, nothing to draw him to this lady." She smiled kindly.

Valerie smiled back. She loved the sound of the woman's smoky, silky voice. "It was really nice talking to you."

The woman smiled. "You're looking a little crestfallen, like you lost the battle. But hey, you've got a great new job to look forward to. I hope you can find your smile again. It's quite nice, what I've seen of it. Just remember–don't be anybody but yourself. And be careful not to look so hard for happiness when you are probably living it."

Valerie stood to leave. She smoothed her dress and smiled warmly. "Thank you, I'll consider that." As she walked away, that sultry voice called out behind her.

"Don't forget to go and eat Parmigiana di Melanzane. Oh – and tell them you want it the way Diana likes it! They'll do it for you."

Valerie waved and walked away. She was smiling for the first time in days.

17

Brian Tobin had decided to come home early. Having this much on his mind was affecting his ability to concentrate. His trip to Toronto had been exhausting and although he'd been back for over a week, he was still struggling with the effects of the time difference. He hated flying and the trip had not been a pleasant one.

The plane ride back to Vancouver had been hell. The couple behind him had argued for the entire trip. First it was Robert DeNiro's first movie. He said it was *Bloody Mama*, she said it was *Mean Streets*. Brian guessed they were likely both wrong. Then, the husband was trying to explain who Rupert Friend was. By the time the plane landed, Brian knew everything there was to know about Rupert Friend. Perhaps the couple should have spent more time getting to know each other. He now understood why people donned headphones and cranked tunes for the entire flight.

He had missed a lot while away. The first news he heard was that a vehicle had plunged off the government dock next to the Albion Ferry terminal in Fort Langley. Police were investigating, eager to find out what happened and how the vehicle ended up in the river. It was a tragic event for the small town. It appeared that one person had died. Brian's first response was to get assurance that neither Valerie nor his half brother had been involved, which was the only good news.

His meetings downtown had finished well ahead of schedule giving him a reason to not return to the office. Instead, he had retreated to the solitude of home and the familiar sounds around him. These past few months had been challenging in more ways than one. He parked his car and sat for a moment to catch his breath. The drive had been a long one, with a few traffic accidents hampering his progress.

It was early afternoon and he was famished, having missed lunch. He dropped his briefcase on the kitchen chair and headed straight to the fridge, where he retrieved the box of pizza and a beer. Heading outdoors to his small patio he savoured the rest of a pizza that had been in his fridge since yesterday. The cold beer helped to wash it down, and he sat back, content. But now it was time to get some more work done.

After putting his lone plate in the dishwasher, Brian grabbed his briefcase and slowly climbed up the staircase. The converted attic consisted of two rooms, the larger one being his bedroom. He crossed the sparsely furnished room to open the window. He had neglected to do so before leaving the house this morning, and the room felt stuffy. After changing his shirt and splashing some water on his face, he crossed the hall and entered his office.

Brian loved this room, with its sloped ceilings, pale blue walls, and hardwood floors. He would often escape here to enjoy the seclusion and to gaze at the view and get lost in his thoughts. At the long end of the rectangular room was a large window that offered a spectacular view of the ocean and of Semiahmoo Resort. The popular resort was situated on a small sandy spit near Blaine, Washington, in the US, and it offered him a glimpse of a lifestyle entirely different from his own.

He also came to this room to work. His concentration was often at a higher level up here where he felt lifted above much of the shit that went on in his world below. His desk, however, stood at the other end of the room, facing the wall. Another small window overlooking the street was situated just to the left of his desk, providing him with some natural light.

This was the view he preferred while working, as the ocean and beyond proved too much of a distraction when he faced that direction. Writing his reports required his full concentration, which is why he chose to write them at home and not at the office. Particularly on this day, and with this report, he wanted the time to think long and hard about what to write.

His files were spread out in front of him. His brain was almost in a fog from cognitive fatigue. He could feel the physical toll this had taken on him, and he was eager to close this case and bring an end to it. How much would he say? His recent findings were not insignificant. Would his actions here bring it all to a close? And what about Miss Russo? Did he feel pity for her, or was it something else? He did feel she became too involved, and maybe knew too much. She called him while he was away, but he didn't return the call-and for good reason. Or was it reason enough?

His silence about past events, he thought, was justified, but at some point these things would surface and he would need to be accountable, but just not yet. He wrote steadily and made certain he included every detail. But he·didn't write as much as he should have. His quandary had a tight hold over his better judgment.

At long last he closed the lid of his laptop. He stood stiffly and walked back to the small sofa that was situated facing the window. Not ready to go back downstairs, he sat down, stretching his legs out over the coffee table. He closed his eyes and waited for the din in his head to subside. The sun was gone, and the stars were appearing one by one. Only when the first bird began his morning song did he drift off to sleep.

But after only a few hours, the blast of a boat horn startled him awake. The sun was shining on his face. His mind was clear. So clear, in fact, that he stood up and with a yawn he returned to his desk. Sitting down, Brian opened his laptop and looked at the report he had written. With one quick click of the delete button, it was gone. He needed to start over again. This time he knew exactly what to say.

Four months later

18

The queasiness had subsided. Whatever Valerie had eaten the previous evening had kept her up all night. While grateful that her twenty-ninth birthday had come and gone, deliberately disregarded, she had quietly celebrated the occasion the following evening by indulging in a couple of extra glasses of wine and some weird food.

She had fallen asleep around three and awoken just after seven, suffering from a headache and a powerful thirst. By nine she felt better. She could hear the world waking up outside–car engines accelerating as the light turned green, horns honking, and children's laughter as they made their way to school. Like it or not, Valerie now found herself living in an area of young families compared to where she was staying in Fort Langley. The positive was that she felt safer.

She sat idly, curled up in the big leather easy chair while watching Barack Obama on the television. He had only months before become the forty-fourth president of the United States and was already hard at work, discussing his fight against the drug trade. He was speaking about an upcoming meeting with Felipe Calderón, president of Mexico. A meeting he hoped would help in their fight against the illegal drug trade, which was a growing epidemic. These cartels appeared unstoppable, and together, these two leaders needed to coordinate their efforts. It was a good sign, and she silently wished him well. She hated drugs and hated having been caught up in them again.

She stood up at the sound of the toaster and went to the kitchen to butter her bagel. Much to her dismay, she was out of cheese, so she ate it plain. She returned to her chair feeling old and listless. She was likely better off without the cheese.

Aside from the vomiting, Valerie was trying hard to figure out what was bothering her. This unexplained lethargy was driving her crazy. She was trying not to think of the looming deadline in Calgary. The two-year mark was fast approaching and she would need to do something about her storage locker. She looked out the window as the wind changed direction and the rain was now slamming against the side of the house. This was the fifth straight day of rain. So this was spring in BC. She wondered how on earth the people here survived this kind of weather.

Her mind occasionally took her back to Garret, and how she had missed the signs. Such as, every time she had a visit from Detective Tobin, Garret visited soon afterwards, asking her what was new. Added to that was the fact that the detective had not returned her last call, which led her to believe he either knew about his brother and chose to say nothing or that he was somehow involved. She had identified the girl from mug shots yet she had never heard any more about her. None of these things added up. The wise thing would be to just forget them all and count her blessings that she hadn't become more involved.

But that wasn't really what was bugging her, either. She missed Fort Langley and that was for certain. Obviously it rained everywhere, but she never seemed to mind the rain there. The winds didn't seem as intense, and she had loved the convenience of being able to walk everywhere.

But here on the water, the winds could be relentless, reaching speeds of sixty kilometres an hour and bringing with them some very large waves. Plus the area was not as accessible, being somewhat isolated, with not many places to shop within walking distance.

Valerie finally had to admit what the real problem was. Sure she missed Fort Langley, but it was more than that. She missed Hank. Hank and his beautiful dog face. Faithful Hank, who was always by her side, without grievance or judgment. Hank, who always made sure she locked the door, reminded her when it was time to eat, and who never let her sleep in. Speaking of eating, what the hell had she eaten last night? It must have been the fish from that terrible place down the street. It looked disgusting while she was eating it. She would need to smarten up and start cooking again.

This new house-sitting job was just outside of White Rock, in an area known as Blackie Spit. The spit was located at the end of Boundary Bay, where the waters were relatively sheltered from storm surges. The spectacular coastline views swept across Mud Bay and eventually came to land's end in the town of Tsawwassen. Different tides transformed the shoreline. But although the bay was sheltered, the winds still came in from Georgia Strait. Across the open waters to the west lay both the Gulf Islands and the San Juan Islands, but she could only see in that direction on her walks to Crescent Beach.

Valerie was living here in an impressive custom-built home, which was situated just off a street called Sullivan, halfway between Crescent Beach and the spit. The area was beautiful, the neighbourhood pristine. The expansive home she lived in was more than she could have ever dreamed of, but outside, the streets were narrow and crowded. The trees were dense, towering and plentiful. She felt more closed in than she had in Fort Langley. Her new home was situated just a short walk away from a nature trail, the off-leash doggie park, and a beautiful beach, which was where she spent much of her time. Here she felt less restricted.

The homeowners didn't live in this country, and the house had been sitting empty for some time. They had purchased it in the hopes of moving in one day, but their immigration papers were being held up and their entry delayed. There was a problem with the wife's citizenship documents, or something like that. After a few break-ins in the area and two reports of squatters taking up residence in nearby vacant homes, the owners became concerned with leaving their home empty. Fortunately it had been furnished, as they had visited a few times on vacation. Valerie had again been fortunate enough to land this position, thanks to Anna.

If it wasn't for the area, she may not have taken the job. But it was working out well; she couldn't complain about the nice house, and she was adequately comfortable. But something about the yard gave her a funny feeling. It wasn't something she had initially noticed, as the rain had kept her indoors for the first month and a half, and she only used the front door for her outings. But once the weather had begun to dry out and she had ventured to the back, she felt almost physically ill. She couldn't figure it out, as it felt like something different than just her intuition. Was it because it was so dark and heavily treed? It was a strangely overpowering feeling, and she knew not to ignore her feelings.

Valerie had no plans on staying here any longer than necessary, as her new job had already started. As assistant coordinator for the 2010 Olympics, much of her preliminary work was, at this point, being done online. Her meeting with the committee in Vancouver had gone very well, and she couldn't wait to go in and meet her team. There was much to do, and planning had already begun. There were the venue setups already in progress, and she would be working on things like the torch relay, the medals table, the opening ceremonies, and the chronological order of events, just to mention a few. The committee was pleased to have Valerie on board; her being trilingual was one more asset. One of her focuses would be to assure a good balance of linguistic duality, as they were concerned with a fair representation from both the French and English sides of Canada.

She knew many aspects of the job would not be easy. There had already been opposition from Indigenous people and their supporters. As well, two BC First Nations leaders expressed concerns over the choice of an Inukshuk as the symbol of the games, saying it inaccurately depicted West Coast influence. They felt it looked too much like Pac-Man. Also the three mascots chosen to represent the Olympics - Miga, Quatchi and Sumá – were proving to be unpopular with many. Miga is a combination of an orca and a "spirit bear," a name used to describe a white-furred Kermode bear. Quatchi is modelled on the sasquatch. Sumi combines elements of the orca, the black bear, and the thunderbird. So these, among other things, were controversial and needed to be approached delicately.

The Olympics were taking place in just under a year and in her mind, she had come aboard late. Ideally she would like to be there from day one of any project, but there it was. Her new focus was now on finding a permanent home for herself, and on making plans to return to Calgary. Suddenly, she had so much work to do in a short space of time.

But one thing was abundantly clear; if she was to survive being in this house, she would need to find a dog-walking job or something, and soon. She found it funny that she now needed the comfort of a four-legged friend. How things change! She remembered seeing a large notice board outside the general store at Crescent Beach. She seemed to recall it was a community board, so perhaps people posted for such things. She would have a look, and if there were no notices, she would post one. She stood up, turned off the television, and headed to her room to get dressed. She needed to do it right now. Besides, the walk would likely do her good.

Leaving Fort Langley had been with mixed emotions but had gone smoothly. Bill and Denise had returned from their sailing trip intact. Their boat stayed in Hawai'i over the winter but she figured by now they would be making plans to move it. Spring was nearly here, and the waters would be conducive to sea travel. Karen and Hamid had planned a welcome home party, and Valerie felt very much a part of it. Denise had been surprised to see the friendship that had blossomed between her daughter and Valerie, but mostly she was surprised at how Hank had cried when Valerie left.

Valerie had spent Christmas Day with Karen and Hamid in Abbotsford. She woke early Christmas morning and after a hurried coffee, she headed out the door. After she had made her way to the freeway, she felt her heart flutter as she saw the sign up ahead for Fort Langley. Then it was as if the steering wheel had a mind of its own as she found herself taking the exit. As she drove slowly down Glover Road she felt a lump in her throat, then she began crying. Tears blurred her vision, adding sparkle to the colourful storefronts, adorned in garland and twinkling lights. All of the trees that lined the streets were laden with lights that glowed under the dark cloudy skies. The place looked magical and she realized how much she missed it here. This felt like home, more than any other place she had lived, and she realized how much she longed for a home of her own.

Christmas had been green but very wet. February had brought cold winds, but the air was now warmer, though no drier. She dressed for the weather and headed out the door. Valerie knew she had to stop wondering about the woman and the parcel. And of course, the nagging questions about Detective Tobin. How much had he known, and were he and Garret involved together in moving cocaine and ecstasy pills?

Since Christmas, Karen had been promising she would bring the kids and Hank to visit her, but she hadn't yet heard from her. Coincidentally, while Valerie was walking, her cell phone vibrated in her pocket. Now properly employed, she had invested in a good phone and ditched the old flip phone, which had been useful only for phone calls. Recognizing the number, she answered.

"Valerie, it's Karen. We miss you! Dani and Ana keep asking about you. Did you know you are now Auntie Valerie? We wanted to be sure you are okay."

"Yes, I'm fine. Wet, but fine," she joked.

"We want to go to Port Moody. The kids want to walk around the bay to Old Orchard Park and then eat fish and chips, and they asked if you would come with us. Have you ever been? It would be nice if you would come with us."

Valerie's face lit up. "You have no idea how much I would love that," she answered. "Just say when."

19

A week later, on a sunny Wednesday, Valerie had her first contact with familiar faces. She didn't realize how much she had needed this until the doorbell rang and she opened it to three smiling faces. The big surprise was the fact that they brought Hank. At the sight of her, Hank wagged his tail and started to whine, jumping up in her direction. She bent down and rubbed his neck, burying her face in his fur. She thought she would cry for joy.

She invited her guests in and gave them a quick tour of the house. Danesh and Anadia walked from room to room oohing and aahing. Karen looked at Valerie in surprise.

"Well done! Look at this place. How could you not be happy here?"

Anadia walked up to Valerie and hugged her around the waist. "Can I see the backyard? Do you have any swings or anything?"

Valerie took them through to the rear of the house. "No, I'm sorry. No swings, but go out and have a look." She unlocked the door. "I'll stay in here," she added, not wanting to explain.

Danesh ran out first, followed by Anadia and Karen. Hank walked cautiously behind them. But to Valerie's surprise, Hank wouldn't stay in the yard. He walked in circles, crying, before returning to the porch. Karen called him back into the yard, but he wouldn't budge. Valerie stood at the back door, watching them through the slider. Hank sat looking at Valerie and whining, his head tilted sideways.

"I might be crazy, but I think Hank and I are both feeling the same thing," she called out to Karen, who was scolding Danesh for trying to climb a small tree.

"What's that?" asked Karen.

"We don't much like the yard," was all she would say.

"That's crazy. Sometimes I think I'm crazy," laughed Karen.

"This is a different crazy. I can't explain it right now. Besides, we are all a bit crazy and it's no big deal. Actually, it's normal to be crazy. But not like this." Valerie's instincts were telling her something. Hank's tail went down and he began barking at the door to be let back into the house. He touched the doorsill with his paw and looked at Valerie. She opened the door, and Hank ran inside. A few minutes later, the others returned to the house.

Karen called the children. "Let's go. Rocky Point is waiting."

As Karen drove across the Port Mann Bridge, Valerie smiled to herself. This was the first time she had crossed the bridge since moving to Fort Langley all those months ago. She felt disconnected from that messed-up person who had moved from Burnaby. It was such a good feeling.

Karen parked along the roadside on Murray Street, near a trail that led to the water. The trails were quiet except for a few young skateboarders and new mothers with strollers. The walk started out breezy but once they rounded the corner, the air was calm. The view of the water made Valerie smile. She ran her fingers along the tips of the bulrushes in the grassy area along the boardwalk on the shoreline trail. In the distance, the mountains looked spectacular, the peak of Mount Seymour was covered in a dusting of snow. The walk to Old Orchard Park took about half an hour but every step was enjoyable. From the old lookout structure she spotted a great blue heron. They walked past pilings in the mudflats, which, Karen explained, were relics of an old mill site. As they rounded the bend, sandy coves and views of the marina at Reed Point came into view across the water.

The children ran ahead as glimpses of the park appeared ahead.

"We can't swim here, of course. It's too cold, but the kids love this playground," explained Karen.

"This is perfect," called out Valerie as she walked towards the water's edge. Valerie and the kids took off their socks and shoes and shrieked as the cold water swirled around their feet. The four beachcombed and played on the swings and climbing apparatus for quite some time. From there they walked back to Rocky Point Park to indulge in fish and chips, arguably the best around. It was a long day, but Valerie was sure she had more fun than Dani and Ana.

On the way home, both kids were soon asleep in the back seat. Karen, without taking her eyes off the road, started talking, and what she said floored Valerie.

"I envy you, you know."

"Are you serious?" Valerie turned slightly to face her. "Look at you, Karen. You have a wonderful life, two beautiful kids, great parents, and you live in a great house."

"Yes, I know. I love Hamid and all, but I kept telling him I wasn't ready for marriage and a family. I was young and there were things I wanted to do. I wanted to study, to travel, and explore my options." Karen glanced in the rear-view mirror to be sure the kids were sleeping. Then she looked over at Valerie, her expression one of embarrassment. "I swear, he poked holes in his condoms. We ended up needing to marry because I was pregnant. When I told him, he had smiled, like he had hoped this would happen."

Valerie reached over and squeezed the woman's hand. It was strange, she thought, how others problems seem insignificant compared to her own; that they would be more manageable, and not such a big deal. But it seemed Karen was dead serious, and distraught about it. She couldn't find the right words.

"I mean, I loved being pregnant, and I loved Dani, but by the second, I felt lost. Empty. He was off running his restaurant, doing his own thing and I was at home being a mother and housewife. He fulfilled his dreams but I didn't."

"But did you talk to him?"

"Sure I did. He'd just pat me on the head and say, 'Good wife, good girl, good mother,' like I was a dog or something." She again checked that the kids were truly asleep, then she continued. "Perhaps this is great in his culture, but not mine. My parents are free spirits, and were totally gobsmacked that I became so docile. I guess I never realized how much our cultures would clash."

Valerie looked at Karen, long and hard. Again she noticed how the woman looked tired and suddenly very unhappy. Not knowing how to respond, Valerie could only offer, "Please don't envy me. How do you know your life would have been better? Maybe it would have been a disaster. What someone once said to me is that the things you don't have may seem better than the things you have, and I suppose sometimes that's true, but not usually."

As she spoke the words, Valerie remembered the lady on the bench in Fort Langley. The lady's words had resonated with her. "I met someone not long ago who told me, 'Don't go looking somewhere else for happiness when it might be right under your nose.' Karen, I wouldn't mind your problems, not to make light of them. But please don't think mine would have in any way been better. My problems I wouldn't wish on anyone."

"What problems, Auntie Valerie?" asked a small voice from the back seat.

Valerie turned around and tickled the little girl. "Where to buy the best ice cream, that's my problem!"

20

Today was sunny and clear. It had rained all night, and the still-wet streets were slowly drying under the sun's rays. The blue skies had not a single cloud and the winds were calm. Valerie had spent the past hour at the doggie park with Max, her new charge. Max was an Irish terrier. Terriers on the whole were not one of her favourite breeds, and it was taking some adjustment. He was extremely energetic and often noisy, but could be quite lovable. She had discovered, quite by accident, that Max loved to fetch a stick, which Valerie had begun to enjoy. And if she chose to not throw the stick, Max happily chased her until she did. This didn't exactly thrill her, but at least he was a happy dog.

While walking along the path towards Crescent Beach, she was more than surprised when she looked up and saw a familiar face walking towards her. It was Detective Tobin she was sure of it. Mortified, she looked around frantically for a place to hide. To the left was a large rhododendron. Was there a chance she could cross the path and get behind it before he approached?

"Shit, shit, shit," she mumbled under her breath. As she was distracted trying to formulate her plan, a giant crow landed almost right beside them, pausing to drink from a puddle. Max caught her off guard, and spun around so quickly the leash wrapped around her legs, and one tug was enough to throw her off her feet. Her face contorted. Her eyes opened wide like saucers and her mouth formed a little O as she went over and fell squarely into the puddle. The sound that came out was more a whimper than a scream, but it was enough to catch the detective's attention. She wished the puddle had been deep enough to drown in.

She looked up to see he was now standing over her. "Miss Russo? I didn't know you lived in this neighbour-hood. What a surprise." He reached out his hand. "It is Miss Russo, right?" She almost wilted at the sound of his voice. She looked up at him, feigning surprise. He was holding back a smile.

"Uh, yes, it's me. I do live here. I'm watching another house for absentee owners." She made no attempt at eye contact as she stood, ignoring the outstretched hand he offered to her. She bent over and tried fruitlessly to wipe the mud from her capris.

He again offered his assistance. "Can I help you?"

"I don't need any help, thank you." She brushed the hair from her face and straightened up. "I didn't know you lived here either." Valerie was still unsure whether or not this man was crooked and was working with Garret. Maybe he was just messing with her head to see how much she knew.

"I don't. I actually live at the other side, near the White Rock pier. I was meeting a friend for lunch." He seemed relaxed and genuinely surprised to see her. He put his hands in his pockets and rolled back and forth on his heels. He seemed to be enjoying her plight.

"It's so beautiful here by the water. How could you live all the way out here and work all the way out there?" she asked, tossing her head sideways in a northerly direction. She had composed herself sufficiently and had drawn Max close to her, holding back a desire to kick the animal.

"I would never move from here. I love where I live. Besides, 'all the way out there' is not so far."

"Well, nice to see you, but I have to get going."

"I can walk with you, if that's okay." He stated this more than he asked.

They walked along together, although Valerie had been certain he was walking in the other direction when she first spotted him. She recalled that Garret had done the exact same thing when she first met him—he had walked with her when she clearly didn't want him to. This was one annoying habit the brothers shared. They strolled slowly mostly in silence, except for the odd time she gave a command to Max. She tried to speak kindly to the dog but she really felt like stepping on him.

Glancing at the detective occasionally from the corner of her eye, Valerie liked how different he looked in casual clothing. His demeanour also seemed more casual. It's true what they say, that one's clothing has a lot to do with dictating their stance, and can have a powerful impact on a person's perception. In this case, she would never have taken this man for the focused, condescending and unsmiling detective she had previously met.

They still walked in silence, the gravel crunching under their shoes. He seemed taller than she had remembered and no more talkative. Valerie found the quiet unnerving, particularly given their history. She sighed deeply.

"I'm not as crazy about this dog as I was about Hank. I actually miss him. He knew things." Again quiet, so she added, "You don't like dogs?"

"I don't understand how people treat them like humans. And how they would have a custody battle over them. I used to like dogs but this new thing is beyond me, and it's made me a little cautious about who matters more," he answered. Valerie noticed the fairness of his hair, when it wasn't slicked back for work. It was soft and wavy and made him look younger.

Finally they reached the small car park, which was at the end of a roundabout. Here, the detective veered off to the left.

"Well, this is where I get off," he said. Turning back towards her, he raised his finger in the air in an afterthought. "Oh–by the way, we got your girl. She was dropping off another package at a high school in Port Moody. The drug squad was waiting for her. It's hard to say what will happen, but she has a chance now to rehabilitate." He rubbed his nose and offered a half smile. "I took what you said to heart, and we are trying to help her. She was put into a rehab detention centre for the time being. Luckily we found her family, and the courts will consider releasing her to their care."

"I can't thank you enough for telling me that." As Valerie was speaking, she was trembling with gratitude. "Will they deport her? She said she would be deported."

"She lied to you. Her family is in Lethbridge. They are coming to get her."

"So maybe a happy ending," Valerie said with a smile. "Thank you again, Detective Tobin."

"Maybe just call me Brian. There's no need for formalities. We aren't on a case here, and there's no official business between us. At least, I no longer believe there is."

"You never called me back," she blurted out. "Why did you never call me back?"

Detective Tobin shook his head and stared at his shoes. "I'm sorry. I was away because of a family medical emergency. Besides, I didn't want to get you involved any more than you were. I had what I needed, and I didn't want to risk putting you in more danger. I did get your message when I returned and I acted on it. So thank you for that. Anyway, see you later."

Max started barking at Brian as he walked to his car. "Are you trying to tell me something?" she asked the dog. Max sat down and looked at her. He cocked his ear, and slowly he started to wag his tail.

As Brian unlocked his car door, he called back over his shoulder, "Maybe I'll see you on my beach one day, near the pier."

Valerie smiled and waved. She hadn't asked him about Garret or about any connection. Running into him had caught her off guard. Hopefully she had been wrong about him, and he had never been involved. She turned and walked towards home, forgetting about her muddied pants. She was still beaming from the news about the girl. She had been given a second chance and Valerie hoped she used it wisely.

As the weeks passed the weather slowly improved. While still cool, the days were getting longer and drier. Valerie no longer woke up to the sound of rain pounding on the roof and the water gushing out of the gutters. She was sleeping well–better than she had slept for a very, very long time.

She woke up feeling refreshed. After putting on the coffee she went to splash some water on her face. Grabbing herself a cup of fresh coffee she made her way to the sofa to watch the morning news show. She was just in time for the headlines on Global TV. Her favourite anchor, Deborra Hope, was just about to announce breaking news. But first the weather, and Wayne Cox promised a dry week, news to which Valerie gave out a squeal of joy. Deborra Hope was back on with her breaking news story. There had been a major arrest of a local cocaine distributor who had been trying to infiltrate the Township of Langley.

When she looked closely at the television, Valerie nearly spilled her coffee. There on the screen were photos of Garret Murphy and the man from the backyard. He was named as Keith Leckie. This Leckie guy, being a key player, was being held without bail until his hearing.

Garret, being his minion, was released until his court appearance. A spokesperson for the RCMP made a brief statement thanking Detective Brian Tobin and his team for their tireless work in the ongoing efforts to clean up Langley.

This was really good news to Valerie, as she hadn't wanted to believe the detective had been involved or was protecting his brother. She sat back, feeling a little safer but dispassionately unmoved. This all seemed so anti-climactic. Just like that, it was all over. She had been more excited about the weather report. Perhaps she had been hoping she was wrong about Garret as well. But she wasn't, and she felt angry with him all over again for using her. He likely brought her along on these drop-offs to cover himself; just two happy people out for the day, as if to demonstrate nothing unusual was going on. His strategy being that as a couple they wouldn't raise any suspicions. She wasn't sure who the bigger ass was—him for being an ass or her, for allowing him to use her like that.

21

Valerie, being nearly bored to tears, needed to get out of the house now that the weather had somewhat improved. She decided this might be a good time to explore the east beach area of White Rock. She didn't like being here at the house, as the backyard bothered her tremendously. The feeling came and went over her like waves. So today she was determined to find an outlet. Up until now she had never ventured outside of the Crescent Beach area. She was surprised to learn that the town of White Rock was actually quite close. And it was lovely! She quickly made her way to the beach area, at the end of Johnston Road.

Finding parking easily, she took a walk along the boardwalk. There were so many people here, she wasn't sure if this was usual or if the good weather was drawing them out of their homes. Here, the views were magnificent, with water extending as far as the eye could see. After walking to the end of the path and back, she then walked to the end of the pier, then to the spot where the big white rock stood. It looked out of place, like a giant snowball. She had no idea there really was a white rock in White Rock.

After studying the rock and where it stood, Valerie wandered back to a small museum she had seen near the pier. There she learned that the white rock was dropped by glaciers some 11,000 years ago and had been used by sailors as a beacon because of its brilliant white colour. As to why it was so white, she learned that seabirds had been regularly pooping on the 486-ton chunk of quartz and mica, turning it white. Bird shit white. She questioned the exact weight and wondered if anyone had actually weighed it.

But legend had it that a handsome son of a sea god had fallen in love with the Cowichan Chief's daughter. Told he could not marry a mortal, he tossed a giant white rock across the Strait of Georgia. It came to rest in this crescent-shaped bay and there they made their home. From the two lovers came the mighty Semiahmoo Tribe, known as the half moon tribe, and they grew in numbers and became a great nation. However, these days they did actually paint it white, which somehow disappointed Valerie. She preferred the legendary, more utopian version.

She returned to her car, walking down Marine Drive, browsing through the windows of the small shops–many of which were closed due to the time of day. Perhaps she would return on Saturday, which was still a few days away. As she had no other plans, she would walk Max early, then make her way back here.

Early next Saturday morning, Valerie returned, this time planning to venture further along the east beach area. It didn't take her long to go through the shops along the main street, and before long she was heading back down to the water. She walked along the path which came out onto East Beach. Walking along the grassy area near Totem Park, Valerie was not surprised when she saw him again; he did say he lived in this area. Perhaps, if she was honest with herself, that was the whole plan.

Brian was walking near the beach. He was dressed in grey checkered shorts, a white sweatshirt and runners. He was wearing sunglasses, so she had to look twice to make sure it was indeed Brian. She smiled and waved, almost embarrassed, as her being there didn't seem as coincidental as their last meeting. He walked towards her, and she couldn't help noticing his muscular, well-toned legs and arms.

"I was just curious about the area," she offered in explanation.

"It's not a problem. It's a public park. Can we walk a bit together? I can show you the rest of the area, if you like."

With a nod, Valerie agreed, and they walked along, mostly in silence.

"You won't find me as charming as my brother," Brian said at last, clearing his throat.

She shook her head. "At first I thought he was nice, but I don't think I ever used the word charming. He was quite edgy. Friendly, yes, but at the same time, overstrung, if you know what I mean." Valerie was glad it was him who brought up the topic of Garret and she desperately wanted to keep up the conversation.

"Whatever happened there? That thing with your brother." She tripped over her words. "I'm sorry about calling you, but I didn't know what else to do. I didn't know if you knew about him."

Brian put his hands in his pockets and looked up as a random cloud briefly covered the sun. "You mean you think you shouldn't have called me? No, you did the right thing. I guess I can tell you." He stopped walking.

"It's true that at one time Garret was involved with these people. But he was lucky that I found out before he totally ruined his life. He did pay the price, got off with probation, but part of the condition was that he check himself into rehab. He did, and he was fine. But before long we found him associating with them again. He pleaded innocence, swore he wasn't doing anything wrong. He told me he could make it up to me by helping us catch these buggers and convict them."

"So what went wrong?"

"At the winery, he did move a small amount. When questioned about it, he said they were testing him, to regain their confidence. I would never have condoned it, had I known. I think they lost trust in him again when he didn't reach the market in Cordova Bay. They blamed it on the fact that you were with him. I was royally pissed at Garret for dragging you along to these outings in the first place. I told him to stop it. I warned him to not get you involved."

Brian started walking again, slowly. "But what we didn't know is that he was playing both sides. He was packing drugs into bike frames and distributing it that way. Garret laughed at the fact that he could move product for Keith right under our noses, almost with our blessing, and our protection. I couldn't believe the operation he had going on there. He moved a shitload of product. But Keith didn't like the fact that you were hanging around. He thought you'd blow it for him, so he may have been genuinely trying to hurt you when he followed you. Garret obviously didn't want Keith to hurt you, but I suspect he only went after him to make it look realistic."

Valerie's heart sank. "So you knew. Why didn't you return my call? And why didn't anyone respond that night after he called 911?" Were you two in on it together? Am I going to, like, disappear or something now?"

Brian laughed. "You watch too many movies. But I have to tell you Garret didn't call the police that night. A neighbour did. That's what triggered me to think that Garret wasn't playing straight. Add to that the argument you saw between Garret and Keith–that's what convinced me. I thought he was telling them he'd had enough. When I confronted him, he tried telling me that their condition was that he'd have to move one more batch. Yadda, yadda. I'd heard it all before. Anyway, that was Garret's story."

"I don't know what to make of that. But I'm so glad you got that man. I'm glad you got him and the girl."

Brian nodded. "That man, Keith-we got a whole different story from him. In truth, Garret was not only moving this shit, but I think he was using again. There were always bikes going in and out of there. So many bikes were moving through such a small shop. Much more than usual, and it drew our attention. How can so many bikes be bought, sold and repaired? That was how we got him and that was his downfall. Not being careful. We got them both, but Keith Leckie was the prize. He was the one we wanted. And it was a huge accomplishment, getting him. The punch in the gut was seeing my brother go back down that road. I struggled long and hard over that, but I had to turn him in. I figured the media would have a heyday with it, once they found out we were half brothers. And they may yet do that, but so far it's not clear that we are related. We had arrested him once before with no backlash, so maybe it will stay an unknown fact. What bugs me is that he had a good chance to get out of it, but I guess he made his choices and I had to make mine."

"So that's why you were so quiet about it all, and so serious." She stopped and looked up at him. "You were almost nasty."

"Brian looked at her with a smile. "You mean, I was just showing you my good side?"

"I'm sorry, I didn't think you heard that," was all Valerie could manage.

"Listen, Valerie, that is my job. I need to be neutral and focused. I can't be all touchy-feely on the job. My loyalty is to the job, not to you and certainly not to Garret. Besides, I got the feeling you were hiding something." He added, "I still think you are."

"Well, like I said, it's private and has nothing to do with Garret or any of that. Maybe some day I'll tell you."

"You don't have to, it's none of my business, like you said."

"So tell me about the drugs. Is the problem over now?" Valerie wanted to change the subject.

"Not by a long shot, but it's a good start. We are sending a good message here. By the way, nice segue. Here's another one for you. How about fish and chips on Saturday? I know a great place."

22

Saturday quickly approached. Brian had given Valerie the option to meet him at the park or at the restaurant. She opted for the park, and she smiled when she spotted him waiting for her. Their hello was still a bit awkward with neither a hug nor a handshake, but side-by-side, they walked to the restaurant. He guided her to a quaint wooden building, situated next to a big tree, a few steps from the main road. The building was painted sea blue, and across the front, the image of a huge orange fish that continued across the door and ended at the other side of the one window had been painted. Other than that she saw no other sign announcing the establishment. On the front walkway, a few small tables and chairs had been placed, protected from the wind by a tall white lattice fence. The pots stood empty, as it was too early in the season for flowers. Valerie visualized it in the summer with the lattice covered in colourful blooms and thought how nice it would be to come back then.

The fish and chips were unbelievably good, and Valerie smothered her fries with malt vinegar. Brian had ordered something called mushy peas, which she had never heard of but was also delicious. They ate outdoors, bundled up in their sweaters, as the air had a chill to it. Nonetheless, as she had learned, in true West Coast fashion, everything goes.

"I'm glad you are okay with sitting outside. Here, we dress for the weather, not the other way around. The weather never seems to cooperate so we have to be ready for anything." Brian gave her an endearing smile, his eyes an icy blue-green. His hair was tousled by the wind, which she again noticed made him look younger. He sat tracing the diamond pattern on the tablecloth with his finger. Were those freckles across his nose? She was remembering the story Garret had told her, about Brian digging up body parts at the pig farm. This man must have his reasons for being gloomy. Today it was nice to see him smile.

Afterwards, as they walked along the waterfront, Valerie was overcome with a feeling of total calm. She trusted this man, and it was a good feeling. It had been a long time since she trusted anyone. Brian had been so open with her, and it probably hadn't been easy for him to reveal the truths about his brother. She wanted to be open in the same way and realized she would need to stop hiding behind herself. Stop being this victimized person. After all, was she? She may have been at one time, but not any longer. She started talking a bit about herself, and how she was able to handle this confusion in her present life. By that time, they had arrived back at her car.

Brian interrupted. "I'm sorry, but I've always found the best way to have a really good heart-to-heart was by walking. Are you up for a good long walk and a conversation?"

Valerie smiled at him. "Actually, I'm dying to go on one. Since I no longer have Hank, I've been getting really lazy. It's just been me and cheese."

"This one may take a couple of hours," he said, with almost a warning in his voice.

"Sounds good to me. What else am I doing?"

Together they walked to the far end of the promenade and on to an area known as the 1001 Steps. Brian wasn't kidding when he said it was a long walk, but Valerie found it worthwhile and the scenery beautiful. They walked and she talked. It suddenly occurred to her that she was laughing and having a good time.

Her thoughts kept taking her back to that day in Fort Langley, by the river. The woman on the bench had told her that happiness might be right under her nose, and Valerie was beginning to realize that the woman might be right. After all, look at how far she had come! She was settling here in BC. She could now call it home. This was what she had hoped for, yet she kept sabotaging her progress with thoughts from the past.

"I had a confusing childhood. I know. Who hasn't, right? I was raised to be independent. But all my life I wished I had some guidance, and I often had to learn things the hard way. Trial and error, you know? Mom said I just never got it quite right, but she'd never teach me what 'right' was. I never knew what direction to go in. As a result, nobody took me seriously. I seemed out of synch. So I withdrew and just found my own way. And whenever I got the, you know, the feeling, my mom withdrew and my siblings laughed, saying I was a basket case."

"Families do that. Sometimes they snap, other times they bite. The snaps can wound but the bites can be crippling. Sometimes their comments are intentional but, try to not give them too much credit, maybe they just don't know any better and they make ignorant remarks."

Valerie nodded. "Maybe so, but we each went about our lives and I never felt I fit in. Mom didn't have time for any of us, having never settled into the move to Canada. It was a life she didn't ask for, and we had all become inconveniences. It was like growing up in a house full of strangers, each of us holding back emotion, living our own lives, not talking to each other, or sharing anything personal. We were nothing more than a house full of roommates.

I went to Europe for a while. I actually went back to Italy, to try to 'find myself.' When I was ready to come home, my mom offered to send me money so I would stay there. I always sensed that she didn't like to be near me. I hugged her once and she backed away, just a little, but I noticed. It was as if I gave her the creeps. So I did stay in Italy, for quite some time. I saw my life as being something I deserved. I guess I was pretty unapproachable in many ways. But the independence made me stronger, and I had long ago learned to see things coming, so it's like I was always ready for anything that came my way."

"Have you tried any counselling?"

"What for? That's the second time you've said that to me. Do I sound that bad?"

Hey, don't knock it. It helped me." His face was very serious. "For example, I was like you. I thought moving away would make everything bad go away. But it didn't. All it did was change the view outside my window."

Valerie took a chance and asked Brian point blank, "Garret told me about the farm. What was it really like, seeing what you saw? I'm guessing that's why you went to counselling. Do you mind me asking?"

He cleared his throat. "I think the VPD really messed up on that one. This guy got away with it for years. They just never had enough on him to go in. He'd been on the radar, but just. He created some stupid charity under the premise of raising funds for groups in need, but I saw it as an excuse to have parties. Piggies something, he called it. But authorities shut it down soon after it started. That was about eight or nine years ago. The problem is, HE wasn't shut down. He was gutting women in his barn and giving away their meat to locals. He used to be a butcher, so he'd grind it up with pig meat and package it. Hell, he was probably eating it himself! People who knew about it weren't talking. It started ten years ago and its just wrapping up now. Horrible things happened there. We still don't know everything, and as for me, I don't want to know."

"Where did these women come from? I mean, why would they go there in the first place?" she asked.

"The addicts downtown were such a mess. There were thousands of them in the downtown east side, homeless and strung out, most of them desperate for their next fix. The really bad ones were falling down in the middle of the street, beating each other up. He'd drive out there and offer them drugs, or ask if they wanted to come to a party or come for a place to sleep. They were just unknown, unlucky women. But none of them deserved what happened to them out there at that farm. The man was a demented sicko. We found body parts everywhere. One victim was hanging on a meat hook, gutted. We didn't talk about it much then, or now. But some weren't as strong as others. I have to tell you, it was tough, digging up bits of hair and teeth, and especially the jewellery. It personalized everything and made it all the more horrific. For Chrissake, we were finding hands and feet stuffed into skulls."

Valerie shuddered. "Why did he do it?"

"I don't even know. I know over half of them were First Nations women, but nobody thought that was the reason. Although it did break open a Pandora's box about missing Aboriginal women. There's a public inquiry going on right now."

"Those poor women. I'm surprised you didn't crack."

"Some of us did. A lot of us had nightmares. Two of my colleagues committed suicide. One guy, Dan, he couldn't stop crying. His life was ruined. He couldn't work any more. The memories stay with you, you know? I remember so much rain. S much mud, and the sucking sound our boots made in the mud during the digging. But I tried hard not to cave."

"You kept up that poker face, right?"

"I just felt so bad for the girls. Bad isn't even the right word. I honestly couldn't believe what I was seeing. My emotions went into shock and I could feel myself shutting down. I have to tell you, it nearly broke me, so yeah, maybe I cracked a bit. But hey, I'm a warrior, right?"

Valerie looked at Brian. His face was painted with an anguish that even his smile couldn't mask. "It must have been a nightmare, being there. I might not know what you were feeling, but every time I think of the girl I didn't help, I silently go mad. And now hearing this from you makes it worse. I hope she didn't end up there."

"I'm just saying that counselling helped me."

Valerie looked at him as if seeing him for the first time. His features were soft, but his expression right now was taut, his jaw clenched. She felt a strong connection. They were both suffering and trying to move on. She thought this might be a good time to change the subject, so she brightened the mood by telling him about her new job for 2010.

"I hope you show up to some of the events. I can keep you in the loop, you know."

Brian smiled at the ground, seeming indifferent to the offer at this point in time. Valerie didn't push the offer. He said he knew a shorter route back, and they were soon walking through neighbourhoods of upscale homes on big lots, neatly lined with mature trees. This place was such a contrast to Fort Langley. They descended onto Marine Drive, and were soon back on the last stretch towards East Beach. On the way back to her car, Brian pointed out some houses that were situated on a ridge overlooking the bay. The driveways were steep and she imagined what it would be like to have to drive down them if they were icy. She could see herself sliding straight into the house.

As she absentmindedly glanced over to the left, towards the shops along the street, Valerie's face lit up with recognition. "Hey, there's that restaurant! This woman I met in Fort Langley told me about it. I had completely forgotten the conversation until just now. She said I must go, and to tell them I want my Parmagiana di Melanzane *'just the way Diana likes it.'*" She gave Brian a big toothy grin. "It's a Sicilian dish. That's what she told me to say."

"How about I take you one day. So you say you started your new job? You will be wanting to celebrate somehow."

23

Valerie had experienced weeks of profound unrest. Something in her very core felt a spine-chilling fore-boding. Although she was not a stranger to this *gift*, as Brian had suggested, it had now invaded her home, and the feeling made her uncomfortable. By the third week, she was jarred awake from her sleep and was absolutely horrified to find herself standing in the middle of the backyard. Never had she walked in her sleep, but there she was. And she heard it-that gut-wrenching silence. And at that moment, she knew. She stumbled into the house, shivering uncontrollably, as if she'd been injected with adrenalin. Feeling nauseous, she drank a glass of water, went to grab a blanket and fell asleep on the couch, curled up in a fetal position. How she wished Hank were here with her.

Valerie slept late and might have slept longer were it not for the sound of a jackhammer coming from some-where outside. Totally unconcerned with what was being repaired or where, she sat numbed by what had happened to her. She was not overthinking, and this was not paranoia. This had actually happened, and she knew what it was. She was determined to do something about it.

Although she had no idea how best to approach this, her first thought was to call Brian. She placed the call around noon, assuming she would need to leave a message, but to her surprise he picked up on the first ring.

"Oh, hi," she stammered. "I didn't think you'd be there. Thought, you know, out catching bad guys and all." She was sure the tone of her voice was giving her away.

"Hi Valerie." He spoke softly, and she noticed right away the change in his greeting from the old days when he had been abrupt with her. She liked this change, from crusty to kind. "This is a surprise."

"It's actually not even important, and I probably shouldn't be bothering you. I'd like to invite you over. Come for wine and see this place I live in. But I have to warn you, it's not without a catch. I really want to run something by you."

"Sure, I can do that. Just tell me where you live and when you were thinking, and I'll be there." There was no hint of suspicion in his voice, no hesitation. Valerie felt relieved.

"Tomorrow is Friday. Can you come after work? Maybe four?"

"Four it is. See you tomorrow." And then he was gone.

Valerie felt her whole body go limp, as though someone had pulled a plug and let her air out. She was not recovered; merely tranquil for the time being. She had no idea what Brian could do, but at least she was being proactive and not running from a feeling. Not this time. She was also comforted by the fact that she trusted him explicitly. She headed out for a walk around the block to clear her head, where she encountered a crew repairing a water main on the side of the road. These were the guys that so rudely woke her up so early in the morning.

Brian arrived a little after four. It was a lovely day, and the house was basking in the glow of the sunshine. She watched out the window as he parked the car and headed for the front door. Valerie had had a week from hell, so she wasn't sure if it was the weather or Brian that gave her this uplifting feeling.

She answered the door barefooted and dressed in jeans and an oversized blouse. She welcomed him into the house, still awkward as to what kind of greeting she should give him. Settling on hello, Valerie took Brian on a quick tour of the house. The sun entered through these south-facing windows, giving the rooms a cheerful appearance. He walked quietly from room to room unsure of what he should be looking at. Afterwards, Valerie invited him to sit in the coziest room in the house, which happened to be the room adjacent to the kitchen. Brian chose the small leather chair, which was situated against the wall, giving him a good view of all the entrances. Valerie noticed and wondered if this was police training. Keep your back to the wall, less chance of being ambushed from behind.

Once he was seated, Valerie padded barefoot through the open doorway and into the kitchen to retrieve the cheese and crackers from the counter. She called back to him, "Can I get you a glass of wine? Red or white?"

Valerie wanted to appear casual and to chat before jumping right into a conversation about the other night.

She came back with the white wine and poured them each a generous helping before sitting near him on the small sofa. Nervously grabbing a cracker and cutting a huge wedge of Emmental cheese, she sat back and shamelessly shoved the big wedge directly into her mouth. Smiling, she mumbled, "I love cheese," as she chased it with an unusually large gulp of wine.

"So I see," responded Brian, with a forced smile. His face then turned serious. "Okay, Valerie. Enough 'Martha Stewart' with the tour and the wine and the cheese. You have bags under your eyes, you've lost weight, and you look like shit. Are you going to tell me why I'm really here? It's not to look at the view outside while sipping Sauvignon Blanc."

Her expression froze and she stopped chewing. "There's something in the yard. I know it," she said, swallowing the last bit of cracker.

"Okay," Brian said slowly. "Can you expand? What is this something you've seen?"

"I haven't seen anything. It's something under the yard, not in it. I can feel it."

He sat back and crossed his ankle over his knee. "Does this always happen to you? Wherever you go, there's trouble? First you carry packages of drugs, and now this?"

"I can feel that something's not right back there," she responded, pointing over her shoulder in the direction of the backyard.

"Let me guess. Crickets."

She was getting angry. "No, not crickets. It's when I *don't* hear the crickets." She looked at him. "Besides, I told you, it's just a way to describe the feeling I get. Don't you listen to me when I try to explain? There really are no crickets. It's in my gut, in the quiet. There's something in the silence that I hear."

The frustration in her voice was apparent. "I don't know if you are making fun of me or if you are just stupid. Besides, Hank felt it too."

"Who's Hank?"

"Don't you remember? The dog from Fort Langley. Honestly, I don't know why I even talk to you." She sat back, looking discouraged.

He had looked amused but suddenly he was serious. He started to stand up but changed his mind and sat back helplessly. He cleared his throat and ran his hand back and forth across the arm of the chair. "No, I'm sorry. I was just teasing because you look so serious, but I wasn't making fun of you. You honestly do look like shit." He leaned forward and looked at her with intensity. "Okay, seriously now, what do you want me to do?"

"Can't you call someone and dig up the yard?"

He again sat back and crossed his ankles. He was trying hard to stay calm. "We can't just dig up the yard, Valerie. I can't get the forensic guys over to dig up the yard because my friend here, and her dog, didn't hear a single thing. I don't think they'd go for that. Besides, Valerie, digging up bodies is not something that has worked well for me in the past. Didn't we just have a similar conversation a few weeks ago? Do you know what you are asking?"

Valerie looked at him. "I'm sorry, Brian, I get that. But *you* don't have to dig, do you? Would you even have to be there? You said the police had people who did the actual digging."

"Well, first of all, we need to have probable grounds. You know, cause for reasonable suspicion. We would need something compelling before we would write a general warrant. Something besides you and Hector the dog."

How about the group you talked about earlier? You had mentioned that Major Crime Unit."

"And what exactly would we be digging for?"

"I think someone is buried there. A body. Speaking of that, can we at least dig into the history? For example, who lived here, and are there any missing people? If someone was missing, that might give someone a reason. And it's Hank, not Hector."

Valerie was trying hard to sound reasonable and sane. She put down her glass, smoothed down her hair and rubbed her eyes. Did she really look that bad?

"I'm not crazy. This is fundamentally who I am and my gut instinct is rarely wrong."

Brian let out an exhale that turned into a lip trill, and he scratched his head. "Okay, let me think. There must be hundreds of missing people. The only ones that came across my desk that I can think of immediately were the cases of the man who went missing on the Island, in Duncan. Bob somebody. Bob Walters. Or Wally Roberts. I think it was last year. And the other is the woman who disappeared from her home in Burnaby. That, I think, was nearly two years ago. I think the name was Madden. Carol Madden. I'd have to check back, but I think that's it. It was an easy one to remember because people in the neighbourhood had organized search parties every day for months on end. Husband said his wife just up and left, and she never came home. But he had waited two days before he notified police. Said they had a fight and she went for a walk in Burnaby Mountain Park. I don't remember much else, but her kids were devastated."

Brian was deep in thought. "Of course, I'm not always in the loop since leaving the Lower Mainland. Another woman disappeared, but I seem to recall she was located, hurt but alive. She'd gotten lost in the bush. Actually, another was lost in the bush and she was found murdered. The names escape me. But like I said, there could be hundreds, Valerie. I'm not up to speed with those things any more. I work in Drug Enforcement now, as you know. Sure, I hear about them, but they aren't my focus or my jurisdiction."

"Well, could you check? Is there anyone you could ask?" Valerie was not prepared to tell him about waking up in the middle of the yard. She was sure he'd think she had lost her mind and might try to have her committed.

"I'll see what I can find out about the ongoing cases," he said, unenthusiastically. "But Valerie, who am I kidding? There could be so many of them, and many more not even reported."

"Well, maybe we can find out about this one, before it becomes a cold case. I think there's someone in the yard, Brian. Please believe me."

"They won't help you, Valerie. Not yet. Not just on your say-so."

"Well, if it's all the same to you, I will try to do a bit of research. I know someone I can call. She probably knows who lived here before."

"I don't know where you would start. Or how much you could find out. I don't know how much I could help, so please don't get your hopes up. I'm sorry Val, but I can't get involved. I do wish I could. This isn't nearly enough for the department to go on."

Valerie would not be deterred. She knew what she knew, and she was no stranger to other people's skepticism about her hunches.

"I understand, really." Not wanting to push Brian any more than she had, she smiled and sat forward. "More wine?" Her wheels were already spinning.

24

While Valerie had told Brian she knew someone who would help her, she was actually uncertain as to whether Anna would want to get involved. Was she asking too much of her friend? She called Anna the next morning. Feeling guilty for not having spoken to her in some time, she started the conversation by asking how she was doing. Anna seemed her usual cheerful self, and after a few pleasantries, Valerie wasted no time in getting to the point. She chose her words carefully.

"I'm getting settled in and thanks again for the job. Hey, I don't know if you mind me asking, but I need some help." Valerie wasn't ready to mention her suspicions about the yard just yet. "Can you find out who owned this house before? I don't think the current owners have ever actually lived here, am I right?"

"Yeah, sure. I think I can find that out. As for the owners ever living there, I don't know if I've ever asked. But I can't see why they wouldn't tell me that. What's going on, Valerie? Why do you need to know?"

"Oh, it's nothing really. I'm just curious about different things going on." She forced a casual laugh. "I'm bored silly, Anna. And it's an interesting house. I'd just like to know about its history. If what I'm doing ends up making any sense, I will tell you."

Anna didn't seem to mind, thinking there was nothing unusual about the request. "I don't know how easy it will be to contact the owners, but I'll see what I can find out from my contact and maybe even the real estate company, and I'll get back to you."

"That'd be great, and thanks a bunch." Valerie hung up, pleased with the call. She was tired of sitting back and letting things happen. It was time to roll up her sleeves and dig in.

Knowing it would take Anna some time to get back to her, Valerie decided to try a few different approaches. First thing, she would start by asking around the neighbourhood. She was familiar with this tactic from working as an event planner. She had often spent countless hours scoping out locations, talking to people and getting up close and personal with their situations.

Unsure what she was even asking, she walked to Crescent Beach. Perhaps someone knew the owners. She drew blanks asking around the local shops and restaurants. "Faces come and go," she was told. "People don't make a habit of introducing themselves and stating their address and occupation," another shop owner snapped back. Walking from area to area, Valerie again found herself missing Hank. This exercise would have been so pleasant with her friend by her side.

Her next step was to speak with the neighbours. The people in the house on the left had not answered the door on any of her walks over, but she did speak with the couple on the right. On her second attempt at contact, she walked over to the house and found them both in the driveway, unloading groceries.

She approached them, a big smile on her face. "Hi, I'm Valerie. I'm the new house-sitter next door."

"Oh, hello, dear," the woman said to her. "So you've confirmed our suspicions. We had no idea someone was staying there until we started seeing lights on at night."

"It must feel strange to have someone next door after the house has been empty for so long," she said, wanting to feel the couple out. "I don't know if you were acquainted with the owners when they lived here."

The woman smiled and shook her head. "I don't think the owners have ever lived there. We've never met them, have we, Ted?" She turned to her husband who had just returned from carrying two bags into the house.

"Never knew them," was his reply. "Seen 'em here a couple of times, but never spoke. At least, I think it was them. Hard to say." He looked away.

Valerie watched his eyes scrutinize her in a way that suggested he was trying to establish her validity to see if she was worth speaking to. Still, she wanted to push a little further. "Well, I know it could feel uncomfortable having a stranger living next door."

The woman handed her husband another bag. "No, it's not the first time. There was another woman who was hired to look after the house for a spell, about a year or so ago. But she was a bit of a strange one. She would never come over, not like you just did. You seem nice." She looked closely at Valerie. "Now I recognize you. I've seen you on the path with a little dog. I hadn't made the connection with next door, though."

"So somebody did live here before me?" As she spoke, the man re-emerged from the house for a second time.

"It's less than a year since she left," he answered. "We weren't too comfortable with her." Grabbing the last bag of groceries, he excused himself. "Nice meeting you, but we need to get inside now. Come on, Kath." He seemed to want the conversation to be over.

Valerie smiled cheerfully. "Nice talking to you. Maybe I'll see you around some time."

The woman, Kath, gave a nice smile and followed her husband inside. Valerie smiled and waved. This was a good start. Her next step was to find out who this house-sitter was. She had no idea where this was going, but supposed she needed to start somewhere.

She called Anna again and left her a message. "Anna, I don't know if you've contacted the owners, but I might have some new information. Apparently, there was someone looking after this house before me. Last year, as I understand. And I don't know if the owners have ever lived here themselves. Don't know if this helps. Talk to you soon. Please call as soon as you have anything."

Anna called her back a few days later, saying, "With the help of the agent, I did reach the owners. They have no idea who the house-sitter was, if you can believe that. The woman was hired through a third party agency, whose name they cannot recall."

"So the owners had never lived here themselves, according to the neighbours."

"Apparently not. They bought the house on speculation years ago, from a developer, but were never able to stay. The house had just been built and hadn't been lived in by anyone."

"Well, how could we find out which agency was used to hire this other woman?"

"I don't know why you need the information or how much it means to you, but I could do a search using the address. You know–the woman would have had utilities listed in her name, or parcels delivered, or something. There must be a paper trail. Leave it with me, Valerie."

Valerie was grateful for her friend's help. She was well aware of how valuable Anna could be, given her previous history in various positions in government ranging from jobs in the areas of laws and statutes, criminal records, and in the Public Services and Procurement department, as well as her current business of running her employment agency

Valerie spent the next day doing a ridiculously thorough search of the house. In true Nancy Drew fashion, she found herself pulling out all the drawers in hopes of finding an envelope scotch taped to the bottom of one of them. There was not a single scrap of evidence that anyone had ever lived there. The house was in pristine condition. There were no papers, no mail left unclaimed–nothing. Valerie could only wait. Night fell, and Valerie found the darkness unsettling. Emboldened, she walked to the back porch. She turned out the lights and wrapped her hands over her eyes, pressing her face against the glass. She couldn't see much, other than a big moon and some fog, over a yard covered in dead debris. She shuddered and retreated. Why were there no curtains on these windows? No wonder she avoided the back of the house.

She was hungry for more information but didn't want to push the neighbours. It seemed to her that Kath was more willing to talk than her husband Ted. If she ever had the chance, she would speak with the woman alone.

The opportunity presented itself a few days later, while Valerie was using the waterside path to take Max home. She saw Kath walking past the small parking lot adjacent to the shops at Crescent Beach. She hurried over to her.

"Hi. Remember me? I'm your new neighbour."

"Yes, of course I remember you. But I don't remember your name." Kath bent down to pet Max, who was too busy moving around, making it impossible for her fingers to make actual contact.

"Perhaps I didn't introduce myself. I'm Valerie."

The woman extended her hand. "Nice to meet you again."

Valerie shook Kath's hand. "I hope you don't mind, but I have one more question about the woman who previously looked after the house I'm staying in."

Kath interjected, "Well, it wasn't just the woman, dear. Soon after she came, a man moved in with her. She said he was her husband. Who knows where he had been. He seemed to just show up one day. No luggage or anything. But he didn't come outside very often and he never spoke."

Kath's husband Ted appeared, a questioning look on his face.

"This is Valerie. Remember her, Ted? She was just asking about the couple from the house."

Valerie lied, "Oh yes, I heard about the woman and now I think I may have known her. You know, these agencies, we often cross paths with each other. Wasn't her name Mary Smith?" She thought to herself. Smith. Seriously? Was that the best she could come up with? These guys would know she was lying, as everything about it sounded phony.

But they took the bait. "No, no. It was White," said Ted.

Kath disagreed with this. "No, it was Weiss. Not White. I think that was his name, but like I said, I'm not sure if they were married, although she said it was her husband."

Valerie again tried to expand on this. "That's it. Weiss. I think her first name was something like Sherry?"

Ted answered with a shake of his head, "It was Audrey. His name was Jay."

Kath's eyes lit up. "Now I remember. She said it was John, I think, but she called him Jay."

"Oh silly me, I must have got her got mixed up with someone else," said Valerie, slapping her forehead with her palm in a mocking gesture. Neither husband nor wife seemed to notice that she had cleverly pried this information out of them. She quickly continued, "Well, she left some things in the house and I'd like to return them, if I could. I don't suppose you know where she went?"

"Not a clue," Ted replied. "Like I said, they weren't friendly. But I think it was Al down the road who helped find her, from that agency he used to work for. They've gone belly up now, I'm sure, but maybe he remembers something."

"So you said Al doesn't work for any agency now?" asked Val as she casually pet Max on the head.

"No," answered Ted. "He's usually hanging around the coffee shop most of the time, these days. That flower place, just by the little park."

"Sunflower," offered Kath.

Thanking the couple, Valerie excused herself. Again, she didn't want to draw too much attention to her questions. "Well, it was nice running into you." She took a deep breath and exhaled. "Wow, it's a beautiful day, right? I suppose I'd better take Max home now. See you around." And she walked away as though the conversation was mostly inconsequential.

That evening, Valerie left Anna a message, asking her to search the names she had been given. Then she searched the web looking for any information or stories about Audrey and John Weiss, but came up with nothing. She went through drawers in the garage and still found nothing.

She knew she would need to patiently wait for news. Anna would search for the simplest things, like a change of address on a driver's licence, or employment insurance payments that were generated, or a number of things like that. She would likely have access to credit card and bank records, and deliveries from online companies. How Valerie wished she could help her. The woman was prepared to dig out of her jurisdiction and reveal all that she found. Valerie loved this edge of badness in Anna and hoped it would be worth the wait.

25

Early the next morning, after a hurried breakfast of peanut butter on rye with a mashed overripe banana, Valerie went for a walk to try to find this Al fellow that lived down the road. Of course, she had no idea what he looked like. She would have to ask every man sitting at the coffee shop if he was Al. Fortunately there were only three men there, seated on their own. The second man she asked was named Al.

"My name is Valerie, I'm a neighbour of Kath and Ted, and they told me I could find you here. I have a friend who needs to hire a house-sitter and you see, I didn't come from an agency, so they aren't interested in me. Do you happen to remember the company where Audrey Weiss came from? These people met her when she worked here and they want to discuss a job for her. They liked her very much."

"I don't know if her name was Audrey, but the name Weiss rings a bell. But yes, I think I do know which agency sent her," he disclosed, seeming not at all concerned to be sharing this information. "I can look into it, but it was nearly two years ago."

He had said yes! "Oh thank you so much. Can I give you my phone number?" Her heart was beating rapidly. Without waiting for him to answer, she grabbed a napkin from the dispenser and scribbled her number down. Smiling sweetly at the man, she added, "This is very kind of you, and I would be so grateful for your help. I'll look forward to hearing from you."

Valerie went home, again feeling optimistic. She didn't have long to wait. Before another day had gone by, Al called her with the name of an agency in Mission. "They won't be in now, but you could try them in the morning. Wait, no. That's Saturday. Maybe try on Monday."

Valerie was pleased with her progress thus far. She mused at how much her life had changed since moving from Fort Langley. There, she had played the waiting game. Waiting for what, she wasn't sure, but here she felt a slow shift back to her old self. She had still been recovering from her previous trauma. Here and now, she felt vibrant, back in the game.

The following Monday she called the agency under the pretence of being an agent for the owners. The woman who answered the phone was very cheerful, which Valerie took as a good sign. She explained that she was hoping to discover the whereabouts of Audrey Weiss.

"They want Audrey back, as the current sitter has to leave."

"I'm surprised to hear they want her. I understood it was a bit of a mess when she left without notice. And she had that man with her, which they didn't know about."

"Who, Jay? Apparently he is her husband, and that was all sorted out. Uh, well, and they've gotten over it. You see, she was, they had discovered, very good at her job. They want to forgive any personal issues that may have caused her to leave early." There was silence at the end of the line. "Good help is hard to come by," she added, unsure if this person was buying it.

"Okay, we'll get back to you," said the woman.

"Would it be okay if I called you back in a day or two? I won't be easy to reach for the next couple of days." Valerie was afraid the woman would discover that she didn't work for an agency at all.

"Sure, give me a day or two." And with that, they ended the call.

True to their word, when she called the agency back they had looked up the information for her.

"Good news and bad, depending on how you want to look at it. We don't know where she went. We don't keep track. All we can do is tell you where she lived before she worked for your client." The woman gave her the last known contact information, which was an address in Burnaby. Valerie wanted to drive by the house, and she thought to ask Brian if he would accompany her. She desperately wanted to get him on board. But her better judgment told her to wait until she had something positive to tell him.

He had gently tried to warn her off. "Valerie, I will not tell you what to do. You've had enough people do that to you. You will figure this out on your own. You are smart, and hopefully will know when to move ahead and when to stop. Only you know why you are doing this."

This was something that was difficult for Valerie to explain. For the past ten months she had been hiding from something. She had spent her time in obscurity, living in someone else's house, walking their dog and whiling away the days. But she had had enough of that. She was tired of being reactive. It was time to come back to being what she really was; strong and motivated, proactive, someone who solved problems and looked for answers.

While disappointed by Brian's refusal to help her, she felt grateful that he didn't make her feel like an idiot or tell her she was wasting her time. But Valerie was not prepared to give up. Each day had brought her a bit closer. As she was leaving the house one rainy morning, she caught a glimpse of the neighbour to the left of her, and she wasted no time in going over. After introducing herself to the young man, she asked her question.

"I'm trying to contact the previous woman who looked after this house. Do you know anything about her?"

"We don't know anything about her. Her husband was a piece of work. A real jerk, if you ask me. I wasn't sorry to see them leave. Some very bizarre things were happening over there."

A young woman came out of the house to join them on the lawn. Hearing the man speak, she added, "You talking about them next door? They gave me the creeps. One night we heard screaming. Well, arguing, I guess, but it gradually got worse to the point it sounded awful.

Memory can sometimes be misleading but I remember that night perfectly. What I heard were bloodcurdling screams. Doors were slamming, someone was howling. After a few weeks, we hardly saw her, but then suddenly he was the one we always saw," she said. "Not her."

Her partner lifted his finger in the air to make a point. "There was an incident. I remember cars coming late at night, then the next day a big truck with a machine came over. He saw us outside and came over to tell us there was a rotted tree in the back that needed removing, and the stump needed to be ground out."

"Yes," the woman agreed. "I remember that as well. And it seemed odd that he took the time to explain, when we really didn't give a shit what he was doing. We hadn't noticed anything sick about the tree, but then again, it wasn't our yard, or our call."

The man continued, "For all the next day we heard chopping, chipping and grinding, then everything went quiet again. My wife says she saw him, but I don't remember seeing either of them much after that. Then again, I work long hours and to tell you the truth, I didn't really give a shit about them next door. I've got my own stuff to worry about."

Valerie thanked the two and went on her way. It was odd that no one had seen Audrey since that night. What had happened there? She also hadn't noticed a missing tree. But there were so many trees in the yard it would likely be easy to miss one. When she arrived home, she stood on the back porch, gazing out at the yard. It wasn't as wide as it was deep, and there were many trees, mostly along the north and east sides. Some of the trees were massive, and old, casting a gloomy shroud over half the yard. Others were more shrub-like than actual trees. She saw overgrown cedar, pyracantha, holly, and even bamboo. A small stack of cut wood covered with moss stood along the fence.

The grass needed cutting, but luckily there wasn't a lot of it. The lawn had been reduced to patchy areas of dirt covered with pine needles, dead grassy patches that had been burnt by the sun, as well as a moss-covered aggregate patio slab. And what lay under the dead grass and pine needles? She whispered, "Are you down there, Audrey Weiss?" As she went back inside, a chill ran up her spine.

Over the next few days, Valerie tried to stay out of the house as much as possible. She spent many restless nights lying awake, reinforcing her notion that it was time to have her own place. Each morning, once she was awake, she would grab a bite to eat and spend most of the day on the beach or parked in her car looking over the water, dozing or reading her book. As the days passed she was getting more involved in her assignments for the Olympics, and she wanted to be really focused. She spent all her mornings at the coffee shop looking at apartments online and in the paper. She wasn't ruling out Port Moody, as she had so enjoyed the trip there with Karen and the kids. She also tried to eat more, as she knew she'd lost weight and was concerned that Brian had said she didn't look well.

Anna finally called her back to say she found nothing nefarious. "I got your message and started searching for that name. There seems to be no record of anyone named Weiss living at that address, or anywhere in the area. As for Weiss anywhere in BC, I found none that seemed connected to anyone named John or Jay, or even Audrey, for that matter."

Valerie groaned. "How can they just vanish?"

"Why is this so important to you? Why do you want to find them?"

"The neighbours here seem to think the man who lived in this house might have been up to no good. And the woman who was with him–the one who had actually been hired to watch the house-had stopped coming around. I'm trying to find out what happened to her."

"But there's no Weiss, so I don't know who they are or where they went."

"Well, what if he had a different name? Look at me, Anna. My name is Katerina and just like that I changed it to Valerie. Nobody ever questioned it. I started using it on credit cards, rentals, utilities, banks, everything. And nobody ever did any kind of search into whether I changed it."

"Well, your second name is Valeria, so it's not exactly the same thing. But you are right, it's easy to change a name, and unfortunately I can't search by given name."

Remembering what Kath and Ted next door had said, about the name possibly being different, Valerie mentioned it to Anna. "So maybe it was White and not Weiss? Can you check that?"

"Okay leave it with me again. And Valerie? I really don't have time for this, but I have to admit, it's fun! I've never dug this deep before. I'll check other sources as well."

Early the next morning Anna called her back. "Guess what, Valerie, you clever, clever girl. The man's name was Pandin, not Weiss. John Pandin. The woman's name isn't Weiss either. It's White, and she isn't really his wife. There was another very interesting thing I discovered. They had moved away from Burnaby months before they moved there to your house. I have no idea where they were in the interim or where they went after that. But he had still used the address for various things, even though someone different was living there. I'm still checking, Valerie. I think I'm getting closer."

Valerie thanked her friend. If she could prove that Audrey was in the yard, all she had to do was try to convince Brian. And she had lots of time to do that. The body wasn't going anywhere. In the meantime, she had enough to do to keep herself busy with telephone appointments and emails. Things at work were suddenly proceeding at a rapid pace. On Thursday, she needed to drive to Burnaby for a meeting, and she wanted to be prepared and appear professional and capable.

Valerie left the house early Thursday morning with a hot carafe of coffee in her cup holder. It felt great to be back in the game. She knew the day would be long and she was looking forward to this new focus. She arrived at her destination, managed to find a parking spot, and hurried inside. As soon as she entered the room, she knew this would be good. She loved the team, and she was well received. Valerie was glad she had done her homework and had come prepared, as she was easily able to join into the conversation and with a good knowledge of what was going on.

One of the biggest issues plaguing the committee at present was that people were already screaming about the cost of the Olympic Village. The economic market had crashed, people were defaulting on mortgages, and building costs were up. The developer had backed out of the project forcing the city of Vancouver to bear the liability. And with building not yet completed, the city was legally obligated to finish the village in time for the games. None of this was sitting well with city taxpayers, who were in an uproar. Politicians were blaming the previous government. Also, there were the rumours of tradespeople making side deals and many suspicions of ulterior motives. And this was just the start. The public was not yet aware of all the details, but they were being discussed at length today.

But even though engaged, it was still difficult at times to stay focused. She couldn't shake the feeling of a body being buried in her backyard. But one thing became clear; it was in fact easy to disappear into a city, or into a crowd. Valerie herself had been concerned about how well she could hide from her past, but she was learning that it was perhaps easier than she thought. This frustrated her, as she had spent so much time afraid to do anything that might draw unwanted attention.

During a brief lunch break, Valerie checked her messages. Anna had tried to reach her. It seemed that while searching her employment databases, she had discovered that a woman had registered for work in the Interior–a woman named Audrey White. She had used an address in East Vancouver.

"That was two months ago. Still, that doesn't mean she's alive. There's the possibility someone is using her name, or that John put the name into the registry so it would look like she is alive. It's hard to say for sure," the message from Anna said. "Another thing to remember, it would be easy to disappear into any of these areas in Vancouver, as many homes have basement units and the high rises are a constant revolving door of tenants. When I checked it out, the unit was unoccupied and had been for quite some time."

Anna could be close to locating Audrey, and apparently she could very well be alive. Then again, she now knew it was not that easy to find someone who didn't want to be found.

26

Surprised to hear that Audrey might actually be alive, Valerie accepted the news with mixed emotions. It's not that she wanted her to be dead, but it would have easily solved her problem about the body in the yard. It would have been closure, knowing it was Audrey who was pushing up daisies. But that now left the nagging question: if not Audrey, then who the hell was in her yard? Now, a sane person would have said there's nobody in the yard, but Valerie knew better. This just meant she'd have to start her search over again. But she couldn't think about that now.

It had been a long day and the traffic was terrible, yet she almost preferred being here in traffic than at the house. She wanted to see Brian and talk to him. Every now and then it troubled her when she reflected on how few friends she had, and how many she had abandoned. Pulling into her driveway, she locked her things in the trunk and, without going into the house, headed for the water. She needed a long walk.

She was well into her walk and beginning to feel calm when Anna called her back. "It's funny, but when you gave me the address, I thought the street sounded familiar. So I did some checking. The Burnaby address for this Pandin guy is just a few doors down from a man named Silas Madden. I remember this man. There was a story about his wife disappearing a couple of years ago, I think. Maybe less than that."

Valerie tensed at the name, but said nothing. "Okay, thank you Anna. All of this has been so confusing, but at the same time, it's starting to make sense. I'll talk to you soon. Please let's get together when you have some time, okay?"

Valerie disconnected the phone, her brain spinning with these new theories. She remembered the name Madden. That day in her house, Brian had said something about his wife disappearing. This had to be the same Madden. Was there a connection between John Pandin and Silas Madden? Could this man somehow have been involved? Up until now there had been nothing linking the couple to anything suspicious, but maybe Anna had just found something. It was definitely time to call Brian.

Having not spoken to him for quite a few weeks, Valerie needed a strategy. She decided to ask if he'd like to walk on Mud Bay. It was an area of Boundary Bay that she had heard of but had not yet explored. She had been hoping to get a glimpse of a bald eagle or perhaps a snowy owl. Someone had told her they could often be seen along the wild, natural shoreline. This, she decided, was a good premise for which to call.

The conversation was brief, and Brian readily agreed. She knew he wouldn't be very happy that she was using this opportunity to trap him into another conversation about the house, but still, she thought it necessary. It would be really nice to see him again, as she really enjoyed their conversations, but didn't want him to feel she had another motive for seeing him.

"If you can wait until next Friday, I can pick you up. How about ten?"

"Sounds good, Brian. I'll be ready." It meant a lot to her that he had never said no, and he was never grumpy. She pushed aside her guilt and hung up the phone. Some things were just necessary. Valerie jotted the time on her calendar, as lately with so much on her mind she had become a bit forgetful.

They arrived at a fairly empty parking lot and Valerie was taken aback by the view. She walked to the water's edge and stood looking across the bay to where she lived, towards Crescent Beach. The bay was aptly named, as the tide was out and before her lay a large crescent-shaped bay of mud. It seemed to her that if she wanted, she could simply walk home across the waterless bed of mud, except that it looked slimy and sticky and smelled of sulphur and seaweed. She could see the small marina at the mouth of the Nicomekl River, where she often walked Max.

They hadn't been walking more than five minutes before Brian began asking about her new job. She chatted happily about her first in-person office visit. Brian was unusually quiet.

Wondering what it could be, she suddenly remembered he had been away. "That time back then, when you didn't return my call. You had mentioned you were away on a family medical emergency. Is everything okay?"

"Oh, that. Yes. It's my stepmother. She'd had a stroke, and it was pretty scary for my dad, but she's actually making some progress. She's not a hundred percent, but she's strong and she's working hard to make a full recovery. I want them to move back here but they aren't interested."

"Where do they live?" she asked.

"Right now they live in Kitchener, but they want to move closer to Toronto. Anyway, they will do what they want. We talked for quite a while, and I guess they are happy doing what they are doing. They are private and love a quiet life, so I'll respect that."

Valerie couldn't wait any longer. "Speaking of living a nice private life, I have a bit of an update, if you are interested to hear about it."

"Sure, let's have it," he responded, a slight smile appearing on his face.

"It's about a man you once mentioned. Madden. The case of his wife disappearing." She wanted to be sure this was the same person he had been speaking of. "Was his name Silas?"

"Yes, I believe Silas is the name of the man I was referring to."

Pleased by this, she quickly told him about the new information she had on the man now known as Pandin and not Weiss. "Did you know the guy that lived in my house was once a neighbour of Silas Madden? So could there be a connection? What are the odds of them being neighbours? Could you maybe check into it?"

Brian looked at her. "I could look into it for you, although I need to warn you that it might be a waste of time. I'm sure he was already questioned."

Valerie touched his arm softly and agreed. "Yes, I could be wasting my time. But really, questioned isn't exactly suspected, is it now? Besides, what else am I doing? I've been sitting around going brain-dead. I'm good at research. It will keep me sharp for my new job. I can't learn much from walking Max, can I?"

She stole a glimpse of him out of the corner of her eye. Was he feeling ambushed? Tricked into having this conversation? She couldn't tell, but also didn't want to think about that right now. Feeling no real objection, she continued. "On the positive side, this might be the connection you need. And I have witnesses that can tell your people about the strange happenings at the house. For example, why would they take a tree down? And what was the screaming about? And where was Audrey? They say she disappears afterwards."

"Yes, I must admit, you've done well. Let's just go slowly and see what develops, okay? Don't rule out that the tree could have been dead."

Her fears of upsetting him proved unfounded and she breathed with relief. He was, after all, a detective and likely enjoyed the hunt as much as she did. They left it at that, and Valerie, not wanting to give him time to change his mind, began chatting about the view over the bay as they made their way back to the car. She couldn't believe they had walked as far as they had.

"Is that Mount Baker over there?" She knew well that it was Baker. She remembered seeing it from Sydney, when she had cycled there with Garret. That now seemed years ago. Brian seemed to not have heard her, as he had his brow furrowed as if deep in thought.

"I must admit you really don't give up, do you? Please don't misunderstand me. I don't mind checking into the name. I agree there's enough here to at least make someone curious. We just don't know if it's anything criminal. That's all I can do."

"And that's all I can ask," she responded. Brian looked deep in thought, and Valerie felt she needed to break the tension.

"Hey, I didn't tell you. I'm working on the entertainment lineup for the Olympics, and guess what? Last week I got Burton Cummings for the medal ceremonies." Brian smiled.

During the drive back from Mud Bay, the windows were open, and the breeze felt good. The radio was playing a song she didn't recognize, and she closed her eyes to enjoy the melody. She loved this shift in their relationship. It dawned on her that Brian was actually her friend, and in her gut, she knew he felt the same. It was comforting. As requested, Brian dropped her off at the small roundabout at Crescent Beach.

"Thank you, it was a really great walk. I hope your stepmom will be okay." She got out of the car and waved as he drove away. Maybe she would just sit here by the ocean for a spell, before returning to the house. She found comfort in the sight and sound of the gently lapping water as it caressed the white, sandy shore. She felt at peace to be in the presence of the people beach-combing, their laughter rising on the breeze to blend in unison with the sounds of the seagulls. Yes, right now, this was where she wanted to be.

27

Brian had promised to call her back, and he did. Valerie was out walking Max, who was needlessly barking at another dog. She didn't hear the phone right away, but she was able to answer just before he rang off. This dog was really annoying her.

"Not good news," Brian reported. "There is nothing on him. Not even a speeding ticket. They may have lived close to Silas Madden, but that doesn't mean anything. It could very well be a coincidence. I think I did tell you this guy Silas was a piece of work. If he's guilty, he was real careful. Maybe you read about the case. He had the entire neighbourhood scouring the area for his wife. People came from all over the region to join in the search party. Her picture was smeared all over the news and on every street post and shop window. He had told police that he and his wife had argued, and that she had gone for a hike on Burnaby Mountain. The police wanted to know why he waited three days before reporting her missing. I don't remember, but it was something vague like, he thought she had gone to a friend's house, or to her mother's."

"So why was he never charged?"

Brian shook his head. "He had this carefully con-structed story but it couldn't be proved nor could it be disproved. Family and friends were angry, kept a neigh-borhood search up for more than a year following her dis-appearance. At least five times they questioned the man, they had searched his house, had him on surveillance-but found nothing to warrant an arrest."

Valerie jumped at the clamour she heard behind her. It sounded like a train roaring down the sidewalk. She turned quickly and moved on to the grass, narrowly escaping being mowed down by a group of youths on skateboards.

"Watch where you are going, you jerks," she screamed at them. Coming back to the phone, she asked, "So you think he is guilty?"

Brian assented instantly. "We all do. But we just couldn't prove it."

"Just because this Pandin guy didn't have a speeding ticket, doesn't mean he couldn't have helped Madden get rid of a body, does it? Okay, so here's another thought. What if this man Pandin knew someone else who knew Madden? Maybe there was another degree of separation?"

"Valerie, there was an extensive investigation." He sighed. "Okay, I'm beginning to understand where you are going with this, so spit it out. You think you have either Audrey White or Carol Madden buried in your yard. Come on now. Don't keep that light under a bucket."

"Here's the thing Brian. I remember what you said about the man on the pig farm. Didn't he get away with it for years? You said people made mistakes. You said people knew but said nothing. You even said the police ignored the signs. There wasn't one single person who could actually prove anything. And didn't you also say if it wasn't for one persistent cop who just wouldn't let go, who kept digging for answers they might never have caught him? Just one guy Brian. That's all it took. You even said so."

She heard Brian sigh. "Hang on, I have to take this call." He put her on hold. Then, "I'm sorry Valerie, but I've been called away. I need to go. Please be careful, and be smart. But I have to agree you have made a very compelling argument. I'll see who else I can talk to on my end."

Feeling mildly elevated, Valerie called Anna. She wanted to know if Anna could dig a little deeper into John Pandin and ask if she'd found anything new on Audrey White.

But Anna wasn't prepared to do anything more. Not this time. Not without getting something in return. "Tell me why you want to know. This is starting to sound interesting."

"What if he was somehow connected to something bad. Maybe even to Silas Madden."

"But wait a minute, I just told you about Madden the other day. Why were you asking about this couple before now?"

"Because I thought they may have done something terrible when they were living here, before I came. I don't know what, or if they even did anything. But now this possible connection to Madden makes things more plausible."

Anna let out a disapproving tsk. "Okay, I'll play along. But I want to be a part of it, Valerie."

Valerie was thrilled at this. "Can you find out things like, where did he work, who did he work for and work with, and who did he hang out with? I think he is the clue, Anna, I really do. And hey, if there's any part of this that I can help with, please let me know."

"I can easily do employment searches and so forth. It helps having his real name even if I don't have a legitimate address. Thanks Valerie, this will be interesting to see where it goes."

Valerie looked down at Max and shook her head as she headed in the direction of its owners. She would need to let them know she could no longer walk their dog. She was just too preoccupied, and she had to prepare to move, and to start her job. They might be upset but she was certain they would understand. Besides, he wasn't really that interesting a dog. He was no Hank.

Anna did call later, to ask Valerie if she was willing to driving to a small business in Mission. Apparently John Pandin worked there around the same time that Silas Madden's wife disappeared. "Valerie, the business is owned by John's cousin Jerry Kowalski. Tell them you are looking for this Pandin guy's wife, or something."

"I can't do that, are you crazy? I might get myself killed. I can try calling, but I'm not going there."

"Okay, call them. Here's the number."

"But what would I say? You should call them, Anna. Tell them you run an employment agency and you have people looking for work. That makes more sense to me. Tell them one of your clients knew Audrey and they had suggested this company as possible employment. Then talk nice, and ask about John and his good friend Silas. Say you were a friend of Carol's and you had once met them together at a neighbourhood picnic or some shit like that. Make something up!"

Anna had reluctantly agreed, as she knew Valerie was right. This was her business, after all. Employment. Valerie waited to hear from Anna; her friend had worked hard and had come up with a lot of information, but Valerie realized it still wasn't enough. She still could go no further until she heard from Anna.

A few minutes later, Anna called her back. The man said they were not hiring, and that while they had no idea where John or Audrey might be. "But get this, Val-he suggested I try reaching her through the equipment rental place out there in Mission, where she used to work. He called her Audrey Bishop, Valerie. Not Audrey White."

"How many names can one person have?" exclaimed Valerie. "So they both worked in Mission at the same time."

"Yes. And it was around the time that Carol Madden disappeared. So what now?" asked Anna.

"I'll get back to you. Thanks for this."

Valerie sat down at her computer to do a search on the equipment rental company. She found they rented small Cat excavators. She was trembling with excitement.

Next she did a image search of Audrey Bishop. She nearly jumped out of her seat when a photo appeared on the screen. Valerie recognized her! It was the girl with the thick auburn braid. She had been at Garret's bicycle shop on more than one occasion, bringing bikes in for repair. It was one of those bulky mountain bikes, with big fat tires and a heavy tube frame. A bike most certainly suited for carrying drugs. Valerie remembered thinking at the time, who needs their bike repaired that often? There was no longer any doubt in her mind that there was a clear connection.

She grabbed a glass of wine and sat down to document a chronological order of things she had brought to light. She had so far discovered that the previous tenant at this house was Audrey White a.k.a. Bishop. Her partner, Jay Weiss, was actually John Pandin, and they were once neighbours of Silas Madden in Burnaby. She had also found out that John had worked for a cousin in Mission at the same time that his girlfriend Audrey, whoever the hell she was, had worked for an equipment rental business which just happened to have nifty little tools like a stump grinder and a cat front end loader. And she worked there at the same time that Madden's wife went missing. But like Brian had told her, nothing up to now had proved anything. Except that now, there was this connection to Garret. Brian may want to pursue this, as it might link Audrey and John to Garret's drug dealing friends.

Valerie was curious about something else. They had both disappeared after that. How do you explain that? Where was the couple now? But since Valerie had just found a link between this house and the Madden guy, just maybe this was now enough to justify a warrant. She wasted no time in jumping to her conclusion. Madden would have had access to this yard without anyone suspecting. And at the mention of Garret's name, Brian just might be a little more enthusiastic about getting involved.

She wanted so badly to tell Brian, and as she spoke to his voice mail she was tripping over her words, asking him to call. She knew enough to leave no detail on a recording. But he had called her back, saying, "Just please don't talk about it now. Tell me on Monday. It's Friday afternoon and you need a break from the case. We are going to your restaurant tomorrow night, okay? You need food."

Her heart was glowing. This was exactly what she needed! She laughed appreciatively. "Thank you, Brian."

28

Valerie could hardly wait for the evening to arrive. By noon she had showered, washed her hair and selected an outfit – her blue calf length summer dress, with tiny white and navy flowers. She had not worn it for years and had long been hoping for an occasion. When she checked herself in the mirror, she approved. While she was a bit thinner, the dress still fit well. The neckline was open, sitting low across her shoulders. The smocked bodice was fitted, opening up to a gently flared skirt, softly gathered in the front.

She pinned her long back hair up and twisted it into a bun. Last, she applied a bit of blush and clasped on her single string of pearls that her mother and father had given to her when she graduated. Her enthusiasm caught her off guard. When Brian had called he had asked her to come early, so they could walk along the waterfront promenade first. She said okay.

"Park at the lot closest to the pier," he had said.

She arrived a few minutes early. Brian stood there waiting by the entrance. He was wearing a blue and yellow check shirt and khaki trousers. His hair partially groomed back, but not the full slick of his day job. When

Valerie got out of her car she raised her head and took in a deep breath. It was a lovely, breezy evening; perfect for a walk.

"I thought we could walk out to the end of the pier and watch the sunset," he said.

Valerie was intrigued with this man, who was soft spoken and reserved, yet tough on the outside. She found herself wanting to know more about him – his core, his essence. His job as well was shrouded in mystery. Curious, she asked again about his work at the pig farm.

"It was not a good time, Valerie. Many of my colleagues were affected, not only me. Not long afterwards, two of them had complete breakdowns and went on long-term disability. Another few took early retirement. I never see them any more, and we were close back then. You see, we reminded each other of things that none of us wanted to remember. Besides, who we used to be is not who we are any more, so there was no point in reliving any of it."

"Trauma can really change a person. I know it did me," Valerie replied, carefully.

He nodded. "I changed a lot. I think I too became withdrawn, and I didn't recognize myself. My wife noticed it. I needed something that she could no longer give me. I was damaged in the worst possible way. Anyway, she left me after that. She absolutely broke my heart and she picked the worst possible time to go. I think we had already grown apart, even before any of the other things happened, but I guess this last thing was just too much. She had already been sleeping in the other room for quite some time. Thinking back, she never really understood me, or my work. And then when I needed her the most... Anyway, soon after, she moved to the Kootenays, to *rediscover herself*, she said. I think she struggled for a long time, not knowing what she wanted. But clearly she no longer wanted me. She found a boyfriend and said she wanted a baby. I suppose that was her rediscovery. But still, she called me all the time. She said she was worried about me, so we'd have brief catch-up conversations. They were good talks, and I was happy for her."

"People can stay close, even if the love is gone. There can remain a friendship and understanding, and familiarity, especially if you are living among strangers for any length of time." Valerie spoke the words, but who was she to utter them? She herself made no attempt at contacting anyone who could have understood her and helped her through any of this.

Brian took off his sunglasses and rubbed his eyes. Putting them back on, he continued. "She went for a run one morning and was mauled by a black bear. Somehow she got between the sow and her cub. She survived the initial attack but not her injuries. Her boyfriend had always begged her not to run alone. She never liked to be told what to do. It had always been a problem of ours. See, I was a cop, and anally disciplined to the core. And she was someone who hated rules and order."

"I'm sorry," Valerie responded, not sure what else to say.

"You have no reason to be sorry." Brian checked his watch. "We'd better go, it's getting to be our time."

They arrived at the restaurant a few minutes early. As their table was not yet ready, they were seated in a small section inside a solarium where they were offered a drink and an appetizer. They ordered two glasses of Prosecco and a bowl of olives.

Valerie held her breath before asking the next question. She didn't want to overstep their individual privacy any more than necessary. "So after you lost your wife, was there anyone else? I mean, is there anyone in your life now?"

"Well, I did like this girl once. It was a few months ago. I met her in Fort Langley, but she moved away, so I guess it doesn't matter any more."

"Oh, really?" Valerie sipped the light bubbly drink.

Brian nodded as he diverted his gaze. "Yes, but it's okay, because she was actually not very friendly. And I don't think she liked me anyway. She seemed to like my brother more."

Valerie's mouth fell open. "That's not fair, Detective Tobin! You were absolutely horrible to me, the way you were acting like this warrior or something, trying to take me down."

Brian looked at her and responded with, "Are you serious? I was doing my job. And what if it had been the girl from the porch that I had come across? Wouldn't you want me to vigorously interrogate her? I didn't know anything about you. And you were, by all accounts, a hostile witness. Wouldn't you agree that I needed to, under the circumstances?" He casually popped an olive into his mouth.

"Okay, fair enough." She felt her cheeks colour. "So, what you just said, is it true?"

Brian had no time to answer, as at that moment they were called to their table. They looked at each other and smiled as if calling a ceasefire. Brian winked at her, confirming all was good. As they made their way inside, the smell of garlic and olive oil made her mouth water. The restaurant was mostly candle lit but for a few glowing drop lights. The décor was very modern with high quality wood, polished cement and lots of red fabric, making it very inviting.

The maître d' asked the two to follow him to a table in the far corner. Valerie noticed autographed photographs hanging on the walls, of celebrities who had visited. On the way to their table, she perused the many faces displayed. She stopped short as she came across the photo of a familiar looking blond lady. Much to her surprise, there staring right at Valerie, her smile revealing those big white teeth, was the pretty lady from the bench in Fort Langley. She wore no hat or sunglasses, but it was definitely the lady with the pastrami sandwich. Valerie's jaw dropped as she read the inscription. It said, Diana Krall.

She looked at Brian in amazement. "You mean I talked to Diana Krall?"

The maître d' smiled. "Miss Krall comes here when she can. She and her husband. Valerie beamed as she again recalled the conversation she had with the woman that day.

She said to the maître d', "I know her. I talked to her." She was stunned with disbelief.

The man smiled again and said, "Are you saying you spoke with her and didn't know who she was?"

Valerie laughed. "That's exactly what I'm saying!"

Once comfortably seated, Brian ordered a bottle of red wine. Valerie really liked the restaurant. Her eyes eagerly devoured the menu as she sipped the bright red Sangiovese that Brian had chosen. "This is very good. You obviously have very good taste in wine."

"I also have excellent taste in women," he said, as he tipped his glass to hers. "And I have to tell you, you look great. Really beautiful."

For the first time in a very long time, Valerie felt a full-on hot blush blanket her face. She coyly looked away. But in truth, she felt beautiful. Here she was, in a fabulous restaurant, in her favourite dress, with a to-die-for police detective. How did this happen?

Shortly after, the waiter came to check on them and to see if they were ready to order. Upon Valerie's approval, Brian ordered a starter of grilled calamari with lemon and garlic.

The conversation revolved around the food and the restaurant. Valerie was very taken with the place, and it took her back to Sicily and to memories of her grandmother. They gobbled up the calamari with the fresh baked bread. Eventually the waiter returned to take their order.

"I'll have the Parmagiana di Melanzane – the way Diana likes it," she said with a grin.

The waiter raised his eyebrows. "Okay! So you know Diana, yes?"

Valerie let out a small giggle. "I know Diana, yes." Brian was smiling at her, his chin resting on his hand, his eyes intensely glued to her.

"Okay, perfecto. I play her music, yes?" And he left.

"You have no idea how long I've waited to say that," she announced proudly.

Someone came to pour them more wine from their bottle. They sipped in silence and listened to Diana's voice as it flowed through the speakers like water bubbling over stones.

"You look great when you relax," said Brian.

Valerie did feel her shoulders relax. Her body loosened up. She had crossed her legs and stretched her arm casually across the table. When Brian said something funny, she gently flung her head sideways and laughed. He made her feel beautiful, and right now she didn't have a care in the world. The ambience was fabulous, enhanced by the music of Diana Krall who was now singing "Charmed Life." Valerie silently thanked the chanteuse for reminding her it was indeed.

"She never said who she was!" Valerie's conversation had returned to her chance meeting with Diana. She had just finished her meal and had patted her stomach, marvelling at the recommendation.

"Maybe she preferred you seeing her just as a person sitting on a bench. Perhaps people treat her differently when they know who she is."

"I'm sure you are right."

Neither wanted dessert, and they finished their wine listening to Eros Ramazzotti singing Ti vorrei Rivivere. This was pure Italian magic.

Leaving a generous tip, Brian turned to her. "Come on, lets get out of here."

29

Wandering back out to the street, Brian asked if she'd like to sit by the water for a few minutes before leaving. Valerie loved the idea. They walked slowly as they searched for a good spot to sit. The sun had gone down and air was becoming quite cool, as it was still early in the spring season.

"I always thought if I just held my breath long enough, all this shit would go away and something new and fresh would happen to me."

"Hold your breath?" asked Brian.

"Yeah, you know. Like a hiccup, or if you lose your temper and then count to ten. Holding your breath – or just the space you create. Its supposed to renew things." Determined to not let the mood get serious again, she quickly added, "But this night has been really, really good for me. Thank you, Brian."

He smiled at her, but said nothing as they made their way onto the grassy flat.

"Know what I really miss?" Valerie knew she was a bit drunk but didn't care. "Those rainy days spent with my school friend Sadie. We'd sit on the floor in her bedroom and listen to CD's, and we'd sing along. Remember when you would buy cd's back then, and you'd open the little plastic case and on one side was the disc and on the other there was a little booklet that included the lyrics? I remember singing along with Jewel, and Natalie Merchant. I loved the Oasis song, Wonderwall."

They chose a bench by a big tree. Under the glow of the streetlight Valerie could see plump new buds that covered the branches, ready to sprout. Brian smiled.

"I remember that. Yeah, I suppose I miss school friends, but I don't think about it a lot. I had a good buddy, Kev. We used to play a lot of hockey back in the day. Kev was a big bugger – built like a tree trunk." Brian's smile grew wider as he reminisced.

"What do you miss most about him?"

"Oh – you know. We'd sit out back on the dock. We were about 15, and we'd have our album covers out and we'd sing along in the moonlight. We sang along to Shaggy. You know – Mr. Bombastic."

Valerie slapped his arm. "You're making fun of me."

"You are right, sorry. I am making fun. What did we do? We'd drink beer while we shot the puck around in the cul-de-sac. I guess sometimes we'd listen to music when his dad wasn't home. We'd smoke a joint and turn the music up in the garage and blast the neighbour-hood. We'd usually play Blue Rodeo. "What Am I Doing Here"–do you remember that one? And anything by the Tragically Hip was good. Love that band. We had our hockey, he and I. And girls," he added, winking at Valerie. "From Grade school right through to college."

"The hockey or the girls?" teased Valerie.

"Oh, the hockey. Girls had no time for us after we finished school. We carried on for a time in a beer league." He looked upwards, and smiled again as he remembered. His enjoyment was obvious.

They were interrupted by the sound of a train coming down the track. Both turned to watch it pass. Valerie was suddenly gripped by an overwhelming feeling of doom - that as lovely as this evening was, things might not end up well.

As the noise from the train subsided, Brian remarked, "You know, I haven't thought about these things in about a hundred years. This has been nice for me too. Really nice." The look on his face, at that moment, stunned Valerie. He could have outshone the moon. His smile changed his entire face, as it was the first time she had seen him with such a real, unfiltered, unguarded smile. She felt a rush go up her spine.

He adjusted himself, turning to face her. "Okay, your turn. What about you?"

It was Valerie's turn and there was no way out. "Going all the way back to Montreal, before Calgary, Alice was my best friend. She befriended me in my senior year, although the move surprised me. I was intimidated by her popularity and dynamic personality. She and I were so different. She was playful and persuasive, while I was bookish and serious. But she said she loved my brain, and was impressed at my choices for post secondary education.

Through her, I met her brother Julian. It was a strong attraction but even at the beginning I had forebodings about the whole thing. It was my one profound error in judgment."

"Alice or Julian?" he prompted, seeming excited by the fact that she was finally talking.

"Both, I suppose. Speaking of Julian, I could see it wouldn't work even before it didn't, so I never really did commit. Somehow his sister – and his family, convinced me that we were so good together, and that I was useless without him. That my decisions were bad but not to worry, because they were there to help me. By then, I don't know how it happened, but we had somewhat promised to marry. I wasn't happy, but he was thrilled. He was still finding his way, and didn't really know what he wanted. The problem is, I did know exactly what I wanted. And it wasn't to look after him."

"So why did you stay?" asked Brian.

"I was so young, and so impressionable. I had no relationship with my own family, so they became mine, in a way. Most of all, I felt sorry for Alice. Her mom was so incredibly manipulative. Alice would bend over backwards to please her. Mom's tactic was to lie in bed and cry until Alice did whatever she wanted. And I guess Julian was the same. So I wanted to be there for Alice, to cheer her up and be her friend, and give her reasons to be happy. But all along I didn't realize that she was doing exactly the same thing to me that her mom was doing to her. I fell for it! Once I was hooked, they convinced me I needed them. That I was incapable of making good decisions on my own. Yet I had always managed. That's when I think about that poor young girl. If I were that controlled by Julian, what would have happened to me if he led me down a path that involved drugs? Would I have done it? There's something wrong with how we humans try to please those who hurt us the most."

"So do you really believe it was that bad? You weren't forced to stay."

"Perhaps not, but I was gaslighted and was losing my confidence. I had been brainwashed, and it could have gotten a lot worse if I hadn't acted. I had accepted this great job, and I wasn't going to let him stop me. Especially since he seemed to be flailing without direction. I mean – I would have stayed if he had been doing something really important, but he wasn't. It's like I didn't even know him any more. He wasn't the same Julian. This guy was big on ideas but had absolutely no resume. So I broke up with him. I told him to sort himself out and then we could maybe try again. Julian was devastated but my best friend Alice was worse – she went berserk. Went totally off the rails. So did her family, mostly her mom. He was very close to his family, much closer than I am to my own. I became so aware of all the nuances that I had missed before-all of those subtle warning signs. So I made my arrangements to move away as soon as I could."

"Calgary," said Brian, playing with a toothpick.

"Yes. Calgary. I know there were other jobs I could have chosen. Closer jobs. But I moved there partly to get away from them – from him. It was only then that Alice told me about his past problems with drugs, and prison. She said it would be terrible if I left him now, as he needed me. They thought they could guilt me into helping him turn over a new leaf. That only I could save him, and whatever happened to him for evermore would be my fault. Running away from them felt like I was running from a cult, like I needed to run for my life. After that, Alice called me constantly, asking me to reconsider. It was crazy. His mom would also call me occasionally. It was almost incomprehensible. I couldn't believe they were serious!"

Valerie looked curiously at Brian, trying to read him. She was so worried that she would lose him over this confession. He seemed okay, his expression curious yet kind. So she continued.

"Anyway, close to a year later, he showed up on my doorstep. He looked awful! But I told him no. I told him to go back home, I was happy where I was. I didn't understand at the time. I was raised with practicality, not with compassion. We were taught survival, not so much feelings. So it was hard for me to understand that he was hurting – that I was hurting him. Things have always been matter-of-fact with me, but this! Afterwards I felt so guilty."

"But Val, you weren't hurting him. He was hurting himself. And you are right, that it wasn't your responsibility to look after him. It sounds like he was overly needy and dependent. It sound like they all were. Guilt is prime in moving us to all sorts of false devotions. Can you imagine your life today if you had stayed with him? So what happened? Did he go back home?"

"No he didn't." She wouldn't look at him for fear her expression would give her away. "Now I had both Alice and her mom guilt tripping me. His entire family wanted me to go back home to Montreal. Back to them, to resume our pathetic co-dependent relationship or whatever it is we had going on. As if somehow I would replace him. His mom said it was my fault because I didn't love him enough. I had no children so I didn't learn how to love enough. Then she cursed me and said she hoped I never had children, and if I did she hoped I would have to go through this as well."

"Ouch," said Brian. "But what about your own family? Would you go back there for them?"

"I could never go back, because there's no 'there' there. Not for me. Even the fact that my own family was in Montreal wasn't enough to make me go back. You see, Julian's family relies on each other to a degree that's almost morbid. My family is almost the complete opposite. Anyway shortly after that, I put my career on hold. I needed a fresh start in life, in a place where nobody knew me, and I came down here, to Burnaby."

"Did you love him, or is that too personal?"

"I remember moments of intimacy, waking up beside him. I remember kissing and smiling, and of caring, in the beginning. But truly, I don't think I ever loved him. He had a way of corroding any affection I might have felt for him. I felt trapped." As Valerie told her story to Brian, she was listening to how ridiculous it must sound to him. She felt completely and fundamentally flawed.

Brian's attention was absolute and his voice was full of concern. "So where did he go?"

Valerie shuddered. "It's a long story. I'd like to change the subject now, if it's okay. I feel like I've talked about it too much."

He started to say something but she cut him off. "I'm all right, Brian." She chanced a feeble smile.

"Maybe that's the problem. Maybe you *aren't* all right. Maybe you just tell yourself you are. You haven't yet dealt with this otherwise you'd be able to talk about it. Is this why you won't go back? You know, Valerie, in life, pain is inevitable but you need to keep living."

"Yes, Brian I know. Suffering is optional. I am trying, but that always sounds so easy."

30

By the following week, Valerie had made some big decisions. She no longer wanted to live in this place. As she
was now making good money, she wanted to be able to
choose where she lived. She grew more excited and at
the same time, agitated. She had already told Anna she
needed to move, that she could no longer stay in this
house. Besides, her job was going well and she wanted
to be closer to the freeway for better access to Vancouver.
Living out here was a nightmare in terms of getting
anywhere. Actually, living here was a nightmare, period.
Anna called again to be certain Valerie wanted to go.

"I want to move, Anna, and I would have wanted to
even if I hadn't gotten the job. I can't stay here any longer.
I need my independence back."

"Where will you go?"

"I don't know, but anywhere but here. This place is
lovely, don't get me wrong, but it's not for me. I've spent
too much time in places where I didn't want to be. Plus I
feel haunted in this house, and if I stayed here, the feeling
would stay with me. I've got a lead on a few places and
I've even started packing! So sorry, but you will have to

tell the owners I am looking for a place to go to, and they should start looking for someone to replace me."

With all of her notes in place and her research being completed, she was now ready to hand everything over to Brian. She waited for him on the front porch as he parked his car, two glasses of wine poured and standing on the small table by the steps. She felt her pulse quicken as he exited his car. It was the first time she had seen him since their dinner date. He climbed the stairs to the small porch and smiled at her as she invited him to sit. She placed a glass of wine in his hand.

"It's all here. I made you notes." She handed him a thick pad of paper, half full of her notations. She watched for a few minutes as his eyes scanned the pages. "Will they now dig up the yard? The Madden woman, Carol, could very well be there. Maybe they can find her after all this time and, hopefully, in the end this guy won't get away with it."

He was quietly reading, making the odd noise, occasionally raising an eyebrow. Valerie was dying to know what he thought. "You are the detective. What do you think? Come on! Please! That woman might be down there." By now, Brian would have realized that her focus had gone from Audrey to Carol in a short space of time, after having discovered Audrey's identity.

"Slow down, Valerie, let me read this." Brian's expression was intense as he studied the papers, his brow furrowed, one hand on his chin. "You are still trying to find this woman." He read on in silence. A few times she saw him nod, at other times he merely shook his head. Then he glanced up at her.

Before he could speak, she defended herself. "This isn't atonement, Brian, this is different. I know I can't save this one, but I can punish the prick that did this to her."

Brian was still saying nothing, but Valerie wasn't finished. "You even said I did good. Answer me truthfully. What I've shown you just now, did your guys know this, or is it new? Did I find something that they didn't?'

He smiled. "Relax, will you?" He held the notes in the air. "You have made some valid points, and I will take this new development to the homicide team. I will, I promise. And I will get back to you as soon as I can. And this part about Garret bothers me, but I can definitely see a connection. I need to go and see him personally. It may be in his best interest if he tells me where Audrey is. I think he'll do it, because it may help him in court if he cooperates." He seemed genuinely impressed with the progress she had made.

Together they sat back and drank their wine. He checked his watch and motioned towards the road. Valerie felt appeased as she walked Brian down the steps to his car. She watched the bend in the road long after the vehicle was no longer in sight. This was good.

She waited on pins and needles for what felt like weeks. It became difficult to think about her job, her deadlines, her commitments . . . all of it. Gone. This was all that mattered. This thing had grabbed her by the throat and wasn't letting go. She had to see it through.

Valerie sat in front of the warming fire. She watched the flames as they flickered, throwing random shadows around the darkened room. Her thoughts wandered aimlessly, often confusing her with nagging questions about her future. Will she ever own a house, wear nice clothing like before, and perhaps have a husband and a family of her own? Was it too late for the family part? Just where was she heading? The sound of the phone made her jump. She was thrilled to see Brian's number on the call display.

"You have their attention. They are sending detectives to talk to the neighbours and to corroborate the stories. Another team will go to Mission to talk to the previous employer of John Pandin. They will be discreet and not yet ask about his relationship to Silas Madden. We are also looking into Audrey Bishop. I'm seeing Garret in the morning, so I'll let you know how that goes. It's happening, Valerie."

Thanking Brian, Valerie hung up the phone, trembling. She had returned to the fire, delightfully elated. Her eyes were heavy, her body was tired, but there was an unmistakable feeling of achievement as a smile broke out on her face.

Brian called two days later to say that, following a visit to Audrey Bishop's previous employer at the rental company, they confirmed the timeline of her employment. Further probing revealed that John Pandin had rented a stump grinder two days before Silas Madden reported his wife missing. As for Garret, realizing it was in his best interest to cooperate, had directed him to a house in a rural area outside of Brookswood where the pair had been staying. Coincidentally, a stakeout of the property had been in place for quite some time, but not because of them. The drug squad had been staking out this house based on reports of drug transactions taking place between there and another location in Merritt.

Months ago, an informant had revealed the property as a place of interest. An assortment of familiar faces had been recorded coming and going, all linked to ecstasy as well as people who were known to be dealing crystal methamphetamine. The informant had been inside and had witnessed drug manufacturing in the basement. Brian had been caught off balance by the connection between this place and Valerie's instincts about her yard.

"All we need now is a reason to search your property. That's another thing. While talking to homicide, I reconnected with an old friend from the VPD. He runs the canine unit. He mentioned there's a cadaver dog in town, Valerie. He's on loan from Washington State."

"Does your friend want to come over for a glass of wine? Maybe he could let his dog play in the backyard for a few minutes," she said cheekily.

Brian laughed. "I could ask him, but even if they came, it would be off the record. Without a warrant we couldn't use it."

She couldn't help but smile at his sober-mindedness at failing to see the humour in her joke. "Yes but Brian, I only want to convince you. After that, it's up to you to find a way to convince them." She did notice that his demeanour changed when he was focused on his work.

"Let's see what these guys come back with. After they are done with their questioning they might be able to connect a few dots of their own."

Valerie was content with this, and she felt free enough to return her attention to her work, which was becoming more involved by the day.

When Brian did call her back, she almost cried with gratitude. He told her that once they had obtained their search warrants for the house, they immediately went in. As suspected, they found a meth lab in the basement. Along with kilos of drugs, they also found firearms which consisted of a Magnum revolver and a few semi-automatic pistols.

"And Valerie, they have taken John and Audrey into custody. I questioned Audrey myself down at the station. She refused to talk, but once I mentioned the name Silas Madden, she broke down. With a bit of coaxing, she gave up what she knew, and she seemed relieved to be telling someone. She said she was scared–that Silas had come over that night. Audrey suspected he had the body of a very dead Carol in his trunk. Audrey admitted she went off the rails that night. That must have been the scream-ing that the neighbours heard. She wanted no part of it, and she told Silas to leave and take the body somewhere else. But John had already arranged for the stump grinder. She thinks they had planned it all in advance, as John had already cut the tree down, and Audrey hadn't been able to figure out why."

"She knew. All this time, and said nothing," said Valerie, then instantly wishing she hadn't. After all, who was she to talk? She held her tongue and said nothing more.

Brian continued. "Well, she didn't really know, but she suspected. Audrey never saw the body. She cannot be a witness to that. Nor did she see them bury her, but she's convinced it happened. They were discussing it when she started screaming. She told me John hit her at that point, so she left. She went back two days later when she was sure the men weren't around, and she went inside just long enough to get her things. That was when she went to see Garret, to ask if he could help her. He took her to the house in Brookswood."

"So does that mean Garret knew about the body as well?"

"He says he didn't. Audrey had just told him that they had fought, and she couldn't be there any longer. But she eventually contacted John and invited him to join her there. I guess she forgave him. She told me again she had no part of it, and that although she didn't actually see anything, she was certain they buried Carol in the yard."

"So this really is happening," she whispered, afraid that if she spoke too loudly she would wake from this dream and the good news would all go away.

Brian concurred. "Yeah, if they will consider this as reasonable and probable grounds they will move forward. The neighbours on both sides of you were inter-viewed and once the guys had put everything together, it strengthened your case. I think they will contact the home owners and get consent to do a preliminary search of the yard."

"Can I give consent? Technically I'm the one in charge, living there."

"I think it has to be the owners, Valerie. Don't worry, about it, it won't take long, I'm sure of it. The guys who have been working on this Madden case want to move quickly, hoping they can finally nail the guy and give the family some closure."

31

It only took a few weeks for Brian to give her the good news. Rather than talk over the phone, Brian suggested they meet for a drink. It was, he explained, an opportunity for him to see her and make sure she was doing okay. He had called it a wellness check, to which Valerie had snorted, but she agreed. As her schedule was becoming much busier they agreed it would need to be a morning meeting. The two had arranged to meet for coffee early one morning, before both had to be at their respective jobs.

Brian was waiting for her when she arrived. As soon as they were seated with coffees in hand, he delivered the news. "Forensics is cleared to go in. They will set it up as soon as they can."

She smiled widely, and he saw some of that familiar spark in her eyes. "Will they use the dog, Brian?"

"I'm not sure at this point. It will either be X-ray imaging or maybe bring in the cadaver dog, if he's still available for our use. But they might not need to. Looking at the yard, it seems clear where the tree had been removed, so if they can go in and do a preliminary dig, that might be all that's needed."

Valerie raised her arms above her head and shouted "YEAH." She felt victorious.

"But Valerie, once they are ready to move ahead, you have to leave the house for a few days. Hopefully not longer. It will be a crime scene. Do you have a place where you can go?"

Valerie laughed. "Here we go again with the friends list. Yes, I think I have one person I can call. I'll call her tomorrow." She looked down at the table and realized Brian was holding her hand. She made no attempt to pull it away.

Within a few days Valerie received word that the team would be starting the following Monday. She called Karen and asked if she could stay for a few nights, and she would explain when she arrived. Karen's delight was immediate and obvious.

"Oh absolutely, Valerie. Please come. I'll have a room ready for you. Oh, the kids will be thrilled to see you."

"I'll see you Sunday afternoon, and I'm sorry for the short notice."

Valerie arrived early in the evening. She hadn't realized it would take so long to pack a few things and assemble her work files. And it was a long drive to Abbotsford from Crescent Beach. It seemed another world away. Luckily traffic was light on Fraser Highway at this time of day, and once she was on the freeway she recognized where she was and made her way easily. Nightfall came early this time of year and she had forgotten that the children had school in the morning. Danesh and Anadia were already in their pyjamas, waiting to say goodnight to her.

Hamid greeted her warmly and then left to put the kids to bed. Karen took Valerie by the hand and pulled her into the kitchen, giggling like a schoolgirl. She poured them each a glass of wine and left the open bottle on the counter in front of them. She was clearly enjoying this evening visit.

"Okay, spill. I want to know why you are here," she said cheerfully, unaware of the gravity of the situation.

Valerie sat on a stool by the counter and told her the entire story, starting with Garret. As Valerie spoke, Karen slowly sunk into a chair. Her smile slowly contorted into a grimace. She covered her mouth with her hand. Hamid came into the room midway through the story. He poured himself some wine and sat beside his wife, intently listening to Valerie. Soon a look of disbelief emerged on his face.

"So Garret was connected? I told you I never liked that guy," was all Hamid would say. By the time Valerie had finished telling her story, Karen had started to cry. Her husband put his arm around her shoulder and she turned her face into his chest, holding back the sobs. Valerie poured herself another glass of wine and explained that while Garret was a total creep, he was only guilty by association. While he was a drug dealer, he hadn't killed anyone. While not defending him, he was Brian's brother and she didn't want anyone to think of him as a murderer.

The next morning Valerie slept in. She awoke to a quiet house, and after quickly dressing, she made her way to the kitchen, where she found Karen sitting with a coffee. The poor woman looked tired, like she hadn't slept at all. Upon seeing Valerie, she sat up and smiled.

"Good morning. Here I just made a fresh pot. Hamid has just taken the kids to school and then he's heading out to the restaurant. We will have dinner together this evening. He said he'll bring a meal home."

Valerie's heart seized up in terror as she realized she might have to endure another difficult meal. She walked over to the counter and poured herself a coffee. They took their cups to the sitting room.

"I was thinking about your story, and I hardly slept. I remember the first time we came to your new place with Hank, and you had said that Hank also felt something strange about the yard. I thought you were imagining it, but wow, you were right. It must have been tough staying there all this time."

"Well, soon it will be over. I am convinced they will find her down there. I'm not even considering a different scenario."

Karen sat and looked at Valerie, her face twisted into a faint expression of horror, which seemed to have been frozen on her face since last night. Valerie was sorry she had inflicted this on her friend.

"Karen, I've been thinking about what you said to me last time we were together. About how you feel your life turned out. It's not too late, you know, if you want to change things. Talk to Hamid! He loves you. The kids are getting older, and both are in school. You have the opportunity to do something for yourself now. I'm sure he will understand. There are so many ways to make changes. Just trust yourself and go with your gut."

Karen looked at Valerie. "I just figured it was too late, but I suppose you are right. I'm still young and the kids are growing up. But maybe I don't even know anymore what I'd want to do. I mean, if I could do it, would it be too late to change anything. Do I know any more what I would want?"

"It's never too late, Karen. Trust me on that one. If you want it, you can have it."

Valerie had accompanied Karen to pick the kids up from school. Fortunately, Hamid came home later that afternoon with fish and chips. He had likely watched Valerie struggle with the first meal they had shared together. Brian called late that evening with an update.

"The team is scheduled to be there first thing in the morning, just before dawn. I'll be there as well, so I will let you know as soon as we have news."

"Thank you again. Who knew when I first met you that we would be here now, doing this?" Her voice was soft and intimate. She was speaking to someone who mattered to her.

"Are you okay?" There was concern in his voice.

"Oh yes, I'm perfectly fine. I'm so glad this is happening, and I'm happy to be where I am right now, with my friend. Thanks for the call and keep me posted." She glanced at Karen as she hung up the phone. She seemed to have recovered from the news, for which Valerie was grateful.

Valerie sat down on the small bench in the bay window, leaning against the stack of cushions. They warmed her back as thoughts of what lay ahead sent a chill up her spine.

"I know I won't feel any differently about the yard, even after her remains have been removed. After all, it's now like a cemetery. I will always have this vision of bad things happening there."

"I know you want to move. Do you have a place yet?"

"I will know next week." Valerie lifted her hand, displaying fingers firmly crossed.

"Don't worry. You know you can stay here as long as you need to. We all love you being here." She stood up. "But right now, I'm going to bed. I need a good night so I can deal with whatever happens tomorrow."

32

Brian arrived at the house early; the forensics team already busy setting up, having arrived a half hour earlier. One officer was busy putting up yellow tape around the property while a group of neighbours had started to collect on the sidewalk. With the use of ground penetrating radar focusing on the areas of obvious disturbances of the soil, the spot had been quickly located, and it proved to be exactly where the stump had been ground out. The men soon went to work digging, and before long, one of the team shouted out. They had found the remains, and quickly. What they found hadn't been buried very deeply, because of tree roots. Within minutes, they had exposed their victim.

The body had been wrapped in a sheet, then plastic, making for an easy extraction from the site. Watching the men working, Brian had a sudden urge to vomit. Signs of PTSD were resurfacing and he fought to hold them in check. Visions of rotting body parts materialized in his memory, and he needed to shake off the feeling. He closed his eyes and turned away. Two men arrived with a gurney and placed the remains into a plastic bag. Brian was relieved that he wouldn't need to see what was in that bag.

Although the body had yet to be formally identified, there seemed little doubt that it was Carol Madden. And the likelihood that she had been killed here was slim. It was assumed Carol was killed elsewhere and brought here for disposal. Nevertheless, the house needed to be cleared. He quickly moved inside, where teams of men were conducting their search, but he knew there would be nothing remaining, unless the infrared could find traces of blood.

Brian found another team in the master bedroom. He felt uncomfortable being here, in Valerie's personal space. To him, this was not a typical crime scene, as he was involved with the person who lived here. He looked around the room as the team worked. Valerie's belongings were meager. There were very few clothes in the closet, but he instantly noticed the dress that she had worn the night of their dinner. A quick search of the dressers revealed drawers mostly empty. He saw only one photograph on the bedside table. He leaned over to have a better look.

It was a photograph of an old couple standing in front of a building. The scene looked like it could be Sicily, and he assumed these were Valerie's grandparents. In the background was a mountain, likely Etna, which eerily looked a lot like Mount Baker. On the dresser stood another photo of the same couple, but this time they were with a small girl with long dark hair in the man's arms.

She had her arms wrapped around his neck. Looking closer, he could see this was, in all likelihood, Valerie.

Brian made his way to the kitchen, where men were conducting luminol tests of the floors and baseboards, looking for any blood residue. He tried to stay out of the way, as he was here only to observe. He opened a few cabinets and saw very few dishes and a lot of empty shelves. He moved back to the main living areas. Looking around uselessly, he noticed that aside from being sparsely furnished, the house looked uninhabited. If he had not been here with Valerie he would have had a hard time believing anyone lived here at all. Even the walls, he noticed, were bare. The entire house contained not one single picture. The place was cavernous and he realized that without Valerie's music, it was like a huge echo chamber. It was awful.

He stood in the doorway of the front room and visualized Valerie sitting across from him-a fascinating beauty, with her full lips, expressive eyes and a mane of black hair. She sat nervously stuffing big chunks of cheese into her mouth while trying hard to smile. Her hair, uncombed, fell around her shoulders. Her dark eyes framed by expressive brows, seemed even darker from a lack of sleep. He remembered the first time he had met her, all those months ago. She had come storming up to the house, dripping wet with rain, and defiantly defended herself, spewing venom in his direction when he had questioned her. Valerie was a frightened warrior who was brave and scared to death at the same time. He smiled remembering that whenever he came near her he was vigilant that at any moment she might come charging and kick him.

What he felt wasn't pity, but rather an overwhelming desire to take care of this person, and to protect her. Not just that, but to be her friend and confidant-her companion; basically, her everything. He had a sudden longing to take her away from all of this and to calm her fears. Brian had known this from the first time he had laid eyes on her.

Life had been profoundly challenging these past few years, and he felt he was on the verge of something new. He had been so busy telling Valerie to get over the past, to move ahead, and until now he hadn't realized the same should apply to him. He needed to get over his past. He needed to leave that behind, move forward and to make a change or two. Somehow this frightened woman had shown him the need to make changes in his sorely lacking existence. Perhaps Brian also needed her to be his confidant and to calm his fears.

He walked outside, not wanting to spend any more time in Valerie's space. As it was, she had just lost what little privacy she had. He walked back to his car, deep in thought.

That evening, Brian drove out to Abbotsford to see Valerie and bring her the news in person. They sat outside together on the covered front porch.

"Was it horrible, Brian?" She realized the impact of what she had asked him to do.

"It was fine. Like you said, I didn't have to do the digging. It might take some time for identification, depending on what they find on the body."

"I don't know if I can go back there. That poor woman."

"You will be fine. You've been there all this time, and now that the body is gone, the terror should be gone with it. I'm sure whoever it is will feel gratitude that you have avenged them. And you can rest assured she wasn't killed there, so the house itself is crimeless, so to speak."

"So can I go home?"

Brian sighed. "I wouldn't hurry, Valerie. If you can stay here a few extra days you might be happy you did. The media is crawling all over the place, and they would likely pounce on you, looking for a story. Something tells me you wouldn't want that."

Valerie hugged herself. Imagine her face on national television, when she had been doing such a good job of hiding. "No, you are right. I would *not* want that at all. I can stay here until after the weekend, if you think that's enough time."

"That should do it. And even then, you may want to keep a low profile in the event some over-enthusiastic reporter hangs around longer than the rest."

The body was easily identified as Carol Madden, as she was wearing clothing familiar to her children and her wallet was in her pocket. The parents, siblings, and other family members had a renewed sense of grief, yet at the same time were overjoyed that they had found her killer and could now have some closure.

As for good old Silas, he had acted happy that his wife's remains had been found, putting his hands together and muttering amen. But before long, the police charged him with her murder. Forensics was able to find traces of his blood on her body. And he had foolishly buried the murder weapon with her-a knife and a small handgun containing his blood and his fingerprints. He didn't get away with it.

Once Valerie had returned to the house, Brian came to visit. While not at ease, she was willing to stay until the move to her new apartment. She didn't want to be a burden to Karen, and she would be much too far from her work. She stayed home most of the time and only went out in her car, not wanting to chance walking into anyone looking for a story.

"But why would they cut down the tree, Brian, when all they wanted was to bury a body?"

"I suppose the premise of a rotten tree would raise less suspicion than digging a hole in the yard for no reason. And to have dug a hole anywhere else, well, there's no guarantee you wouldn't be seen by anyone."

"Better not to have done it at all."

"But you did well, Valerie. You did really well. You should come work for our canine unit. You'd make a great police dog." He sat back with his legs outstretched and crossed at the ankles. Taking a sip of his beer, he winked at her.

Valerie snorted. "I hope you realize that you are not at all funny."

"To the contrary, I think I'm very funny." Then furrowing his brows he added, "I have to thank you for being so insistent about this. You solved a years old case. I'm just hoping that you are done with these vibes of yours."

"But how tragic for Carol. She didn't deserve that, no matter how bad the marriage may have been. I hope her family can move on now."

"You need to move on as well, Valerie. I hope this is your last-how can I say it-adventure? You have a job and you need to focus on that. Maybe I can do something to help you get over it. I have an idea."

To celebrate, Brian took Valerie to an outdoor concert by the pier in Port Moody. This was the first outdoor concert of the year. The band was very good, and Valerie was riding high on her accomplishment. It was getting towards the end of the show, and they'd both had a few drinks, but the night and the breeze and the music were more intoxicating than the wine. And Brian. He was most intoxicating of all. As they danced, they suddenly locked eyes, and in the worst of clichés they each took a step closer until their bodies were inches apart, and they kept rhythm, both moving in the same way so that their bodies remained close but never touched. Their eyes were glued to each other.

When the song ended, he took her by the arm and led her to a tree, where he wrapped his arms around her and held her tightly for a long time. She closed her eyes and rested her head on his shoulder. Oh how she had wanted to do that, for so long. How she had longed to feel those arms around her.

Drawing away to look at her, Brian said, "So you have now atoned twice. Are you ready to tell me the real reason?"

"I'm afraid to tell you, because it will change things. It will change everything. Our relationship. How you see me."

Brian looked at her tenderly. His arms were still around her waist. "Well, maybe if you don't tell me, it will change our relationship also. Valerie, we can't even begin a relationship without honesty. You know that yourself. We've both been there."

Valerie squeezed her eyes shut and took a deep breath. She nodded, now compelled to let it out.

"I killed someone," she cried.

Julian

I walked forward, into the fear. Was I walking towards something I should be running from?

33

Brian had grabbed her arm and steered her to his car. Valerie had felt his hand shaking. He then drove to the other side of the park where the gravel lot faced the water. There was no one else around. The treed area was dark and quiet. He put the car in park and shut the engine off. "What's going on, Valerie? Let's hear it," he said, an uncharacteristic tremble in his voice.

Valerie nodded nervously and began speaking right away. "I told you I was being manipulated. I think Alice really only wanted me to be his keeper–that was the family's master plan. They knew he was off the rails. He had been to prison, and he was a dealer and a user, for god's sake! Nobody told me that. So what was I supposed to do? Or be? His saviour, the one who would keep him clean from drugs and out of prison?"

Valerie looked at him. She knew she was finally ready to tell him everything. "When I think back, it feels like I was cherry-picked. Even when we met, Alice insisted on calling me Valerie. You see, her mom was Catherine, and I think she didn't want to find a woman with the same name as Julian's mother. She grilled me, tried to steer my decisions. And when she finally introduced me to

Julian, she had it in her mind that we would be a couple. She grocery shopped for me!" Valerie was shaking, her voice wobbly.

"They took three years out of my life. I slowly started questioning my sanity, and I was losing my ability to make any decisions on my own. They had gradually convinced me of so many things, like what I was and wasn't capable of. Alice would talk me into doing things, then she would secretly sabotage them and come back telling me I screwed up. I would be devastated and argue with her, but she'd act hurt and tell me I was just embarrassed that I screwed up and was trying to blame her for it. She worked so hard at pointing out my faults.

When I think of all the times I had wanted to leave. How many dream jobs I had turned down. Somehow, between Julian and Alice, they always came up with reasons why I shouldn't. I didn't know who I was anymore. To me, a new job was never going to be a problem. I had credentials! We were living together and I loved my work, but he was unemployed. We could have relocated. Lived anywhere. But he wasn't willing to leave his family. So once I started feeling trapped, I applied to Calgary. I just didn't tell anyone. I was ready to leave, with or without him."

Brian sat very still, unable to move. Valerie kept talking, seeming anxious to be getting it out.

"One day, my instinct was working in full force. I don't know why, but in the middle of my day, I had to go home. Something just told me to go. As soon as I walked in the door, it hit me, hard. I walked upstairs. There they were, in our bedroom. He was sitting on the bed with a girl who didn't look to be much more than a teenager. They were both naked, and he was injecting something into her arm. I kept the scream down as they looked blankly up at me. While I waited for them to dress, I grabbed a bag and calmly filled it with his stuff. I opened the door, told him to get the hell out and then locked it behind them. I didn't look at his face but I could feel his panic. I couldn't take my eyes off the girl."

Valerie's eyes locked with Brian's. "My atonement. I let her go with him. I should have thrown him out, not her."

"I know you want to imagine you could have saved her, but the truth is, she probably would have gone with him no matter what you did. I speak from experience."

Valerie shrugged her shoulders. "Maybe. But if people can help, they should try, and I didn't. How many cases did I hear of in the years that followed, of young people dying of an overdose because they had been experimenting for the first time? Of being introduced to drugs by someone else, like River Phoenix. And I keep thinking of Amy Winehouse and why is nobody helping her. I have a bad feeling about her as well, and I can see her being another tragic statistic. It will happen, and soon-wait and see."

"I just don't want you to live with the notion that you could have changed her mind."

Valerie cleared her throat. "Okay, well, maybe you are right. But Julian disappeared after that. Nobody knew where he went, and I really didn't care. I was just glad he wasn't with me anymore. A few months later, I took the job in Calgary and left. I told no one I was going."

Valerie felt a chill and wrapped her arms around herself. Seeing this, Brian put her window up. She kept her eyes on the floor as she continued.

"Anyway, Julian's family became needier, like leeches stuck to me. Once they found out I had left, they called me weekly, and before long they were calling me every day, asking where he was. They assumed he would follow me to Calgary. His family was close, but now they were as close to me as they had been to him. I became him. I hated it and I hated Alice; these people were not my family. I stopped answering the phone, which further affected both my work and me. I felt so guilty, but not for him, oddly. My guilt stemmed from leaving the girl.

After many, many months, his mom still wasn't getting out of bed. Alice called, saying I had to go find him. By that point I suppose I wanted to find him too. I had been having bad premonitions. The thing is, I never disliked him. I had very strong feelings for him as a person. I just didn't love him enough to stay with him. I wasn't prepared to take a chance on what didn't feel right. And now I was so happy in my job, but it's like I couldn't even be free to enjoy it. I told Alice not to be so stupid. How could I find him if I didn't know where he was? I told her *she* should go find him. It was *her* brother, and it had nothing to do with me."

Valerie could feel the effects of the alcohol and it made her brave. She had needed to say this for so long. She swallowed hard before continuing.

"Eventually she heard from him. He was in Quesnel and he needed money. And get this—they wanted *me* to go get him. I refused for as long as I could. But they were driving me crazy. They said this was my fault, and I had to make it right. Alice said she hated me, saying, after all they'd done for me, how could I treat her brother this way. His mother said his fate rested on my shoulders, because it was my fault that he had gone."

"Okay, so you went, did you?" Brian was barely breathing.

"So I went. I had to. He's a human being and he was in trouble. You see, the big mistake they made was in making him impotent and needy. Actually, making us both co-dependent on each other. Luckily, I was strong enough to overcome it, but poor Julian wasn't. They made us like this, but then I abandoned him. I think the closer I got to finding him I was actually looking forward to the prospect of seeing him again, of making sure he was okay. Anyway, it doesn't matter. I found him, and it was a disaster."

The car was quiet. Valerie leaned her head back and closed her eyes. She felt so tired. Brian spoke. "So did you talk him into going home, like his mom wanted?"

"Not exactly. I drove to Quesnel in one day, and I found him in a pretty shitty area of town. I had asked around the shelters and the soup kitchens, and then there he was. He was walking down the street. It was more like staggering. I left my car in the middle of the road, and crossed the street, and walked towards him. I called out his name. He looked a mess, Brian. It was really difficult for me to see him that way. He stared at me like he didn't know me. Then when he recognized me, he looked at me with-I don't know what it was–disgust? And he just ran away. He literally ran away. '*Go away, I don't want you here,*' he said. Then I knew how rejection felt and how it must have felt for him when I pushed him away. I tried following, but before I could catch up he had disappeared around a corner.

I ran back and asked at the kitchen where I could find him. The staff told me where he was living, and I drove there. I eventually found his room, and I knocked on the door. I knew he was distressed, and I knew he was home because I could hear him moving around. I heard him kick something, and I heard him muttering under his breath. I knocked again and heard him mutter, '*Go away, go away.*' I had to leave, I had to get out of there. I couldn't breathe. Once I got outside, it suddenly hit me, right in the gut."

"The cricket thing?"

"Sure, let's call it that. Thinking back, I can't believe I didn't know exactly what was happening the first time. I arrived back at the rooming house and walked up the stairs. There was no light coming from under the door. I put my ear to the door, and I immediately felt sick all over again. I must have known all along, before I walked back to the car and sat there waiting. Waiting for what? How could I have waited so long and not dialled 911? He had hung himself, and I knew it. I had left, even after hearing the grunt of the noose tightening and the thump of him kicking the chair out from under him. I heard him choking, Brian. I heard him thrashing on the end of the rope. The beam was squeaking, for Chrissake. And I let it happen. I made another error in judgment, and I allowed him to die."

Valerie looked down at her arm. Brian was squeezing it. "Valerie," he whispered. "You are shouting." She sat looking at him, stunned. He released his hold and looked into her eyes.

"You didn't kill him."

"Don't you see? They sent me to help him. To bring him back safely. Not kill him. I was to stop him from doing this, not to help him do it."

Brian said to her, "Stop giving yourself so much credit. How were you to know, Val? There's not one of us who hasn't, at some point in their lives, said the same thing. I should have known. I must have known. Why didn't I do anything? But what I don't understand is why do we choose to live with misguided guilt and deluded self-blame? It wasn't your fault, it never was. Let me put it this way. If you walk into a convenience store and an armed gunman follows you in and shoots the clerk, is that your fault?"

"I really wasn't sure why it happened, and I didn't want to know, I suppose. But I imagine it was because he saw me. I drove him to it. I think I will always be haunted by his death, because I killed him. I have this feeling that something bad should happen to me–karma."

"You need to know that you didn't kill him. Hey, maybe you could have stopped him, I don't know. I'm fumbling here. I don't really know what to say. What I mean is, even if you had broken the door down, it might have been too late. By the time help arrived, it would have been too late. Or he might have waited a week and tried again."

"You know, he was smart. He could have done anything he wanted to. He could have really been somebody. I imagined him being successful somewhere but I guess it just wasn't in him. But still, I think if I hadn't left him, he wouldn't have died."

"That's batshit crazy, Valerie, and you know it. You were not responsible."

"Anyway, I turned as someone opened their door, and I told them to get help. And then I freaked out and ran. Disappeared. Vamoosed. I ran away with his life, his soul, rather than stay and fight for it. I drove all the way back to Calgary without being aware of the road. I have no recollection of the trip, and I don't know how I made it. I stayed in bed for a week. I felt sick, I felt guilty. I wanted to vomit. I didn't shower or answer the phone. I needed to suffer. I was finished. His mom had already cursed my offspring, if I ever had any."

Valerie was biting her lip, fighting back the tears. "You say I had no way of knowing for sure what happened to Julian that day. But I felt it. I could have tried to help, but I chose flight over fight. At that time, giving up was really my best option. I have never told this to anyone before today. You tell me it wasn't my fault. Once Julian was dead, it's no longer his fault, but it has to be *some-one's* fault, doesn't it? The other bad thing is that I fled the scene. I was a witness to a crime, and I fled the scene.

They'll be looking for me, and I could be charged and go to jail."

"For what? Did you see any crime being committed?"

"Well, no. But I knew it."

"You knew, but what did you know exactly? You saw nothing, you were frightened, and so you ran. I don't think that argument has any basis to it. The only crime was his drug habit. That's what killed him. I think Alice saw goodness and strength in you. She figured if anyone could save her brother, you could. But a person has to *want* to be saved. You didn't see him dead, did you?"

"I guess I assumed he was. It was the uncertainty at that moment that kept me sane."

"Okay, let's look at Audrey. Did she know Carol Madden was dead? Did she know she was buried in your yard? Did she become guilty simply by not saying anything? Why is it you can see things clearly when they involve someone else but not yourself? Besides, how do you know he died that day? It could have been the next day."

Valerie looked at him flatly. "I know, Brian. The news report even said so. It was a week later that Alice phoned me. She saw it on the news. The couple I spoke with had called the police and they broke the door down. He was dead. Alice called and started screaming at me. She said he was dead and it was my fault. I started to explain, but then I said to myself, screw it. It wouldn't make any difference anyway. So I hung up on her instead. I'd had enough of them and their manipulation."

"Valerie, look at me. I'm a cop and I'm saying you did nothing legally wrong. You didn't kill him. You are not responsible. Morally, you had no obligation either. You could not see through that door. And you were definitely messed up."

Valerie looked at Brian with an indescribable look of seriousness. "I was under their spell for years. In their opinion, I was incapable of anything. They were questioning my abilities and making me question my own. So I did the most sensible thing that anyone would have done. I ran away." Her voice was laced with sarcasm.

"You see, I'm the kind of person who always has everything planned out. Precise. I always know where I am, and if not I will formulate a plan and have things in place, but not this time. I was drowning. Within a month I had put my stuff in storage. I literally quit my job. I walked out on them and I left. I disappeared. And now I don't want them to find me and start that crap all over again. I left because I didn't want that terror to be the only thing I had. There was a whole other life ahead of me, and I decided to live it."

"I think you did the right thing," offered Brian. "You might not believe me right now."

"But it hasn't ended. Not for me, anyway. They continue to terrorize me. Julian haunts me many nights in my dreams. Even in death, he won't leave me alone. None of them will."

"But the dreams are not them haunting you. It's you haunting yourself. As long as you feel guilty they will continue to plague you and drive you mad. You need to forgive yourself in order to feel absolution. This reminds me of Crime and Punishment – the guilt is making you feel crazy and paranoid. I guarantee, once you stop feeling guilty about it and can move on, the dreams will go away."

Valerie tried to say something but Brian stopped her. "Don't interrupt please. Yes, they will go away. You are a different person now. You are a person with nothing to feel guilty about. Christ, the way you tell it, all you did was try to help them, do all of their bidding. Who does that? But look at you. You've changed, even since I've met you. You are who you want you to be, not someone else's puppet–some mutant who would just obey."

"I'm not really Valerie, I'm Katerina."

"Well, I kind of like Valerie. I didn't know Katerina. What's she like?"

She rolled her eyes. "I don't know if I remember any more," she said with a laugh.

"It's only your name, Valerie. And you are just fine the way you are." Brian started the car. "Come on, let me take you home. You've had a tough day."

34

Valerie was not in a hurry to get out of bed. This was her last day in this house, and although she was glad to be going, she didn't want to ruin a perfectly good sleep-in. She had spent the previous two days cleaning the house and packing up for the move. Anna was arranging for her belongings to be taken to her new apartment within the next few days.

Her confession to Brian, while difficult, had gone well. Better than expected, and she felt renewed and, strangely, reconciled. She had felt a welcome stillness ever since, and the weeks had flown by peacefully. The phone rang and she beamed when she saw it was Brian calling.

"How do you feel today?" The sound of his voice brought on strong emotions.

"I actually feel pretty good. But now that I'm going back, my stomach is in knots. I know I'm not there to stay, but just the thought of going is tough. I do need to apologize to my bosses and to empty out that storage locker. I had paid for two years, and now that time is almost up. I need to clean it out and get on with it. I will leave Calgary behind for good, in my heart and in my head. It will be closure. Every time I close my eyes, it's real-those feelings I had when I left. It's time to change that."

"Like I said, I will come with you if you want me to. Just say the word."

"No, no. I need to do this alone. I will be fine, honestly. The best thing that could have happened to me was getting this job for the Olympics, so it's all I'm focused on. I want to get back here, get settled in my new home and get back into my work."

"I'm coming over to say goodbye, if that's okay. I could be there in a couple of hours."

"I'd be upset if you didn't. I really want to see you before I go." As Valerie spoke, she clambered out of bed, knowing she needed to hurry.

By the time Brian arrived, Valerie was packed and standing by her car.

"I can't wait to get back. In my mind, I'm already on that plane. I don't want to be anywhere else. I want to stay here. I like it here and I think I found a place where I can be happy. I want to go hiking on Grouse and Hollyburn Mountains. I want to go wine tasting in Naramata. And I want to learn to ski. But please don't ask me to get on a bicycle any time soon." Valerie smiled, and so did Brian.

"And I might want to get a dog," she teased, checking for a reaction.

"I've heard home is not where you are from but where you are wanted," he answered. "I have no comment on the dog thing," he laughed.

Brian's tone grew serious as he stood by her car. "When did you say you will you be back?"

"Probably within two weeks. I am not sure how long it will take to empty my locker, and do I want to get rid of everything there. I don't really want to bring the stuff back here."

"I'll be waiting for you. Please send me a message once in a while."

Valerie looked up at him, and she was struck by an overwhelming desire to stay. To not get on the plane and just say the hell with everything there. She really didn't need to do this.

"I won't be later than that. Two weeks, tops. Maybe even sooner. I have a bit of work I can do remotely but they do need me here."

He stepped closer. "You are going to be okay. Remember, you don't have to see the whole staircase, just take the first step. And you've already done that." Brian stood quietly as he waited for a response.

Valerie fell against him and buried her face in his chest. Her hand found his. Her fingers fit into his like threads through cloth, like they belonged there. Oh how she didn't want to leave.

"I'm going to be okay. I believe you," she whispered to him. She wanted to believe him, but the thought of Calgary gave her the creeps. Maybe she should just forfeit her belongings and start fresh.

Brian stepped closer. With his finger, he lifted her chin up towards his face. "I can't get you off my mind, Miss Russo. Ever, it seems." Taking a step closer, he bent down and kissed her on the mouth. There was no silence this time, just the sound of the blood rushing to her head. The sound was deafening. The first kiss and it was gentle and powerful at the same time. The kiss was sensual and unhurried. It could have been the worst kiss in the history of kisses, but to her it was perfect. When it was over, Valerie pulled him to her and kissed him back. He held her tightly, and his hug was different this time. It permeated her entire being. She had never been hugged like that before. She got into her car, tears in her eyes.

Brian leaned over into the car. "I have to tell you something before you go. You see, I think I've fall-"

"No!" she said, placing her hand on the doorsill. "Please don't tell me now. If you do, I won't even make it out of the driveway, and I need to go. I want you to tell me when I get back. Please?"

He touched her hand and smiled. "Hurry back, then," he said.

Valerie drove away slowly, feeling trepidation like she never had-apprehension, fear and excitement at the same time. As she entered the freeway heading towards Abbotsford airport, she wondered what the future held. The secret of Julian was now in the open, and hearing she was not a murderer had lifted a huge weight from her shoulders. It still bothered her that she hadn't tried to help the young girl, but she had twice atoned and had inadvertently solved a cold case. So what now? Would her new job be enough? She knew Brian would.

As she drove, she reflected on the past year. It had been a profoundly troubling year, and the only source of real joy and contentment she experienced was from a dog and a tortured police detective. Would the happiness still be here when she returned? Valerie smiled. Although flying to Calgary brought back memories of Julian and Alice, she also realized she had not thought of them in a very long time. She was well aware of the significance of this. She was thinking of them now but even so, the thoughts didn't have the same impact. Simply telling her story to Brian had reduced her past trauma to merely a story.

"So onward and upward," she said to herself as she entered the terminal.

Valerie sat on the plane, her seatbelt buckled tightly. A young girl took the seat next to her. She had dark hair and a fresh innocent face, and she reminded Valerie of herself. That seemed so long ago now. The girl smiled at Valerie, then put on a set of headphones, closed her eyes and leaned back. Valerie, too, closed her eyes and waited for the thrust of the engines that would take them into the air.

She heard a sound and opened her eyes. Before her stood Julian, a noose around his neck, a string of vomit running from his mouth to his chin. Beside him stood Alice, her black eyes piercing into Valerie's very soul. She was holding the end of the noose.

"No more!" Valerie growled. "No more. It's finished." She raised her hand and suddenly they were disintegrating into distorted pixels and then they were gone. Valerie's head was spinning. She heard a loud sound, and it was overpowering.

She felt something grab her arm. When she opened her eyes again, they were gone. The young girl was touching her arm. "Are you okay? You were making sounds."

Valerie realized the loud sound was the plane taking off. She exhaled and smiled.

"Yes, I am okay. Actually, I'm better than okay. You see, it was so loud. And then it was quiet."

"You think this is quiet?"

"Never mind, it's a long story," Valerie said, waving her hand dismissively. "I'm okay now."

The girl, obviously uninterested, shrugged her shoulders, repositioned her headphones and closed her eyes again.

Valerie looked out the window and watched the ground below get smaller and smaller. She looked at the fiery sky. The combination of the setting sun, the denseness of the cloud cover and the electric charges mixed with the coming darkness created a truly unique tapestry of colour.

The roaring in her head was gone. She felt unusually calm. Maybe Brian was right. Maybe simply saying it out loud would make it go away. It was time to move on. A whole new story awaited her, and maybe it had been there all along. All she had to do was look a little deeper.

The End

Disclaimer

This is purely a work of fiction. Most of the names, characters, businesses and incidents are either the product of the author's imagination or are being used in a fictitious manner. While some events, places and incidents may be real they are used in a fictitious manner as it relates to this story. Any resemblance to actual persons, living or dead, is purely coincidental, except, of course, Diana Krall. I would like to extend my warm thank-you to Diana and her agents, particularly to Sam, who helped me keep Diana in my story.

In the Willie Pickton murders, Commissioner Wally Oppal's final report from the public inquiry identified a list of "critical failures" in the various police investigations. Those included poor report taking, a failure to take proactive steps to protect sex workers, the failure to pursue all investigative strategies, and poor co-ordination between Vancouver police and RCMP, among others.

At the inquiry, the forces urged the commissioner not to judge their actions with the benefit of hindsight, insisting officers did the best they could with the information they had at the time.

The Vancouver police and the RCMP also spent considerable time at the inquiry blaming each other. Vancouver police accused the Mounties of botching their investigation into Pickton himself, while the RCMP said the Vancouver police weren't passing along information and resisted forming a joint investigation.

The Vancouver department released its own internal review in 2010, which identified a number of problems with how the force's management handled the case while also laying considerable blame at the feet of the RCMP.

But the saving grace was that Willie Pickton was behind bars, leaving everyone involved to deal with their own trauma and recover the best they could.

I dedicate this book to the memory of my best friend,
who sadly lost his battle with cancer.

Frank Robert Giampa
February 15, 1940 – March 19, 2023

Closer than a heartbeat, further than the moon
There is a time to come and a time to leave
This I read but how will I ever understand it?

Laurika Rauch
Stille Waters